RACING

TO LOVE

BOOK ONE
CARTER'S TREASURE

Amy Gregory

Sapphire Star Publishing
www.sapphirestarpublishing.com
First Sapphire Star Publishing trade paperback edition, June 2012

ISBN-13: 978-1-938404-08-5

Cover Image by Heidi Cantrell

www.sapphirestarpublishing.com/amygregory

About the Author

Amy Gregory leads an incredibly active lifestyle in Kansas City with her husband and their three fantastic kids who keep them running in three very different directions. When she's not rushing her oldest daughter to tumbling, her youngest daughter to music lessons, or sitting track-side watching her son practice motocross, she's taking the few minutes in between to scribble the next pages in her Racing to Love series.

When asked, "When do you have time to write?" Amy Gregory giggles. "In bits and pieces," she says.
Amy is known for her snarky, off the cuff sense of humor, which you'll find shining through in the characters she's created. Her debut novel, *Racing to Love, Carter's Treasure*, is set for release June 7, 2012.

I've spent my whole life trying to figure out what I want to be when I grow up, and now I've finally found it. – Amy Gregory

Dedication

I have to write a shared dedication. These people are equally responsible for my dreams coming true!

For my husband, Brian. Thank you so much for your enthusiastic and never-ending support. I'm so lucky to have you by my side to share this incredible journey with. Thank you for always understanding, for your patience, and for your love. Thank you for welcoming Carter, Molly, Jesse, Brody, Eli (and their coming friends) into our lives...they are so real to me. Thanks for getting me and the crazy world inside my head. And most of all, thank you for giving me the ability to reach for my dream.

For Amy and Katie. Thank you so much for taking a chance on me. Your support and love are amazing, and I will be forever grateful for the opportunity you've given me. My SSP Family has become so much more than just publisher - author. It's my own treasure that I hold very dear to my heart. Thank you both for making my dream come true.

Acknowledgements

To my husband, thank you for reading, reading and reading some more! I love you dearly.

To my children, thank you for your patience and understanding. I love each of you so much. I hope you see that no matter what, always keep dreaming.

To Kim C. & Chris T., my early victims—I mean readers. Your friendships mean the world to me. I trusted you with my baby, thank you for your support and encouragement.

To all of my friends and family, for all your love and support. It's been amazing and more than I could have ever asked for.

To Blue, my forever twinny, we started on this journey strangers and you've become my Thelma.

To Mari C., Renee D., KE S., and Jane I., my new friends that have given wonderful words of wisdom and encouragement.

To Heidi Cantrell, thank you for my beautiful cover photography, you're amazing. To Chad L., thank you for my gorgeous cover design, it's so perfect. To Kelly, thank you for your edits, I greatly appreciate your work.

To R & J and the wonderful track we lovingly call home, and for all you've done for our racer. You're amazing people who've become part of our family.

And…to my dear friend and editor. Amy, words just can't express my love or gratitude. You took a chance, going above and beyond on a very green writer. I have learned more than I could have ever hoped. Your time, support and enthusiasm were all amazing, but it was the friendship that came from it all that I am so honored to have. I love you friend.

Molly cowered, shaking in the dark. Her heart was pounding so hard she could feel it in her ears. She tried to stay quiet, tucked in the corner so he wouldn't see her. Molly knew he would hear her breathing, it was so out of control. She knew that he would find her — again.

She could sense him getting closer. A wave of fear rippled across her skin in a rush of heat. The scream she had tried desperately to contain erupted from her. It always made him madder when she screamed.

"No. Please. Please, I'll be good."

Light flooded the small space. She squeezed her eyes shut and shielded her face from the blow.

She jumped with the hand on her shoulder.

"Molly...honey...it's okay...calm down. I'm right here, kiddo."

She drew in a ragged breath with the familiar voice. She was sweaty and panting, but finally coming out of the nightmare. Her hair stuck to her neck and face, her t-shirt drenched. When he wrapped her in his arms, she realized where she was and she began to cry. She was safe.

"Oh, Brody."

Sagging against his strong chest, she silently thanked him for being there and cursed herself at the same time. She hated crying—hated the stupid dream that sent her hurling head first toward an anxiety attack every time.

"It was bad this time, huh?"

"Yeah," she whispered in the tight space of the motorhome. Even though Brody had turned on the bathroom light on his way to the couch, she was used to being on the road and it didn't take her long to get her bearings. Now, if she could just get her breathing under control. "I'm sorry I woke you. Is Erin still asleep?"

"She's fine, don't worry about us. That's what we're here for, Mom and Dad too." Brody pulled away to look at her face, those knowing gray eyes sympathetic. He knew her better than anyone else. "Hey...I'm right here," he said. "I'll never let anyone hurt you. You know that, don't you?"

Molly looked at her brother's face. Well, the only brother she'd ever known, even if it wasn't technically by blood. Molly figured your family was those who loved you. "Yeah," she replied quietly. She did know. It was just that these nightmares took so much out of her.

"Mol, you know he can't ever hurt you again, right?"

She nodded again. She knew she was safe as long as she was awake. It was when she fell asleep that her world flipped upside down.

"I'll always be here for you." Brody hugged her tight and then pulled away. In the dim light she could see his sad smile as he ran his thumbs under her eyes, wiping the last of the tears away.

"I know, Brody. Thanks. I love you."

"Love you too, sis. You think you can get some sleep? We'll pull into the stadium tomorrow afternoon."

"Kay." She laid back down and took a deep breath as she felt Brody run his hand over her head.

Chapter One

Carter stood with the guys from his team in front of Brody Noland's bike trailer, hoping to get the first look. They'd all heard rumors that George Kapp, the circuit promoter, had set up something special for the rest of the season, something entertaining to draw crowds and even more attention to the races. That something special had turned out to be Molly West. *The* Molly West. In all of his years of racing Motocross, he'd never had the chance to meet her, but he knew she'd broken about every women's record out there. He also knew she was retired and he, like the rest of the guys, was anxious to know why George had brought her on.

George headed their direction. He was probably in his fifties and kept fit by walking around the stadium and pits week after week. "Hey guys."

Everyone in the group grinned and said hello.

"I've got some people I'd like you to meet," he said. "I want you to make them welcome around here. They're going to be with us the rest of the season." George turned his attention to the couple who were walking their way.

"Morning," George welcomed them when they made it up to the group. Both waved. "Everyone…you all probably know who Brody Noland is, and this is his girlfriend, Erin." He turned to gesture to the circle of racers. "This is Eli Hunter, Carter Sterling, Jesse Frost, and one of our rookies this season, Cody Stark."

"I saw your bike trailer over there," Eli said to Brody as he took his turn shaking his hand. "I wondered if you were riding or something this weekend."

"Oh, hell no, not me." Brody shook his head. "Not anymore. Got a hard enough time being stiff and sore these days." He shrugged his shoulder at the truth. "Just too many broken bones over the years."

"What, are you all doing some kind of promo then?" Jesse jumped in to ask.

"He brought in my girl for me." George grinned.

The guys all chuckled at the older man. It was pretty obvious to Carter that George was just as excited that Molly was there as the rest of them.

Carter was the first to notice the petite girl walking their direction. He'd seen pictures of her in her riding gear over the years, but that couldn't have prepared him to see her now. In riding gear she was completely covered head to toe, but not today. Today she wore tight jeans, Nikes, and a fitted little tank top. He could tell by her arms alone that she was ripped, definitely athletic, but she had some curves to her, too. They were there, barely, and he couldn't help but imagine running his hands over them. Long, golden hair hung down in a thick sheet past the middle of her back, and in the sun it glinted with a hint of red.

Carter let out a slow breath. *Damn, I wish she'd take off those aviators so I could see her eyes.* He'd just have to wait. Waiting was something he was used to. He'd been waiting for the right girl for years.

Carter tried to pay attention to the conversation happening around him, but he couldn't take his eyes off the absolutely gorgeous girl talking on the phone a few yards off from them.

"There they are," Carter heard Brody say. "That's Joey, our mechanic, and of course, Molly West. She rides for my dad." Carter was more than happy to have an excuse to continue to stare.

"There's your pre-race entertainment." George's excitement was obvious as he clapped a hand on Brody's shoulder. "I can't wait for you boys to see her ride."

Pre-race entertainment? Holy shit. This little thing was a trick-rider? A sudden swell of protectiveness rushed through Carter. He tried to shake himself from it, knowing he was being absolutely ridiculous. From what he knew, this girl had been a rider her entire life. Who was he to say that it was too dangerous, that she was too small, or that she was too much of any of the other million reasons he could come up for why she shouldn't be on a bike? He cut an eye back toward her, watched her swaying as she talked on the phone, her arm moving through the air animatedly. Still he couldn't shake the gut feeling he had that he somehow needed to protect her.

Their mechanic Joey walked toward the group. "Hey, man" He slapped Brody on the back. "By the sounds of it, you're next."

"Aww, shit. Is that my dad?

Carter inclined his head to listen to Brody and Joey's conversation. He'd been silently praying she wasn't on the phone with a boyfriend. His heart wasn't the only thing that jumped when Brody confirmed it was his dad. He shifted in his sudden discomfort that wasn't entirely unpleasant.

Damn.

He was going to have to get himself under control. His mind and body were getting away from him, and he hadn't even met her yet.

"What's going on? You guys do something to piss him off?" Jesse asked.

"No, my dad's just a bit of a control freak, mainly when she's involved."

"I can see why. She's freaking hot," Jesse laughed and raised his eyebrows, jerking his head in Molly's direction. Even though Jesse was one of his closest friends, Carter had the urge to punch him.

Apparently, Brody didn't like the statement any more than he did. "Hey man, that girl is like my sister. Do not fuck with her, do you understand?" Brody glanced around the group. "That goes for all of you. She's off-limits."

Everyone took a collective step back from the sudden fury radiating from Brody.

Carter tore his attention from Molly and placed it on Brody, trying to read to him, sensing a whole lot more to his warning.

Carter watched as Molly ran a hand through her side sweeping bangs and mouthed, *Oh my God,* to Brody, shaking her head in frustration. Brody mimicked her, obviously teasing her. Rolling her eyes, she flipped him off.

Carter couldn't help but laugh at the two of them.

"Yes, James…I know…I know…You already told me that…yes you did, twice! You're making my brain hurt." She rubbed her forehead. "I'm not being smart with you, James, you're really making my brain hurt." That sent Brody into a laughing fit and Carter found himself laughing, too. "I know, James, seriously."

Molly had been so focused on getting James off her ass that she hadn't paid a bit of attention to the group Brody was standing so close to. The sudden laughter caused her to become acutely aware they were all not only watching, but listening to her.

It was typical for her to be really uncomfortable around groups of guys, which was really *great* since she'd spent her life around groups of men. At least Brody was there.

As she talked, she looked over each of them individually as she continued her conversation.

Then she saw him.

He had short sandy blond hair, the ends at his neck curling just a tad. Lightly tanned and lean with a racer's muscular build. He was standing there in low-slung, well-loved jeans and a plain white v-neck t-shirt, just watching her with a lop-sided grin on his face. She could tell he was a good head taller than her, but that was nothing new. She was only 5'2", so just about everyone was taller than her. He had Hollywood good looks that could have landed him on TV, and gorgeous ice-blue eyes with long eyelashes that would make any girls heart start pounding on the spot. He must have known she was staring at him from behind her sunglasses, because he flashed her this killer smile that did something funny to her stomach.

She swallowed hard. She didn't notice guys except to figure out which ones to avoid, and she had no idea why she was suddenly fixated on this one. "Um, what did you say, James?"

Then the guy winked at her.

"Um…James, Brody wants to talk to you, so gotta go, love you, bye." She spit out the last part as fast as she could and shoved the phone into Brody's chest.

"Dad…okay…I know…yeah…I know."

Molly couldn't help but snicker. James was the biggest pain, always worrying more than he should. She knew why, but still, it was hell to get stuck on the phone with him.

"All right, well, George is here, so we've gotta go," Brody said before he rushed out a quick, "Okay, bye." He hung up and smiled at Molly. The phone didn't ring back, meaning James had apparently given up for the moment. The tiny victory was theirs. She mouthed a silent *thank you* to her partner in crime.

George crossed to Molly with his arms open wide, the smile making his warm eyes crinkle. "Hey, sweetheart, how's my girl?"

"Hi, George." He hugged her tight, picking her up off the ground for a second. "I'm good. How about you? You still like running the big boys circuit? Wasn't it way more fun with the kids?" Still in his arms, Molly grinned with the tip of her tongue barely touching her top teeth. She remembered how much fun they had with good ol' George. Well, mainly Brody, but the two of them were never separated, so she always got blamed too.

"These boys aren't nearly as entertaining or as maddening as some racers I know." He laughed and patted her back the way he'd done when she was young. "So, I see James is still as overprotective as always."

She had missed sparring with George. "Oh, he means well." She smiled up at him briefly before she raised her eyebrow in defense. "And maddening? I never gave you a lick of trouble, old man." Brody and George both laughed as if that was the funniest thing they'd ever heard, and she threw her hands up. "What? Did I say something funny?"

"Sweetheart, your ass is the reason for most of the gray hair I have."

Molly rolled her eyes to disagree. "It was all Brody and you know it, George. I was only guilty by association."

"So how much of that conversation was about riding?" Brody cut in.

"Roughly three minutes out of about twenty," she said, shaking her head again at Brody, sure the pink in her cheeks gave away that she was embarrassed by the guys snickering at her.

Jesse grinned. "So, I'm going to venture to say your dad is more than a little worried about his little girl being surrounded by all these boys?" Molly didn't answer him, but Brody gave him a look that told him to drop it.

George's laughter died down to a light chuckle. "All right…all right, let me introduce you to these guys. This is Cody, Jesse, Eli, and Carter. This is my girl, Molly West."

She politely shook hands with each of them, Carter being last.

When he took one of her hands in both of his, she immediately felt tingles everywhere and her heart started beating faster. She looked down at her hand, then back up to his face. She watched a slow, sexy grin come across his face, and she started to blush as she tried to pull her hand back away.

"Um—" It was barely more than a whisper "—you still have my hand." She bit the right side of her bottom lip, grinning shyly.

Confidently, he smiled back. "Yeah, I do, Gorgeous."

Oh God. He was sunk, hook, line, and sinker. She'd lowered her sunglasses with her free hand, since he wasn't about to let go of the one he held, and now he was looking into the most beautiful deep blue eyes he'd ever seen.

She blushed and looked down.

"Well, Sterling's smitten," Cody teased.

If it was possible, her ivory-skinned cheeks flamed even more.

Yep, he was done for.

Carter squeezed her hand before letting it go.

Those innocent smiles and blushing cheeks were a welcomed change to the constant offers he got, but continually denied.

When they all headed over to sit outside Brody and Molly's bike trailer, he made sure to sit in one of the chairs closest to her and patted the other one for her to sit next to him, hoping she'd take it instead of one of the empty ones by Brody.

Molly had just started to pull her sweatshirt over her head when Dylan, a rider from another team, walked up. Carter groaned.

Dylan Martins was such an asshole. When Dylan whistled, Carter's stomach clinched at the thought of her with him.

"Damn, what a hottie," Dylan said, walking up close to Molly as she pulled her head through the sweatshirt. "And a very pretty face to match. Hey, babe." He grinned at her like the jackass he was.

The protectiveness Carter had felt earlier came swooping back. He bit his tongue.

She pulled her hair out the sweatshirt with one graceful sweep. It fell almost to her waist.

Carter was shocked when she raised her eyebrow and squared up to him. "Excuse me?" she said, "you may want to back up." Her blue eyes were locked on him, her head tilted as she gave him a look that said *you've got no chance in hell.* Molly let out a disgusted snort.

"Come on, babe...come hang out with me. We can go back to my trailer." He ran a finger down her arm.

She yanked her arm away, stumbling back as she glared at him. The back of her legs hit the white plastic chair he now had her backed up against. "You don't even know me."

"I want to get to know you, all of you."

Carter was on his feet before he knew it. "Back off, Martins." Carter put his palm against Dylan's chest and physically backed him up a couple of steps.

"Come on, I'm just messing with her."

"No, you're not. Are we clear?"

Dylan backed away, laughing. "Whatever. See ya, babe." He gave her a creepy wink before he turned and walked away.

Carter looked back at Molly after Dylan disappeared around another trailer. "You okay?"

She nodded and said, "Yeah," but he knew she was shaken up.

Molly took a breath as she looked around the pits. Underneath the stadium was nothing but concrete, the floor, the ceiling, and the walls. But what they could transform it into to make the pits a fun place for fans to walk through on race days was something she'd always loved. She had missed this. The vendor trailers and factory semis completely covered in sponsors' names and logos, all parked close together, the camaraderie of the various teams, mechanics yelling back and forth in moments of panic, the smell of exhaust from the bikes, all of it. She missed being in the pits just in general, indoor or outdoor, it didn't matter what series. She had missed hanging out with other riders. It was a different world and she fit in there. Well, she missed most of the riders.

Usually the riders were fine and didn't mess with her— treated her like one of them. But then there were always guys like Dylan that James and Brody tried to protect her from. She could usually back them down with the glare she'd perfected, but some guys just couldn't take a hint. She was fine until they tried to touch her.

"I'm sorry about that, kiddo." George ran his hand through his hair.

She shrugged and put back on the hard exterior Dylan had managed to crack. "Ah, no biggie, George, occupational hazard."

"That's why Dad taught her how to box," Brody said proudly, glancing over at her. She knew he was checking to be sure she was okay, though he played it off for the guys. She said a *silent thank* you as he continued on. "Pissed Mom off, but I've seen it come in handy several times. You can't see it very well—" He looked around at the guys, then at Molly who still stood by Carter. "—but she's got enough red in her hair to have an attitude."

"Bite me, Brody." She couldn't help but laugh and was thankful he was trying to lighten the mood.

"And the temper to prove it, huh, little girl?"

She grinned and shook her head.

Carter sat down and Molly sat down in the open chair next to him. She didn't know why, but something about him felt safe. She guessed it was because he'd automatically jumped up to help her when that pervert Dylan had hit on her.

It definitely *wasn't* that wicked grin.

"So," Eli said, "seems like you know who we all are, what about you? Tell us more, you obviously know George here."

"Yeah." Molly lovingly looked up at George and he winked back at her. "We go back a few years, huh? I don't know. I raced, went pro, retired, did freestyle, retired again, now I do paying jobs. End of story."

"I hate to say this out loud, but you don't hear much about women's racing in the media," Cody added.

"No, it's definitely not as big as men's racing, but that's okay, it cuts down on the stalkers that way." She laughed, more out of nerves because Carter had just rested his arm on her chair, touching hers. She let out the breath she was holding and bit her lip.

"How many wins did ya end up with?" Jesse smiled.

She could feel the heat on her cheeks. "I don't know. I didn't keep track," she answered, then mouthed *help* to Brody, but he just grinned at her.

"I'm not buying you don't know your own stats! Nice try, girl! Fess up," Eli said.

Her chest heaved as she sucked in an uncomfortable breath and then looked down. "Seven."

Carter patted her leg and then just kind of settled in to rest on her thigh. She couldn't take her eyes off the spot where his large palm engulfed her leg, the heat from his hand burning through her jeans and spreading through her.

What in the hell? She should have been freaking right about now.

"Seven wins is awesome!"

His answer barely registered with her.

"Um....not...wins." She finally looked around bashfully then quietly answered, "Titles."

Eli choked on his beer. "What?" Eli asked, wiping his chin from the beer he just spit everywhere. "Did I hear you right? Did you say titles, as in seven AMA Pro Titles? Not amateur, but we're talking pro?"

"Yeah, well, women's, so WMA, but yeah," she answered shyly.

Molly had never bragged about her career; the titles, the medals, the winning. She competed because she loved riding. The winning came easy because she loved being on a bike. Plus the fact that it made James and Brody so proud, that was all she ever cared about, except for one. The first year she went to the X-Games was Brody's last. They both won gold that year, and to stand with her brother with matching medals and wearing his number on her jersey—that was the highlight of her career as far as she was concerned. She had that 8x10 framed on her dresser at home; they were hugging, his cheek resting on top of her head, both with the biggest smiles they could produce, showing their matching medals to the camera. That one moment was worth more than the other eighteen years of motocross wins combined. That one picture was more precious than all the trophies, medals, jerseys, and plaques James still had displayed with all of Brody's.

"That's my girl!" George boasted. "You boys don't even want to ask her about the amateurs."

"Whoa, I knew you were good, girl, but..." Jesse said, his Texas accent thick with embarrassment.

"Should've paid more attention to those girls, huh, Frost?" George joked sarcastically. "If it makes you feel better, James wouldn't have let any one of you within fifty feet of this one."

George winked at her. "So really, what do you have up your sleeve for me? Did you bring the big ramp?"

"Maybe. It'll depend on your track and if Brody can get the ramps situated properly. So…speaking of which, when can I get on your track?" She batted her eyes at him.

"For you, tomorrow afternoon, but don't tell these guys."

Carter put his hand on her arm. "What's the ramp for?"

She glanced down at her forearm that was resting on the arm of the chair. He was lightly holding it and stroking it with his thumb. She knew there had to be sparks shooting from it because she could feel them, even through the sweatshirt.

"Um, what?" She was dazed and he only made it worse when he flashed her that perfect smile again. "Oh," she finally said, gazing up at him, "um…a flip."

"A flip," Carter said in a tone Molly didn't quite understand, he's eyes narrowed as he looked at her.

Eli slapped Carter on the shoulder. "Hot damn girl, it's gotta be crazy at your guys' house." He laughed.

Molly shook her head in disagreement. "No, for two reasons. We were homeschooled so Karen was almost always around, and two, James would never allow that. And Brody learned everything the hard way, either by being taught tricks by people who could do it but didn't know how to really teach them or by working on tricks with his buddies and teaching themselves, which didn't always turn out very well. I just have to do what he says, and he's good at explaining exactly how to do stuff so I don't get hurt…usually." She raised one eyebrow at Brody. "And since he had to retire completely from competing a few years back, let's just say I get his undivided attention," she said flatly with her head cocked to the side. Brody just smiled back innocently. He knew just how hard he worked her, but she knew it was for her own good.

"So how do you get up one day and say, I want to do this trick or that trick?" Jesse looked between the siblings for an answer.

"By getting up and wanting to be better than you were the day before."

"Ah, a philosopher, huh?" Jesse grinned at Molly's comeback that she had laced with just a hint of sarcasm.

"Nope, a realist. Gotta make a living somehow."

Jesse raised his beer. "I'll drink to that."

"Me too, bro," someone else said, but she didn't notice who because Carter was still rubbing her arm. To top it off, he'd crossed his leg so that his knee was touching her thigh as well. Every time he moved, he touched her.

Each time her stomach would drop and do flip-flops and her heart would begin to race. She was also pretty sure he had to have scooted his chair closer to hers when she wasn't looking.

This was all so foreign to her.

She had always been around guys. It was her career and it was male driven. She'd learned to tolerate being around men.

But never had she felt like she had electricity running through her from head to toe when a guy brushed by or even just gave her a simple smile.

God…that damned smile of his and those eyes.

Molly tried biting her lip to keep her reaction to herself, but she could feel her cheeks warming up.

"Don't let her fool you," Erin teased, "she likes the adrenaline rush just as much as the rest of you."

Molly just shrugged off the remark. But as she glanced in Brody's direction, she knew he understood. They had always been able to read each other perfectly.

George stood and stretched. "Well, I better get back and check the track and make sure things are moving along. You boys better play nice, she could out ride any of you."

Molly stood to hug George. "It's so good to see you again. And you better tell Eileen hi and give her my love."

"Well, tell her yourself, she's coming in Saturday to see you."

"She is?"

"Are you kidding? Sweetheart, she wouldn't miss it for the world!"

Brody grinned. "Told you I had a surprise for you if you were a good girl."

"Bite me!"

"Brody." George shook his head at Brody while Molly was still tucked under his arm. "She may be a good foot shorter than you and probably doesn't weigh a hundred pounds soaking wet, but son, if you remember right, I've seen you two go toe-to-toe before on more than one occasion, and well, it's a pretty even match. You two couldn't act more like brother and sister if you were actually blood related."

"Are you kidding?" Brody laughed and stood to shake George's hand. "She's the most stubborn, bull-headed brat around."

"Me? Seriously?" She gave him an eye roll. "Well you are an over-protective control freak just…like…James." Molly unleashed a big, satisfied smile, quite proud of her retort. She kept that one in her back pocket for when he deserved it most. She knew how much he hated it when she compared him to his father.

"Brody," George attempted his warning again, "I'm leaving and I think you're gonna get your ass kicked."

"Na, I wouldn't want to embarrass him in front of all these guys." Molly laughed, then laughed even harder at Brody's exaggerated sigh of disbelief.

"All right then, if it's safe, I'm walking away." George looked around at the men watching her, "I mean it boys. Be good. I've seen you all ride, and I've seen her. I'd hate to have to put you in your place by making her race against you. She'd whip every one of your asses." George hugged Molly one last time and patted her cheek. "Oh…it's so good to see you sweetheart."

"You too, George." Molly sat back down, only to realize that Carter had moved his arm to the back of her chair. The breath she sucked in was automatic. She snuck a look his direction to see if he heard it, praying he hadn't.

"So, you're a bad-ass, Molly." Eli put his arm out. "Will you marry me?"

Molly's head dropped. "I'm not a bad-ass, James had his reasons."

"Besides, Eli—" Jesse nudged him. "—I think you're a little late." Jesse cleared his throat and nodded toward Carter and Molly. Everyone looked their direction. Carter's knee was still touching her thigh, but the hand that was on the back of her chair was now playing in her hair. Molly blushed as she continued to look down, avoiding their questioning eyes.

She was so out of her element.

She bit her lip as she gazed up at Carter. He squeezed the back of her neck lightly and left his hand tucked in under her hair. She snuck another look up at him, and for a second time he caught her, making her blush all over again.

"Damn it, Sterling." Eli smacked him as he got up to get another beer. "I find the girl of my dreams and you swoop in."

"Just grab me a beer, Hunter. You want one?" Carter asked her.

"Na. Thanks, though. I've still got to run."

"Besides, she can't handle her liquor. Can you, sis?"

If at all possible, Molly's cheeks reddened even more. She bit her cheek to keep herself from embarrassing herself further with a nasty retort, and from laughing. Instead she leveled him with her laser pointed glare. Unfortunately, he just cackled more.

Chapter Two

If she looked up at him with that blush one more time, Carter was going to lose it. The tingle that radiated up his arm from his hand buried in her hair was bad enough.

There was just something about this girl. Yeah, she was gorgeous—obviously. But there was so much more than that. She was sweet and funny and shy all at the same time. She was herself. No games. And he didn't have to peel her off because she was clinging to him like glue. She was just...Molly.

Carter had spent his whole life on the track. As a boy and then as a teen, it was his whole world. But as he slid closer and closer to thirty, he was beginning to find the track and his career empty.

Like all serious racers, there was never a time when he was young and partied, at least not to the point of being wild. He, Jesse, and Eli always had a good time, but they had careers to worry about. Now at twenty-eight, he realized exactly what was missing. Sure, he'd dated over the years, but no one made his heart race like the girl sitting next to him. "All right, boys." She glanced around the group. "I'm going to get my run in."

"How long are you going to run for? I'll go with you. If you don't mind, that is?" Carter asked her, squeezing her neck again. He wasn't ready to give up his time with her yet.

Joey looked at Carter and shook his head. "Dude, don't embarrass yourself in front of her. I'm begging you as a fellow man. Don't do that to us. I don't know you that well, maybe you run regularly, but she'll kill you."

Brody put his hand on Joey's shoulder, laughing. "Oh my God, he's right. You know she's going to kick your ass out there, don't you?" Brody looked at Carter, his head tilted to the side. Brody was laughing, but it was forced, Carter got the feeling there was something more to it.

There had been silent warnings all afternoon and evening. They were under the radar and seemingly unnoticed by Molly, but Carter was hearing them loud and clear. Brody protected Molly more fiercely than he would consider normal for a sibling. He grew up with brothers, so not having a sister, who knew? Maybe it was different. But he'd always had a pretty keen sixth sense and he definitely was reading something in Brody's narrowed eyes.

"Oh, Lord have mercy, Brody," Molly said as she started to stand up, "you have shit knees, a bad hip, a bad back, and a laundry list of other problems. You couldn't keep up with a three year old." She looked down at Carter and raised an eyebrow. "Have you been drinking all afternoon?"

"Na, this is only my second," he replied, holding up the empty bottle.

"It's up to you, then," she said with a smirk and a shrug before she turned and crossed to Brody and held out her hand. "Can I have the keys to the motorhome?"

Carter shook his head. Molly West was something else. Brody stood up to pull them out of his pocket. "You going to take it easy on him?"

She looked back over her shoulder just as Carter climbed to his feet. "Why would I?"

"Ah, that's my girl."

Eli nearly choked on his beer. "Oh my God, I adore her! You and Brody are going to make the weekends a whole lot more fun."

She smiled mischievously at Eli and Jesse, then back at Carter with a question on her face.

"I want to go, if that's okay?"

She turned to walk to their motorhome. "It's up to you, Hollywood," she hollered as she walked away without looking back.

"Hollywood?" Carter yelled after her. She didn't answer, but he could see her shoulders move as she snickered to herself.

He looked at her friends. "Hollywood?"

A tease of a smile lit Erin's face. "I think she thinks you're hot." She winked at him. "But I can't believe she said that out loud, in front of all of *us*. She never gives any guy the time of day…much less admit it like that."

He sucked in his cheek hard as he tried not to blush, but failed. He shook his head, turning bright red as they all started to give him shit. "Oh, you all laugh now, but she thinks I'm good looking," he laughed and flipped them all off as he left to go change.

Carter rushed to his motorhome, quick to throw on a pair of running shorts, a t-shirt, and running shoes and was back in less than ten minutes. Maybe it was ridiculous that he was so into this girl so fast, but he couldn't help it.

"Dude, you are whipped." Joey chuckled as he approached. "She ain't worth that kinda pain."

"I think she is," Carter mumbled as his jaw dropped open.

Molly had changed into a pair of short spandex running shorts and a tiny tank top. She pulled her hair up in a long pony tail as she walked then tossed the keys to Brody. "Here."

Carter watched as Brody forced out a heavy breath as he looked at Molly, muttering, "I really wish you would've put a t-shirt on."

"Why?"

"Never mind." He shook his head. "It's too late now."

She frowned, then turned and grinned at Carter. "You ready?"

Uh, yeah, he was definitely ready.

Brody watched the two heading off toward the stadium, completely on edge. He dragged in a long breath through his nose. What the hell was Molly doing taking off with a guy she didn't even know? This was *so* not Molly. His dad would kill him and Carter both if he found out.

"Hey, relax." Brody glanced over at Erin who reached out to rub his back. "She's a big girl, Brody. You need to learn to step back and give her some space. She's never going to heal completely with you and James suffocating her all the time, and she's sure as hell never going to learn to trust anyone. She has good instincts, Brody."

Brody sighed and shook his head in worry as the two disappeared. "She doesn't even know that guy. Hell, *we* don't know that guy. That isn't like her, and you know it, Erin."

"And that's a *bad* thing? You should be happy she's found somebody that she seems interested in. He seems really nice."

Brody looked at his girlfriend who squeezed his shoulder, trying to encourage him. He wished he could just relax and watch her go, but protecting Molly had been his job since he was fourteen. He wasn't going to stop now, especially with some cocky rider who was obviously just playing the nice guy. He wasn't about to let him take advantage of his little sister. She wasn't the only one who still lived with the nightmares of her past.

❧

Sweat slicked her palms, and she tried to casually wipe them on her spandex shorts. Her heart was racing before she'd even started warming up. Molly just couldn't figure out why she was drawn to this guy.

Yes, he was hot. And he was nice. Okay, he was funny, too. But he was still a guy. A stranger.

He'd been showing her light affection all afternoon, which he was a damned fool to be doing in front of Brody. That right there proved he was a crayon short of a full box. On one hand, the girly side of her wanted to giggle and bat her eyes. It plain pissed her off that her heart was doing its own thing. Her head, on the other hand, told her to keep a safe distance.

She let out a shaky breath, racking her brain for something to say. Normally she could laugh and joke with the guys she'd just met when she was around Brody and Erin. But now? Alone with him, she was clueless. She didn't know what to say, she didn't know how to act. She felt like a silly middle-school girl who got a note slipped to her by the cutest boy in the class.

"So? Do you like to run or are you just trying to earn points?" Molly asked Carter as they walked.

"Earn points?"

"With me."

"Well, it's not my favorite form of exercise."

Her brain was right. She stopped dead in her tracks. Here she really liked this guy and he was just like all the rest. *Damn it.* She should have listened to Brody when he warned her to never trust a rider.

Carter stopped and looked back at her. "What?"

She closed her eyes and shook her head.

"Oh, I'm sorry, Gorgeous." She felt him approaching. "I didn't mean it like that. I meant I'd rather ride bicycles or lift weights, stuff like that."

Wait, what? Molly took a deep breath and silently berated herself. "Sorry," she said quietly as she started walking again. There were just so many guys like Dylan she'd had to deal with over the years.

Karen, Brody's mom—well, she considered Karen her mom, though she'd never called her that—had been telling her for years she couldn't assume all men would be like Dylan. She'd told her that one day she'd meet a guy she could trust, someone good like Brody or James. But then she'd had James and Brody talking in her other ear, telling her that men were *all* like Dylan. Time and time again, James and Brody had been proven to be right, an unfortunate event on both counts.

What if? What if this was the guy? Man, she needed some space to get her thoughts in a row.

"What are you sorry for?"

"Automatically assuming something, like I told George, occupational hazard."

"Ah, don't worry about it, Gorgeous."

She rolled her eyes at his apparent nickname for her, her cheeks flushing. She averted her attention to the ground.

He slowed and she could feel his eyes burning into the side of her face. "You don't see it, do you?"

She peeked up at him. "See what?"

"You are absolutely gorgeous and you have a killer body." He looked her up and back down, smiling.

"Whatever." She turned away. Maybe he was just like all the rest, only caring about what she looked like and how fast he could get her in bed. Little did he know the nickname she had been given years ago—she earned that one. Even after the silent treatment, the brush off and any other avoidance tactic she could employ, a few guys took the challenge. All she ever had to do was mention it to Brody or James and those men were never allowed to ride the Noland track again. No, she didn't mind her nickname at all. As a matter of fact, it seemed to help. *Ice princess.* She snickered silently to herself.

Well…James *did* treat her like a princess.

He chuckled. "See…that's what makes you even more beautiful."

"What's that?"

"I can tell it's just who you are, that you aren't trying to impress any of us with your looks. Yeah, you've got a killer body and this face." He brushed the back of his hand over her cheek. Molly gasped, not expecting the jolt she felt with his touch. "But it doesn't even matter to you." His smile was gentle. "That's what."

She changed the subject. "We're here."

"Where here?"

"Here, the track," she said as they walked through the rider's entrance and out onto the dirt track. Smiling, she eyed the hills and let out an *I'm home* sigh. She breathed in, forgetting her discomfort of a few moments before, excitement taking its place. "You ready?"

Carter looked around the track and back at her like she was crazy. "Seriously? We're running here?"

Molly nodded, rubbing her hands together in anticipation, chomping at the bit for her runner's high.

"Okay...you mean like the perimeter of the track, right? You know, nice flat surface."

She laughed and bumped him on the shoulder. "C'mon. You're in shape, Sterling, I can tell."

Maybe she hadn't been as obvious as he had been, but she couldn't help but check him out when she'd come back from her motorhome. She could tell by his muscles that he worked out hard, too. She knew he had to so he could keep up his endurance to race. Working out for him was as much a part of the job as winning races. She could appreciate that. Molly took off at a pace a little more than a jog, grinning happily at the thought.

Carter caught up easily, only because his legs were longer. "So, I thought George didn't want anyone on the track until tomorrow?"

"On a bike, and that's to stay out of the way of the builders, but they're pretty much done and we'll stay out of that corner where they're still working."

"And..." he drew out, grinning at her.

"And what?"

"And...George will let you do pretty much whatever you want, huh?"

"Um, sometimes." She tried not to grin.

"So how long do you run for?"

"Normally or tonight?"

"Is there a difference?"

"Usually I go for about two hours or so. Then I do weights or Pilates."

"Are you serious?"

"Yeah. I usually run our property line and it takes about two to two and half hours, depending on the weather. Then move to the gym for the rest."

"What about tonight?"

"Well, you're kinda cute, I don't want to kill you."

"So, you think I'm cute, huh?" He grinned.

She turned red instantly. *Oh my God.* "I didn't mean it like that."

"Yes you did. You think I'm cute." The way he smiled at her was so adorable, with this little dimple in his cheek that appeared as he teased her.

She couldn't believe she just said that. Oh my God.

Yeah. He was cute. But, oh God, she was so out of her element.

What the hell was she thinking? She didn't know how to flirt.

She didn't want a boyfriend, but then why did her cheeks feel like they were on fire and her heart feel like it was going to pound out of her chest? Why didn't he just stay back with his friends? Where was Erin when she needed her? *Why, why, why?*

"Well, now you're just fishing," she said, gathering up all the courage she could to play his game. Maybe then she wouldn't look like captain innocent.

"Fishing?"

"Yeah, fishing…for compliments." She cursed the giggle that escaped. Could she sound stupider if she tried? "You're such a guy."

He nudged her shoulder and took up a pace beside her.

The gentle pounding of their feet on the dirt and the grinding of the dozers in the background were a relaxing god-send. They ran for a long while, each in their own thoughts. This was okay. Running with him was enjoyable. She could almost relax, at least enough to be herself.

She broke the silence and even teased him. "I'm impressed. You drank two beers and you're still upright."

"Don't be. It was two too many. You're about to kill me." Out of breath, he slowed down. Way down.

"Ah, the truth comes out. So you did want to run with me just to continue flirting, eh?" Molly bit her lip, taking herself by surprise that *she* was the one who was flirting.

"Yeah." He dragged in a breath. "You gonna take pity on me now since I'm being honest?"

"Sure, you go back and I'll be there in a little while." She grinned, but she would have to admit she was a little disappointed. She had really enjoyed being alone with him like that. No pressure, just two people that were running. And it hadn't even been *that scary* without her brother to protect her.

Carter bent over with his hands on his thighs. He looked up, his blue eyes meeting hers. "I'll stay."

Her lip and eyebrow both went up in confusion. *Huh?* "You're going to hang out here…bored?" Why in the world would he want to sit in the dirt, in the middle of the track, by himself?

Carter didn't do fake. It was what turned him off about most women he met. They only cared about their looks, his fame, and what he could do for them.

Molly obviously cared about none of those things.

She stared at him now as if he were crazy for wanting to stay.

He smiled at her. He was crazy all right—crazy about her. The last few hours had been the most fun he'd had in, well, he couldn't remember how long. There was no way he was going to pass up spending time with her, even if she had just tried to kill him with her so called *running*. When people said they were going running, it usually meant a nice, even pace, easy to chat through. Oh no, her special kind of hell meant they were booking it, and with those damn hills to boot. But one look at her body and he could do nothing but appreciate her effort.

"I won't be bored."

"Whatever." Molly rolled her eyes and grinned as she took off running even harder than she had been with him. He snorted in slight embarrassment as he realized she'd been holding back for him. Chuckling to himself, he let out the deep breath he'd finally caught. She was something else all right, a walking, breathing contradiction. The most beautiful girl he'd ever seen and as sweet as she could be. He certainly had never met another woman with those two qualities combined. Plus she had a childlike innocence to her, he found it refreshing, and very frightening.

She made her way back to him about forty-five minutes later. "Okay, you just look lonely sitting here."

He'd been sure that he wouldn't be bored, and he'd been right. He'd watched her the entire time, lost in his thoughts, trying to figure her out.

Most of the time she seemed so free, so fun, and at other times it seemed as if a wall suddenly went up around her.

She smiled down at him, toying with her ponytail, red-faced again.

"Nope, just watching you, Gorgeous."

Her blush grew. "I don't know if I should feel flattered or…creeped out."

"You're not even breathing hard." He patted the ground beside him. "Have a seat."

"I do this every day. Ugh, I'm sure I smell great."

"You smell fine. Besides, you owe me."

Her head cocked to the side at the same time her hand flew to her hip. "For?"

"Because I protected you from all the boogie men."

Standing twenty feet up on top of the hill of the finish line, under the framing, she looked around at the empty stadium. They were completely alone except for a handful of workers putting the finishes touches on the track and the sound of dozers.

"Oh, I guess those track builders are a pretty scary crew, huh?" she replied sarcastically.

He patted the dirt again, laughing. "I won't bite, well...unless you want me to."

She backed up a step, her eyes wide and her smile instantly wiped away.

Shit.

"I'm kidding. I'm kidding. I'm sorry. Come sit, please?"

She looked at him for what felt like ages before she hesitantly sat down beside him. He bumped her with his shoulder and lowered his voice. "Hey...I'm sorry. I was just joking around."

She drew her knees to her chest and nodded.

He ran a hand through his hair, feeling like an idiot. He should've known better than to have said something so overtly sexual to her. He got the feeling that she was really...innocent. *Damn it.* He should have seen it, but it just didn't make any sense.

Carter sat beside her for as long as he could without touching her, until he just couldn't stand it anymore. He brought his finger up under her chin to raise her face to his.

"Are you nervous?" he asked quietly when he heard her breathing catch.

"Um." Big sapphire blue eyes blinked up at him, wide with emotion.

He'd never wanted to kiss anyone more than he wanted to kiss Molly in that moment.

Carter watched her eyes as he leaned in, still holding her chin. She shivered and turned her head toward the ground, biting her bottom lip.

Sighing, Carter pulled away. "I'm sorry," he barely whispered. He really was an idiot. The first girl he had ever really wanted, and he had to ruin it by pushing her when obviously she needed time.

"I didn't mean to scare you," he said as he reached out to turn her face back to him, those eyes now sad.

Molly brought her hands up to hold his wrist. "I'm so sorry," she said as she released a shaky breath. She tightened her hold when he tried to scoot away to give her room. "Don't go," she begged. "I don't want you to go."

Carter brushed back the piece of hair that had fallen from her ponytail and smiled softly at her. He could feel the war going on in her. He could see the pulse tick in the triangle at her throat, he could hear the choppy breathing she couldn't control. "I want you to trust me, Molly. I won't hurt you. I'm not like other guys." He knew she probably had to deal with a lot of men like Dylan, but he was pretty sure it was more than that. "I won't hurt you, I promise you, Gorgeous."

Molly's eyes wandered over his face as if she was searching for the truth. He hoped desperately that she would believe him. He could say the words all day long, but he'd learned enough in the short time he'd known her to know he had to prove it to her. The only way he could do that though was if she gave him the chance. And he'd walk through fire for that chance.

She leaned in slowly and kissed him softly on the cheek, just barely grazing the skin on the side of his mouth. "We'd better get back," she whispered, "before Brody sends out a search crew for me."

"You're probably right." He stood first and then helped her up, pulling her into a hug. He felt her suck in a deep breath. Kissing the top of her head, he tucked her in close, feeling her breath on his neck. "I don't want to let you go," he said.

He ran his palm up and down her back, stroking her gently for a long minute before reluctantly releasing her. He reached down to lace his fingers through hers. "Is this okay?"

She squeezed his hand and nodded.

"So?" he said as they started walking back, hoping to lighten the mood.

"Yeah?" She grinned nervously up at him.

"You gonna give me a chance before you go get married?"

She looked at him, puzzled.

"You know, before you go and marry Eli?"

"Oh. Yeah. Oops." She smiled this sweet little smile, swinging their hands between them. "You think he'll be disappointed?"

"I bet so. He's a pretty good judge of character. You fit right in with our group."

"Well, you all are pretty cool."

"Especially me, right?" He winked at her. He liked this carefree part of her, even if he only got to see glimpses of it here and there.

She squeezed his hand. "Especially you."

Chapter Three

They continued to walk back toward the pits, but he stopped when they were in the darkened hallway, just before they would have rounded the corner and been seen.

Molly's heart sped.

He was still holding her hand, but turned to face her as he placed his other hand on her waist. She sucked in a breath when he stepped forward. Her first instinct was to be anxious, to cower back, but something in those ice blue eyes told her she didn't have to be afraid.

When he had leaned in to kiss her when they were sitting on the track, she'd panicked. And then when he had started to move away, she'd panicked again—for a different reason entirely.

Those flip-flopping emotions were about to drive her crazy.

Now, in the dimmed corridor, Molly closed her eyes to catch her breath and to search for a decision. He'd been rubbing his thumb on her waist, but his movements stopped when her eyes dropped closed. The soothing strokes didn't continue until she finally reopened her eyes and dragged her attention up his chest and past his Adam's apple. She continued up until she locked her gaze with his. When she offered him a hesitant smile, he began stroking her again with a warm smile on his lips.

Staring down at her, he let go of her hand and skimmed the back of his over her cheek. She felt her heart thundering, her pulse racing when she ran her hands up his chest, feeling each and every rippled muscle. She'd never purposely touched a man like this before. Sure, she'd felt Brody's muscles when she'd smacked him for one reason or another. Or when trying to push him off of her after he'd wrestled her to the ground being an ornery brother and all. But this? This was foreign.

Her eyes were back on her own fingers, taking everything in. She stopped at his heart and could feel it pounding hard beneath the soft cotton t-shirt.

"Just so you know…" he started in his slow, sexy voice.

She could tell he was waiting for eye contact again before continuing. "Yeah?" she whispered.

"I'm going to fall in love with you."

What? The world stopped and her eyes went wide for a brief second before they narrowed. Her head tilted, her face questioning him. "But you hardly know me." Her words came out on a barely caught breath. "We just met a few hours ago."

She was just beginning to work out in her head the fact she was touching him and that her instinct to run away was non-existent, trying to decide if she should allow him to kiss her, and he was talking about falling in – *love*?

She knew she was out of her element. But this was like trying to win a SuperCross Championship race when you've never even had your ass in the seat before.

Up to this point in her life, her heart had always been well guarded, only letting in a few special people. And that circle of people had kept her shielded, vowing to never let her be hurt again. But there was something about Carter that was she was drawn to, something different. A connection she'd never felt before with anyone.

Her pulse quickened again and she swallowed, unable to look away from his overpowering gaze. It was commanding, yet she felt cherished at the same time.

"I know you well enough to know you feel it too." He inclined his head, increasing his hold on her waist. "I *know* you feel it, this *thing* between us. This is it, Gorgeous."

He pulled her to him and held her. She closed her eyes and listened to his pounding heart. Finally, she attempted a deep breath. "I've been hurt a lot in my life, Carter, but I've never had a broken heart. I won't be able to take that."

He squeezed her tightly, then let go to cup her face in both of his hands. "I promise you, with all my heart, I'll never hurt you." He leaned down and softly kissed her lips. "I promise."

She reached up and placed her fingertips to her lips, still feeling the jolt from the feather soft kiss. The light touch had been just a hint of what was sure to come, something that sent her stomach to the ground in both fear and anticipation.

Somewhere deep in her own heart, she could feel his truth, but it didn't mean she wasn't terrified. She looked up at him, biting at her lip, and finally nodded.

"Come on," he said as he stepped away with a smile, reaching for her hand as he began to walk. He brought it to his mouth to kiss her knuckles, his demeanor shifting from heavy to light, as if he understood she needed time to process it all.

Carefree, he swung her hand, teased, "You're quiet now. I have a feeling that once you get to know people, that doesn't happen often."

"Hey."

"I'm joking." He wrapped his arm around her, pulling her close. His smile was so untroubled, his touch so warm. It wasn't difficult for her to melt into his side.

She glanced up at him. "I'm just trying to figure this all out. We just met, Carter, and...and I don't do *this*...I don't flirt with guys. And I sure as hell don't go around kissing random men. Normally, I do what I've come to do, get paid, and that's it. I don't sit around talking. I don't try to meet people. I do my job and get out. And I guess it's because, for the most part, I've only been around guys that are trying to be...ugh...I don't know...*men*."

"What do you mean?" He pulled away and took her hand again, regarding her as if he really had no idea what she was talking about.

"You know braggy, perverted, show off. Like your buddy, Dylan."

He chuckled. "We all are, Gorgeous."

"You included?" She looked at him, unable to hide the disappointment.

"Well, it takes the right girl to make a man want to act better than a twelve-year-old boy." He squeezed her hand.

"So...I'm the right girl?" she asked softly as they walked up to the group. Like she'd told Carter, she didn't flirt, didn't play games. She wasn't going to skirt around questions or assume answers. And though it was dangerous, she wore her heart on her sleeve.

He leaned down to whisper in her ear, "Yeah...you're the one, Gorgeous."

෨෴෨

"How come she's sweaty and flushed, and well, you're not?" Jesse laughed as Molly and Carter approached the group.

"Screw that. That's my fiancé." Eli hopped up and put his arm around Molly's shoulders. "Damn it, Sterling, how come you're holding hands with my girl? You're not going to fall for this guy, are you? I proposed already, you and me, we got something going girl."

"Sorry, E." She looked up, smiling between the two men who were standing close on either side of her. "I kind of already did." She grinned when Carter squeezed her hand.

Eli let out an exaggerated breath of disappointment as he squeezed her shoulders, then kissed the top of her head. "Well at least it was Sterling and not Martins. That'd have been a real blow to my ego." Laughing, Carter fist-bumped Eli as he pulled Molly close to his chest.

"Hey, jackass, I'm sitting right here," Dylan piped up.

"So?" Eli asked, not hiding the look of extreme annoyance written all over his face.

Carter sat down in a chair without letting go of Molly's hand. "Sit by me?" There was no way he wanted to lose the connection they'd made. He could tell Erin was her safety net, and even more so, Brody. Call him paranoid, but he was more than a little scared that they'd talk her out of pursuing this *thing*. Even though he knew with every bit of his soul that she was special and the woman of his dreams, he could feel the way Brody's eyes narrowed in concern as his eyes roamed over her, the way those same eyes filled in suspicion and doubt when he looked at Carter.

Molly settled into the chair beside him and he wrapped his arm around her shoulders. He met Brody's stare but didn't back down. The guy was intense and he probably scared off other men on a regular basis, but Carter thought Molly was worth putting up with the big brother bully treatment. And he didn't scare easily.

"So, did he keep up?" Jesse asked, grinning.

Carter could tell Molly was trying not to laugh, which was obviously a wasted effort. She snickered under her breath. He reached across and tickled her with his free hand. "Hey, that was our secret." His voice was low, but teasing.

Laughing, Molly answered, "I didn't say a word."

"You didn't have to." Even in separate chairs, they were close enough that he could pull her tighter. Carter looked at her friends. "Well you all could have told me she intended on running on the track and not just around it."

Brody threw Carter a cocky glance. "I knew you couldn't keep up, so why bother with a warning?"

Carter felt Molly stiffen under his arm. He glanced down to see her chin come up in a defensive stance. Even without knowing her subtleties yet, it was clear that it was a silent warning to her brother, telling him to back off. He kept the smile to himself. He could tell she was a spitfire. Carter could only assume when they got into it over something, it got ugly.

Cody winked at her. "So how far did he get?"

Molly giggled and pretended to zip her lips. Eli slapped Carter's arm. "Well that answers that, doesn't it, Sterling?"

Carter tickled her again. "Thanks a lot. You're a brat."

Carter noticed even Brody chuckled under his breath, before he said, "Go get your dinner and bring me back a burger."

"Bossy, bossy."

"Just go, kid. And bring me back a beer, too."

She rolled her eyes. "Geez, I'm going, I'm going."

She climbed to her feet, stretching her arms above her head. Carter couldn't help the grin that danced across his face when her tank top rose up, revealing a section of flat, toned abs. When she put her arms back down, he looked up at her face and caught the blush that had reddened her face. When he winked, she bit her lip. He couldn't help but love the way she was so easily embarrassed. Not that he wanted to purposely cause her discomfort, but he found it so endearing. Just another nod to how innocent she seemed to be. Another reason he felt like he needed to be the one to protect her.

Carter stood up and put his hands on her shoulders. "Come on, Gorgeous, I'll go with you."

"By the way, smartass, they don't have a salad bar. I already checked," Brody hollered after her.

She didn't even bother to turn around. Instead, she simply held up her arm and flipped him off, making the rest of the group start laughing all over again.

Brody watched Molly walking off with Carter toward the grills. He didn't trust Carter at all. He knew his type, the nice guy who plays it sweet, makes a good girl like Molly fall in love with him, and then takes off the second he gets what he wants. Over the years, he'd seen guys do it again and again, and he wasn't about to stand by and watch it happen to Molly. She was so naïve to what he saw plain as day.

Jesse nodded toward Brody. "So, what's the story on your girl? I bet she's a real heartbreaker, huh?" Jesse grinned. "I mean, look how fast she had Carter and Eli falling at her feet. You've got to have men crawling all over your house."

Brody snorted.

"Oh, *hell* no." Brody shrugged. Not those that valued their life and their family jewels.

"She's just kinda what you see is what you get. She's pretty easy going most of the time, and she works harder than anyone I know. But she really isn't one of those flirty girls. She doesn't date really at all, actually. She works too much now to have a social life. We'll be on the road with you all for the next several months. For us, it was a last minute contract. I found out Sunday night, had her out on our track Monday and Tuesday, and then hit the road to be here by today. No guy is going to put up with that shit." *Which is the way dad and I prefer it.*

"Then you add guys like him." He motioned toward Dylan and shook his head. "She has absolutely no tolerance for guys like him. Besides, Dad keeps anyone that hangs out at our house in line. They know not to mess with her or he'll kill 'em."

He rubbed his palm over his face. "The problem is we've kept her so damn sheltered that unfortunately she can be kinda naïve sometimes."

Really naïve. He rolled his shoulders. They were just going to go get dinner. Innocently. But running through his mind were pictures of his sister with Sterling's hands all over her. Brody shook his head. *Oh God, I'm losing it.* He definitely preferred when she was younger. She was easier to protect then.

Erin was right, though. At some point, they had to let her find someone. It wasn't fair that his mom and dad had each other and he had Erin. Sometime, they were all going to have to let her trust her instincts. She'd been taught how to defend herself, but God, when he thought of what could happen to her, it made him physically ill. What she'd been through before, it skewed any man's chances with her, at least in his mind.

"But you aren't actually related, though, right?" Jesse asked.

Brody shook his head. "No. She moved in with us when she was fourteen, almost fifteen, and Dad took over her training. She's a hell of a rider." Brody tried to shake himself from the worry that was eating at him.

"You okay?" Jesse asked, obviously sensing how serious he'd become.

"Yeah." Brody lowered his head. "Just a lot of history."

As they walked back with their dinners, Carter's question finally bubbled to the surface. Maybe it was stupid, but he couldn't help the little nagging in the back of his head. "So, are you and Brody always at each other like that?"

"Oh, yeah sorry." Molly snorted quietly. "We forget we're out in public. It can get kind of uncomfortable for other people who aren't used to being around us."

"No, no, it's just funny. You guys act like an old married couple."

Molly laughed out loud. "You know, he's been with Erin for years."

He did a little happy dance in his head. "Really?"

"Yep. She started hanging out around us about twelve years ago. A friend of a friend type of thing, and now they've been together for almost five years. I think. It could be more like six...hell, I don't remember."

"I would never have guessed they're together at all. They don't act like it."

Molly just shrugged. "I guess maybe they've just been together so long? I don't know."

She glanced up at him. "Why?"

He'd never considered himself a jealous person before. As a matter of fact, he'd prided himself on being a pretty easygoing guy, never minding when a woman he was dating danced with another guy or had guy friends she hung out with, even if he wasn't around at the time.

But now, with Molly? Here he was...jealous...and it was of her own damned *brother*. Even if he knew it was insane, absolutely certifiable, he was just having a hell of a time keeping that part of him that was apparently more caveman than acceptable in check. Talk about a way to scare the absolute shit out of the girl.

"No reason."

She bumped him with her shoulder. "Wondering if Brody and I were ever anything?" She grinned up at him, shaking her head as if he was completely crazy.

Cringing, he couldn't help the slight redness from coloring his cheeks. He was embarrassed she'd figured him out so easily. He couldn't help it, though. He really liked her. *Really* liked her, and he wasn't blind. He saw the way Brody kept glaring at him. Brody definitely didn't want him anywhere around Molly. He didn't take it too personally. He got the feeling Brody took the initiative to scare away all men, growling if they even looked at her. He was definitely going to have to check for knife wounds from the daggers Noland had been shooting his direction since they'd met.

She sighed, thankfully cutting him a break. "No. Never. We were practically raised together, pretty much like twins since our birthdays are so close. Half of the year we're even the same age. It's very much a brother-sister thing. It's a long story…I'll get into it sometime. I just…I owe him a lot."

They were nearing the group again so he let her comment drop. Carter snuck a look at her and smiled. "I've never met anyone like you before."

"Is that a good thing or a bad thing?"

"You're unique."

She rolled her eyes at him. "That's about as good as 'you've got a great personality, but…'"

She was grinning when she looked up at him.

"Unique is good, Gorgeous…very, very good," he said quietly as they came up behind Erin and Brody. Oh, so good. Finally after years of putting up with the wrong women, he finds the most perfect girl. He wasn't going to factor her possessive control freak of a brother into the equation or that small, minor little problem that what she did on a bike scared him to death.

"Here, Erin, exactly the way you like it," Molly said, handing Erin her food.

"Oh baby, you're my angel, I'm starving."

"Where's mine?" Brody asked her.

"Probably back at the grill, I would imagine."

This time Carter laughed when Molly did nothing to disguise the smug look she shot at Brody. He figured he'd better get over the two of them being so close if he had any chance of making this work.

"That's the thanks I get?" Brody fired back. "Rearrange my life for the next four months, drive your ass clear across the damn country, and then no dinner? Seriously?"

Molly looked at Brody with her head cocked to the side.

"Rearrange your life? *Really*? Need I remind you…I *am* your life?"

There were a few chuckles from the guys. Brody just raised one eyebrow at her response. Carter did his best to hide his pride. That would only make things worse with Brody. He had a feeling that if she'd stand up to her brother, she was definitely no doormat.

Carter had seen bits and pieces of that spunky attitude. She was going to be a challenge. And that attracted him all the more. Sweet, caring, and fire all wrapped into one. He didn't want a *yes girl*. That was half the problem with being famous. Molly on the other hand, she didn't need him like that. She was famous in her own right. She was his perfect match, all right.

"Here's your beer, now shut it." Molly smirked.

Carter could tell she loved bantering back and forth with Brody. He had watched them torment each other all afternoon, but it was plain to see how much they adored each other, too.

She shrugged. "It's not like you won't eat the rest of mine anyway."

"Then what are you going to eat?" Carter asked, suddenly concerned, and then caught himself. *Damn it.* He had this compulsive urge to be protective of her. He knew he was going to have to tamp it down or he could screw *this* up before *it* ever got off the ground.

"Oh, Lord. He's making me sound like I'm high maintenance."

Erin smacked Brody for Molly's sake. "He's just being an ass. You just eat a little healthier than most."

"Anybody that doesn't chug four energy drinks a day eats healthier than him," Molly shot back.

Carter squeezed her leg, giving in a little to that compulsion. "So what do you eat?"

"Damn it, Brody. You're making me sound like a salad picker." Molly eyed her brother from across the space.

Eli choked on his beer as Jesse and Cody came back with their dinners. "Dude, you okay?" Cody asked as he plopped into an empty chair.

Eli pointed at Molly while still laughing and half-choking. "What's a salad picker?"

Jesse grinned. "You know, one of those girls who won't eat in front of a guy. She orders a little tiny salad, then sits there and just picks at it."

Molly giggled and finished Jesse's answer, "Yeah, and then goes home and pigs out on anything she can find because she's starving."

Eli crossed to give Molly a high five. She took one more bite and then got up and crossed the group, handing Brody her plate.

Eli, still grinning, looked at her. "So what's the difference between you and a salad picker, since you ate…what…two bites off that plate?"

"I can polish off a salad. Besides, all that fried food…I can't run if I eat that crap. I'll just grab something from our motorhome later." She gave Brody a shit-eating grin. "This really was his plate. I just wanted a couple of bites."

Carter chuckled proudly.

"Speaking of running." Brody snatched the plate from her and gave her an evil eye. "Don't wake us up in the morning."

"Do I ever?"

"I'm just saying."

"Whatever." All she could do was roll her eyes. Brody was in a foul mood. One could only hope Erin could fix that, *however* she had to do it. Molly knew he was concerned about Carter. And she had no explanations for him, at least not until she could wrap her own head around it. This was new for both of them and he was going to have to back up and give her some space to figure it out.

She let out an impatient breath, blowing her long, draping bangs from her eyes. She sat back in her chair, crossed her feet at her ankles, and took a very relaxed stance. She wasn't going to fight with him about it in front of these people. They'd just met. It would take a saint's patience, but she refused to embarrass herself.

"Don't wake them up?" Cody looked at Molly. "What time do you get up?"

She shrugged nonchalantly. "I'm up usually by four or so."

"A.M.? Are you *crazy*?" Jesse asked.

"What the hell are you doing up that freaking early?" Carter looked at her, his eyebrows scrunched, mouth parted.

"Running." Her simple answer floored the guys around her. It made her all the more proud of how hard she worked. She grinned at Carter who was shaking his head. "Don't worry, I promise not to wake you up, either. I'm used to it. I only ran this afternoon because we've been on the road and I couldn't get it in before then."

Jesse looked at her, still in slight shock. "So what time do you go to bed then?"

"Well, pretty quick here."

"But…" Carter chewed a bite of food quickly and put his plate down. "You can't go yet. It's only, what, seven?"

"More like seven-thirty and that's Pacific Time. I'm running on East Coast time…you've got to remember the time change."

Carter wrapped his arm over her shoulders again, squeezing her tight to him, obviously not wanting to let her go just yet. The fatigue was setting in, and she took a deep breath and rested her head against his shoulder. She looked at Erin for support then closed her eyes to block the shock on Brody's face.

"Okay. I know this is so rude and you're not supposed to ask a woman her age, but with you curled up beside him like that, you look like you're about fourteen. I've just got to ask, are you legal?" Jesse chuckled.

"Ha ha ha, Jesse. Yes, I'm legal. I'm retired, remember? I'm twenty-six, if that makes you feel better."

"Almost twenty-seven, by the way."

She didn't even lift her head to argue with Brody's smart ass answer. "Younger than you brother." She knew he was getting sensitive about starting to feel his age and getting closer to thirty, especially when it was added to the aches and pains he'd had the last couple of years. He'd dealt his body a lot of abuse over his career.

"On that note," Erin said as she stood up, "I've got to go to bed, you boys be nice. Mol, call me if you need anything, honey."

"Thanks Erin," Molly said, yawning.

Brody stood up to get the keys out of his pocket and leaned in to kiss Erin goodnight. "I'll be there in a bit, babe."

Jesse looked between them. "Aw, look at you two," he teased, obviously making note of the chaste gesture. Erin winked to answer, before turning to walk away.

"Yeah, well, we aren't quite as into the PDA like our love birds over there," Brody said sarcastically, gesturing to Molly and Carter.

"Oh, bite me. Joey remembers what it was like four or five years ago, don't you, Joe?"

"Oh Lord yes," Joey answered with his hand covering his mouth and pretending to throw up.

"It was awful." Molly rolled her eyes as she tried not to laugh. "They were all over each other. You had to be careful walking around corners or you'd walk in on them making out. Especially in the shop when James was at work. Joey and I both saw way more than we ever wanted to see…and on separate occasions." She could see Brody smile to himself. She laid her head back down against Carter's strong shoulder, liking the safety she felt next to him, something she definitely needed to think about. Maybe tomorrow, when she wasn't so tired.

"Speaking of PDA," Dylan said as he looked at Molly, snickering as he tried to be funny, "I thought you said she wasn't that kind of girl. Are we sure? You said she wasn't a flirt, but I think she passed flirt a long time ago."

Oh my God, will he not shut up? Molly had taken several deep breaths throughout the afternoon and evening to block out his remarks and nasty comments. She had been flirting with Carter, but she had done nothing to deserve the crap this asshole had dealt her at every turn. Even she had a breaking point. She sat up and eyed him with a glare. Before she could open her mouth to speak, Carter was out of his chair and in Dylan's face.

"I sure as *hell* hope you're joking."

Jesse smacked Dylan hard. "Dude, you looking to get your ass handed to you tonight? If so, keep talking." He scanned the circle. The joking and laughing had come to an abrupt halt and both Brody and Joey had immediately flanked Carter's sides.

"You know what, jackass, you've been making snide and rude comments all night. Everything that has come out of your mouth has been a slap at her. I've tried to let it go and to ignore you. But dude, you just went too far."

"Oh yeah, Sterling, what are you going to do about it?"

"Carter!" Molly pled as she tried to calm him down.

"How old are you?" Brody asked with a laser pointed glare locked on the man.

Dylan looked Brody up and down. "Why? What's it to you?" Dylan continued to glower back at him, but he finally answered, "nineteen."

"Okay, so let me put this in perspective for you."

"Oh yeah?" Dylan stood and crossed his arms, then sneered back at Brody.

"She started racing, *not riding*, but racing when she was four. So she'd been racing for two, almost three years by the time you were even born. She put her time in and retired the best of the best. Then I moved her into freestyle, trained her hard, day in and day out, and she competed for two more years. Now she works. She's worked hard her whole life to get to where she is today. She's never even so much as had a boyfriend, so I don't know where you get off being a dick. She rode when she was sick, she rode through every holiday, hell she's ridden with broken bones more times than I can count."

Molly gasped. She couldn't believe Brody had just said that. That was something she didn't want brought up. It was the last thing she wanted to explain to complete strangers.

"Brody!" Her heart began racing.

"She's getting paid to be here, so don't you ever compare her to those little girls who drool all over you guys. You are a cocky little shit with a God's gift to women complex, and you're just pissed off that she didn't fall down at your feet."

"Yeah, well I can't help it if she's been all over him like a tramp all..."

Carter came across his nose with his right fist faster than Dylan could finish his sentence. Dylan bent over, blood gushing all over the concrete floor. "Son of a bitch. You broke my nose."

Molly froze.

"Don't you *ever* talk about her like that again. You got me, asshole?"

"You broke my fucking nose."

"I don't give a flying fuck," Carter spat out the words. "You will never talk to her like that again. As a matter of fact, you'd best do your damnedest to avoid her, or I'll finish your ass."

"What the fuck?"

"I mean it, Martins. One more nasty word out of your mouth and I'll beat the living shit out of you."

"Carter!" Molly tried to wiggle loose of Eli's hold. "Just Stop. You're going to get into trouble with George. Eli, please...let me go!" She flung her arms, fighting the hold. She knew Eli was trying to help by keeping her a safe distance from the possible brawl, but she hated behind restrained. A couple of other riders had joined in on Dylan's side, but Jesse, Brody, and Joey had Carter's back. At this rate, if this got out of hand, it looked like it was going to be an all out mess. Because *of her.*

"Oh God. Carter...stop! Eli!" she begged as she continued to fight the arms around her, but he was so much stronger. *Oh my God.* "Stop." Panic engulfed her before she could stop it. She went limp, except for the racking sobs coming from deep within.

"Noland!"

Brody turned at Eli's startled yell.

"Oh my God, Molly!" Brody forgot all about Carter, Dylan, and the fight. Eli had sunk to the ground with Molly crying in his arms. Brody dropped to her side, scooping her up.

This was the last thing Molly needed. When she calmed down a little bit, Brody knew she was going to be mortified. He whispered to her, letting his voice bring her back down while he cradled her in his arms and gently rocked her. He slipped his phone from his back pocket.

Handing Eli the phone, he rocked Molly while giving him directions. "Erin is number one on speed dial, call her. Please."

Eli nodded, stood, and stepped away with the phone.

Carter was on his knees across from them, his expression shocked. "What's...?"

Brody ignored him, continuing to whisper to Molly as he rocked her.

"Brody." The choppy whisper tore his heart up.

"It's okay baby. I've got you. It's okay. Shh...it's okay." He held on tightly to her middle, but never constricted her arms.

"Carter?"

Brody cringed, but answered, "He's right here, sweetie...don't worry."

The crowd parted for the loud voice.

Shit. Could this get any worse?

Brody heard George coming before he could see him.

"What the hell is going on here?" George dropped to his knees when he saw Molly and Brody on the floor. "What happened? Is she all right?"

Brody nodded. "You need to get everyone away from here. Wait." He swallowed hard, trying his best to keep his composure and his voice calm. "Sterling, Frost, and Hunter can stay."

Chapter Four

After she'd had to give George the gory details plus a long phone call to James, Carter could tell Molly was exhausted. When she announced she was going back to their motorhome to go to bed, he jumped at the chance to be alone with her and offered to walk her back. Brody had scoffed, but Carter watched out of the corner of his eye as Erin quieted him down. It looked like he had an ally. That was a helpful piece of knowledge to keep tucked away.

He walked at a slow pace with her pulled close to his side, wanting to make the minutes last as long as possible, wanting to keep her with him.

And he really did, he wanted to keep her in his arms, permanently.

He sucked in a quick breath as the meaning seeped into him. He knew he felt like she was the one, but the force of that word hit him like a two-ton truck. All of a sudden he felt lighter than he had in years. Even after the last forty-five minutes of hell, he all of a sudden felt amazing, like he finally had the answer to one of life's hardest puzzles.

She snuggled into his side and he could feel how relaxed she was with him. It made his heart swell even more. She'd fallen to pieces during that whole fiasco. Brody had brushed it under the rug as a reaction to violence. No big deal. *What the hell*? It was a big deal, a very big deal. But she had pulled herself together within minutes and with such grace, he had to admire her strength.

"Come here, Gorgeous." Carter pulled her closer to him.

"Hey Molly." He tightened his grip on her in case she should try to pull away. "I heard what Brody said, but sweetheart, there's more to this story. Even if you are opposed to violence, it was *one* punch. I sure as hell didn't mean to scare you, but I have a feeling it's way more than what Brody let on."

He felt her stiffen, but she didn't say anything, so he continued, "I won't pry, but if you ever want to talk, I'm here. I want you to know that. I'll always be right here, I'm not going anywhere."

With her body next to his, he felt the deep breath she took. After several silent moments, she nodded.

He knew she wasn't going to tell him anything tonight. But that nod was an admission. He had a feeling tonight's episode had to do with how skittish she was and how protective her brother was. And after hearing her and Brody on the phone with their father, he knew Brody was a walk in the park compared to James.

As they walked out of the large, dim walkway toward where the motorhomes were parked, he kissed her head. They wound their way around to hers. He glanced up at her door. He'd hang onto anything he could to keep her from walking through it. Knowing he wasn't getting any information tonight and that he wanted to keep her in his arms just a little longer, he changed the subject. "So? Who'd have thought I'd meet the girl of my dreams today?" His tone was playful.

Molly looked up at him. "The girl of your dreams, huh? Are you *crazy*? Were you not there and *involved* in a fight? Over *me*?" She paused. "I talk like a trucker and I ride a dirt bike for a living. I'm not exactly the girl you take home to mom."

"Oh, yes you are, you're perfect...perfect for me," Carter said in a low voice.

Suddenly the jovial mood he was going for went serious. With one hand on her waist, he pulled her closer. He ran his finger under her chin and brought her face to his. So much had happened since the last time he'd tried to kiss her. But he was caught up in the moment and wasn't thinking. Before his brain could warn him to give her space, he bent and kissed her gently on the lips, so light it was almost a whisper.

He pulled away a few inches to look at her...waiting for her to stop him, but hoping she wouldn't. Her shallow, jagged breaths gave her away. She wanted him. He leaned in to kiss her again, cradling the back of her neck with one hand as he slid the other to her cheek, stroking it with his thumb. When he felt her put her hand to his heart, he prayed like hell it wasn't to stop him. Instead, she parted her lips just a little, and he took the invitation, tilting his head to the side to deepen the kiss. He slipped his tongue over hers, just slightly, instinct telling him to take it very slow with her. The deep breath was necessary as they slowly broke.

He watched her eyes flutter open and he grinned at her. She still had her hand on his heart and he still had her face in his hands. Carter gazed into her deep blue eyes—the deepest sapphire blue he'd ever seen.

"Please, Molly. Tell me you felt that too," he begged desperately in a low voice. Carter didn't care if he was begging, he'd get on his knees if he had to. He'd been immediately attracted to her, but he knew something was different. That wasn't *just* a kiss.

"Yes," Molly whispered. She touched her tongue to her top lip, wanting to taste him again, her breathing still shaky. Pure habit when nervous, she bit her bottom lip again. As she did, she heard him suck in a sharp breath.

"Between listening to your breathing and the little lip thing you're doing right now, you're about to make me lose my control, Gorgeous."

Her mind was spinning, almost as fast as her heart was racing. She'd been kissed before, she wasn't a complete moron. But not a toe curling, stomach dropping, sparks shooting kiss like that. Oh, wow. Wait, what did he say, *lose control*? Her breath came out with a whoosh.

"Um."

"It's okay. I'm teasing, I promise. I didn't mean to make you nervous," he said softly while rubbing her back to keep her calm.

You mean more nervous?

"I'm…I'm okay," she said with as much confidence as she could gather. She took a deep breath. "This seems surreal. I like to know what's going to happen next, to be in control. You know, have things planned out."

"Sometimes," he whispered, "there's a bigger plan out there and we don't have the answers to it."

"Sure feels like that, huh? It's kinda scary, don't you think?"

"Why's that?" He stroked her back. "You're not scared of me, are you?"

"No, no, not at all. It's *this*. I mean, twelve hours ago life was very different. I was missing home and my family and I wasn't ready to be gone for four months."

She couldn't help the sickening feeling she just had. James. Ugh. She'd thrown the equivalent of a temper tantrum before they'd left town. She had just gotten home from one contract job to find out that two days later she had to leave for another. And this was a long one. When he found out she not only wasn't mad anymore, but that she was excited about being here—God, he'd never let her live it down. Then he'd lecture her on men.

She had that one memorized, probably because she'd heard it regularly since she was fourteen years old. She only mimicked it verbatim when his back was turned. She loved the man with all her heart, but she had to admit she was a teensy bit worried about how he'd take the news of Carter. Well, more than a teensy bit. She was more like scared to death for Carter's safety. She bit the inside of her cheek to keep the smile under control. She didn't want to scare the man off by explaining what was going through her mind at that moment, especially since he'd stuck out the panic attack.

"But now?" he asked in his low, sexy voice, hugging her to him.

He continued to rub her back and rested his cheek on the top of her head. He didn't know it, but his voice was such a comfort to her. When he lowered it like that, it could almost slip her into a peaceful trance.

"But now, I want time to stand still." She pulled in a breath of his cologne, his scent like a magnet.

"Me too."

"We're moving really fast, Carter."

She knew it was one kiss, a hell of a kiss, but—*one* kiss. But combined with other comments he'd slipped in here and there? She knew what he meant when he said she was *the one*. He was talking about something much bigger than just a weekend fling. She wouldn't have done that anyway, but he was making *this* into *more*. Way more.

Plus, if she had to be honest, he deserved points. Most men would have run like their ass was on fire when they saw her in a heap of tears on the floor. He hadn't. He'd been sweet, nurturing, and if she wasn't mistaken, scared to death. He also hadn't pushed her. He hadn't made her feel bad when she denied his earlier kiss, he hadn't pushed her to talk when she wasn't ready, and he wasn't pushing for more right now. He seemed happy to go at the pace she was setting.

"Fast is relative. When its right, you don't measure it, and we aren't teenagers." He laughed lightly. "You can't even consider us *young adults* anymore, Gorgeous. And look at the thousands of people who go to bed together the first night they meet or have one night stands."

"That's not me," she said softly, then shut her eyes.

"I know, baby." He had figured out that she was only confident and out-spoken around their big group. When he was alone with her, she was quiet, sweet, and vulnerable. He grinned to himself, completely in love with both sides of her already, but also proud that she trusted him. Seeing first-hand how fast she could throw a wall up against men that wanted to be with her.

"Carter, I have never really had a boyfriend before." She took a deep breath at her admission.

"Never? I find that hard to believe."

"No. There was never anyone worth the effort of a long distance relationship. We grew up on the road. Hell, I'm still on the road a lot. You live the same way, you know what it's like. So why bother? I have been on a few dates over the last few years, but just a date and usually just once. It doesn't take long to figure out that they're all just the same. But here…tonight…with you? I've been acting like a ditzy, flirty girl. I've been hanging on you all night. Uh…your friends are going to think I'm easy."

"I knew you were the kind of girl to worry about that."

"I do. Look, it started a fight."

"There was nothing you did that started that fight. I promise you, Molly. That was all on Martins. He's a jackass. Don't you dare feel guilty over that. Please? And as for you hanging on me, you weren't. But I'll admit, I like it. I like having your hand in mine, my arm around you. I love your head on my shoulder. I could tell you were able to relax around me. If you consider all that hanging on me, I'll take it."

"That's a *man* answer." She softly chuckled.

With her still in his arms, he whispered in her ear in an even lower voice, one with an edge to it, "I am a man."

Her stomach did another flip flop, but then her mind caught up and her heart dropped. *Like you need to remind me?* She looked up at him with an eyebrow raised. "Yeah, and I'm sure you've got women throwing themselves at you."

"Not really."

"I don't believe that for a minute."

"I don't."

"Carter, you are incredibly good looking and you have killer eyes. So no, I don't believe you." A cocky, slow grin danced across his face. "Oh, don't you look at me like that," she teased. "You know you're absolutely amazing, don't play innocent with me." His hands slid down to her butt, pulling her as close as he possible could.

"Oh yeah?" He raised his eyebrows up at her a couple of times.

"Yeah." Her eyes were as wide as saucers, but she wasn't minding that his hands were on her, and she was loving the crooked grin on his face. It made him appear almost boyish when just seconds before he was—almost—hungry. Boyish she could handle. Hungry scared the shit out of her.

"So…"

"So?"

"Am I worth a long distance relationship?"

Her heart went from zero to sixty from the excitement and the fact he really did like her. Karen had always told her there would be someone. She felt her insides go gooey and her cheeks get warm.

Feeling a little braver, she said, "Depends." She grinned up at him, getting a small thrill off the control.

He squeezed her butt. It was a total possessive move on his part and she knew it. "Oh yeah? On what?"

"On how long it takes you to kiss me again."

"That I can do, Gorgeous."

She slid her arms up to his neck and smiled at him. Then she bit her bottom lip. He smiled his slow, sexy grin that kept driving her insane. There went the control, back to Carter — she had no power against that smile. "What? You're staring." She giggled nervously. She gave herself a mental slap upside the head for sounding like a goofy teenage girl.

He smiled down at her and she melted all over again. "I'm just…"

"Just making me nervous," she finished for him.

"I just can't get over the fact that I get to be the man holding you. I get to be the man to kiss you."

"I was thinking that I'm the lucky one."

He leaned down to kiss her and she slid one palm to his cheek. With her other hand, she threaded her fingers through the back of his hair just as she parted her lips to kiss him. When he pulled her even closer to him, she sighed. The move was intentional. He needed her to know how much he wanted her — to feel how badly he wanted her. A part of him needed her to know how hard he was struggling to keep himself under control, to silently prove to her she was safe with him.

He broke the kiss and pulled her tight to him, the man in him wishing she wouldn't object to going back to his motorhome. But he knew she wasn't ready for that. He drew back. "Oh my God." He breathed heavily, just standing there holding her, willing himself to behave. Carter finally caught his breath and pulled away a few inches to look at her before he leaned his forehead to hers. "Oh girl, what you do to me."

She looked up at him and graced him with the sweetest smile he had ever seen. "I don't want to let you go," she whispered.

"So…" he replied just as quietly, "Don't. Tell me I'm worth it, that you'll do long distance. Please."

She reached up to kiss him gently. "You're worth everything."

Chapter Five

"He should have been back by now. I'm going to go check on them." Brody started to stand, but Erin reached out to stop him.

"Brody...don't. Let them be. She's fine."

"Erin. You don't understand."

"Excuse me? I don't understand *what*? That she's a twenty-six-year-old woman? That she has a drop dead beautiful man following her around like a puppy dog. That he's probably kissing her goodnight. I get it Brody." She rubbed his leg. "I also get that she's a grown woman, one that deserves this. You have to let her be. If not now, when?"

"But Erin."

"She's lonely, Brody."

"She has us. She has Mom and Dad."

"You're forgetting I've been around the last twelve years. I know why you and your parents are so protective. But she talks to *me*. I know she's lonely because she's told *me*. I know she wants what we have because she's told *me*. And she can't find it because *you* won't let her."

He didn't need to stick around and listen to this shit. He was going to go check on his sister. *Probably kissing goodnight.* Hell. He'd watched Sterling all night. There was no *probably* to it. Just the thought of that had his blood starting to boil. He stood up.

"Fine, Brody…go. But that guy has sat here all damned afternoon and evening, putting up with your shit, without even one nasty remark. We could all see and feel it…you've been a jackass to him. The closer he got to her, the bigger ass you became. Add to it that he defended her honor and risked getting in trouble without so much as a second thought. He deserves some respect. You need to cut the guy some slack."

He stood holding the back of the chair, his knuckles turning white from gripping it so hard. He narrowed his eyes at his girlfriend, took a breath in, and gritted his teeth even harder. Erin was right. But it didn't make it any easier and Molly was still his to protect, whether Erin or Molly liked it.

"You're suffocating her. You have to let her go. She *needs* space."

"She needs *me*," he slapped back.

Erin stood and walked around to face him. He loved and hated the way she stood up to him. She never backed down from a fight, but as much as he loved her, he wished she wouldn't square off with him, not here. Not on this subject.

"Brody, she'll *always* need you." Her voice was calmer, but he still heard the force behind it. "Just not the same way as she did when she was younger. She's made a lot of progress today. The fact she's even giving Carter a chance, that's a good thing. We're here. Nothing's going to happen to her. I promise. If he hurts her, I'll kill him myself. In the meantime…space. You *have* to give her space."

She tried to wrap her arms around him. He held stiff for half a minute and finally cracked. Pulling her to him, he took a deep breath. He knew he could trust Erin's judgment. If she was so adamantly defending this…whatever this *thing* between Carter and his sister was, then he should listen. It was just a damn shame that his sanity went right out the window wherever Molly was concerned. What could he say—he'd learned from the best. He pulled away and patted Erin's arm.

"I'll be back."

"Don't you embarrass her, Brody Noland, or pull the bully treatment on him. I have no problem killing you, either."

He nodded at the threat and turned to walk toward his motorhome. He chuckled nervously to himself. He wasn't scared of Erin killing him, he was more nervous of what she'd do prior to the long, tortuous death. She didn't fight like a girl, she went straight for his balls and squeezed until she got what she wanted. It was too bad they didn't see eye-to-eye on this subject.

He rolled his shoulders, trying to shake some of the unnecessary panic. After Molly was safely tucked in the motorhome, he needed to call his dad. There was no way around it. It already sounded like his dad had picked up on something earlier when they spoke to him after the fight. But he had to lay it out there. Brody was done dealing with *this* by himself.

He rounded the corner and his jaw dropped. He stood stock still, he legs suddenly heavier than concrete as he watched his sister. She had one hand up Carter's neck, her fingers in his hair. The other was on his jaw. Sterling's hands were of course on her ass. Of course. Where else would they be? He watched as they kissed…intimately. His heart started pounding almost as hard as pain in his head. *Oh my God. What the hell?*

They both looked at him. Shit. He wasn't aware he'd spoken out loud. He took a breath and walked closer. The pain in his forehead spiked when he clenched his teeth even tighter. He blinked a couple times and forced his mouth open to relieve the pressure.

"What the hell is going on here?"

"Nothing, Brody. Goodnight."

"Ah-huh. Goodnight is right. Go on in the motorhome. I need to talk to Sterling."

"No!" She turned around, shaking her head.

"What do you mean no? Go to bed."

"I'm not a little girl. You don't just dismiss me and send me to bed. Bite me, Brody. Go back to the pits with Erin."

He watched Molly as she took a defiant stance. She stood taller, her eyes narrowed. But she hadn't let go of *him* yet. And Sterling still had one arm around her waist keeping her close to him. Oh, they were pissing him off more and more. Standing there like some united front against him. He let out a shaky breath and lowered his voice, but even he could hear the anger in it. "Good. Night. Molly."

"Don't do this, Brody. You don't want to start this."

"Try me."

"It's okay, Gorgeous." Carter's voice was calm and soothing. And while Brody watched his sister melt into it, it grated on his nerves.

"You go, you're so tired. It's fine. I'll talk to Brody. It's time we had a few words, anyway."

"Carter."

"It's okay, really, honey. We'll meet in the morning and have breakfast together. Okay?"

Brody stood silent as Carter talked his sister into the motorhome. The pain in his forehead made him wince and he realized he'd been gritting his teeth again. He waited none so patiently with his arms crossed as she finally conceded. It pissed him off even more that she'd only done so when *Sterling* told her to.

"I'll apologize for my brother's attitude. I love him, but he's being an *asshole*!"

Molly's blue eyes were almost black when he looked in them. He never had her anger turned on him before. Not like this. He was completely taken aback by it. But he wasn't backing down. She was naïve, innocent, blind, and didn't know what she was doing. He did. He narrowed his gaze, but kept his retort to himself.

"Gorgeous, its fine. I understand where he's coming from. Everything will be fine, no worries. You go on, get some rest and I'll see you in the morning."

Brody's anger was fanned as he watched Carter stroke his sister's cheek, then lean down and kiss her again. A peck on the lips, but a kiss nonetheless. The man had balls. He was going to have them on a platter if the guy didn't back away from his sister.

"Night, baby."

Carter shut the door and took a second to himself before turning to face her brother. "Listen."

"No. You listen. I very distinctly remember telling you and your buddies she was off limits. And yet, here *you* are. And now, I walk up to see your hands all over her. In my book, that makes you no better than that Martins prick."

Carter narrowed his eyes. "Don't you *ever* compare me to him. You got me?"

"You don't even know her. I'm not going to let you take advantage of her."

"I *am* not and *will* not take advantage of her. And no, I don't know her inside and out—yet." Carter let the single word hang. The smoke billowing out of Brody's ears meant he understood. "But...I am getting to know her little by little. I know she's sweet, funny, beautiful, and from watching her with you and Joey, I know she's got quite an ornery streak. I personally find that hysterical. I know she's timid and shy and I get the feeling she's fairly innocent."

"Which," Brody interrupted, "is why you're going to leave her alone."

"If not me, then who, Brody? You going to chase off every man that comes along?"

"It's been working up to this point."

"Maybe for you, but what about her?" When Brody didn't answer, Carter shook his head. "I'm not going anywhere."

"You don't know what she's been through."

Brody was right. He didn't know, and the scenarios that ran through his mind all made him sick to his stomach. He had dated enough women who had brothers to know this was not a common reaction. Something about the whole night was off. The melt down she'd had during the confrontation with Dylan, the way Brody had been treating him all evening, and now this? Something was way off.

"You know what, Noland, you're right. I don't know what she's been through, and I told her when she was ready, she could tell me. I'm not going to push her, but I'm not stupid. She's been through something obviously traumatic, and I'll be here for her when she's ready. I won't push. Just like I won't push her for anything else. *Ever.*"

"I'm not buying that shit."

This guy was a real piece of work. Luckily for Carter, one of the many things he'd learned from his parents was *patience*. It was a necessity on the track, but in this situation, it was a godsend. He blew out a breath and looked toward the door Molly had disappeared through moments ago. He could imagine her sitting close to the window, even though the blinds were closed. He pictured her listening to every word through the thin walls. It wasn't as if either one of them was trying to keep their voices down.

Carter had heard the story of his parents' whirlwind relationship a thousand times. How they met and it was love at first sight. How his dad fell madly in love with this beautiful girl in the library while in college and offered to walk her to her dorm when she was finished studying. They were engaged a month later. Married three months after that. But he never heard anything negative from his grandfather. Surely he must have been a little nervous, like Brody. But Carter knew he had never heard of any knock down drag outs over it.

Love at first sight could happen. It worked for his parents and they'd been happily married for over thirty-five years. He felt it with Molly. With every fiber of his being, he felt she was his. His, as simple as that. Carter's heart swelled and his anger faded. His to cherish. His to protect. His to love.

He took another deep breath and turned back to Brody. "We can play this however you want. You can fight me all you want or we can get along, but at the end of the day," Carter waved his hand toward the door, "It's still her choice. And I'll do whatever I have to do to prove to her how much I care for her. It might be quicker than rationally possible, but I'm falling fast for that girl. And like I said, I'm not going *anywhere*."

Carter nodded toward the door and snickered out loud. "Now I'm willing to bet money she's sitting right inside that door, listening to every word we've said. And there's only one of us that looks like an *ass* right now."

Carter patted the door to the motorhome twice. "Goodnight, Gorgeous. See you at breakfast." He turned back around. "It's your call, Noland."

As he walked past Brody, he gave him a hard pat on the back. "Night."

જ∘ઉ

Molly and Carter sat together the next morning, eating breakfast at a plastic table outside Brody's utility trailer. Carter's hand was on her thigh, lightly stroking her skin with his thumb as she drank her protein shake and happily chatted with him. She sneaked a look over at the man sitting so close. She could feel the heat radiating off his body and her heart skipped a beat—again. She might have to look into getting a medical device to keep it regulated, because, hot damn, the man was killing her.

Brody came trudging up from the motorhome and pulled up a chair beside them with Erin following close behind. "How in the hell can you drink that shit?" Brody said as he plopped down into the chair.

Well, apparently Brody was going for round two. Molly had seen him make an ass out of himself around guys before and it never bothered her. And if she had to be honest with herself, she was always thankful he ran interference for her. This time he was taking things to a whole new level. Somewhere along the way, he'd bypassed crazy on his way to flat out insane.

"Geez. Good morning to you, too. What?" Molly held up her bottle. "This tastes good. I really like the chocolate. The vanilla is nasty, but this one tastes fine."

Popping the tab on his energy drink, Brody took a drink. "And you argue with me all the time on the modeling contracts."

Damn. He's just trying to start something. Molly blew out a breath, taking her bangs with it. "That's because I'm no model," she said through gritted teeth.

"Yeah, well, working out two to three hours a day and drinking that crap and living off that nasty grass shit you pass off as *salad* is what makes you a photographer's wet dream."

"Damn it, Brody," she said in almost a snarl. "Don't be so damn crude. That's gross. Why do you always say that?" She took in the scowl and tempted the fates above. "Did you not sleep well or something? What's wrong with you this morning?"

Brody almost growled. "Bite me."

"That's my line."

Erin stood back up and held out a hand for Brody. "You want to go walk around for a little bit?"

Oh thank God. At least Erin was going to get him out of there. Molly smiled at her in appreciation. Erin rolled her eyes and shrugged. Molly knew that Erin thought Brody was out of line and was doing everything to help. She mouthed *It's okay,* and winked as she pulled Brody's arm, trying to tug him out of the chair.

"You sure you feel up to it?" Brody asked Erin as he looked up at her.

"Yeah, I just need some fresh air."

Brody eyed Carter and Molly still sitting at the table. "You two stay out of trouble. That's the last thing I need."

They started to walk away and Molly hollered after them, "Hey, Dad, I'm not fifteen anymore."

Erin turned back around to smile. "That's exactly what he's afraid of."

When they disappeared around the corner, Molly lowered her head to her hands. She waited a few seconds before running her hand through her hair and turning to see the lop-sided grin of Carter beside her. He had no anger, no embarrassment. He seemed to be taking this all in stride.

"I'm sorry, Carter. I really am."

"Don't apologize, Molly. It's not a big deal, I understand."

"You shouldn't *have* to understand. That's my point. You shouldn't have to put up this."

"So, when are you practicing today?" Great. A subject change. Completely new to this *guy thing,* she couldn't help but wonder what that meant. "George told me three."

"The guys and I are going to come watch, if that's okay?"

"Yeah, no biggie."

"So, modeling huh?"

Molly rolled her eyes but stayed silent. She loved being on a bike, but she knew her skills, like her beauty, were fleeting. Someday she'd wake up and she would be the *has been.* Not a comforting feeling, but a real one nonetheless. In the meantime, she did the exhibitions and modeling to cash in on her name. She didn't need the money now, so she tucked every penny away for the future. She hated the modeling, especially the shoots where she wasn't covered from head-to-toe in gear, but they paid damn well.

She had grown up on a track. She and Brody were homeschooled so they could travel. She hadn't made it to college yet because she'd been too busy winning. So far as much as she hated to admit it, her pretty face along with her name in the sport were earning her much more than she ever could working nine-to-five in an office building somewhere.

"What? It's no big deal. I'm just not a model, no biggie."

Carter raised an eyebrow, completely serious. "You've got to be kidding, right? Have you looked in a mirror?"

"Um, yeah." It was the mirror that was her second biggest enemy these days. Her memory was her arch nemesis. *I have muscles, whoopee.* It was the scars that she couldn't hide that floored her. A real model needed perfection and that was something she simply couldn't give, no matter how well she controlled everything around her, to make her body perfect. The hours spent sweating in the gym, the miles she logged running, it would never be enough. She absentmindedly snaked a delicate hand up to her shoulder. "Yeah, that's why I know I'm no model. I don't like people staring at me. With an ad, it's you on the paper that people are looking at. Put me in gear and I'm fine. Put me on my bike, even better. Anything less makes me cringe. Paycheck or no paycheck, I just don't like it."

"But Gorgeous, we all saw you last night, you're beautiful."

She looked at him as he hesitantly finished, her eyebrow slowly rising.

"What do you mean, you all *saw* me last night?"

"When you and I ran. Your workout clothes are….well." It seemed as if he let the description hang open-ended on purpose.

"Well, normally no one is ever up when I workout. But it's still different than when people are truly staring at you."

"And you don't think that every one of us wasn't staring at you last night?" he asked, grinning nervously.

With blinding speed, her jaw dropped. "Like *staring,* staring? Eww!" She tried to cover herself up with her hands. "No, not until you just said that. You all are just...*eww*...a bunch of nasty boys."

"Look at the bright side...you're freaking hot."

"Whatever."

"You do know that, right?" His face and voice had turned sincere.

"Well, if your idea of hot looks like a boy, then okay."

Carter turned to face her as they sat at the little plastic table. He squeezed her leg again and rubbed her arm with his other hand. He gave her a sweet smile. "You do not look like a boy, you're ripped. I mean seriously, you're muscular and toned from head to toe."

"Yeah, and have no boobs. I'm not stupid, guys like big boobs."

"You have no body fat on you. You're not going to have big boobs, I know you know that."

"Well still."

"Well, I think you're perfect, and you have an amazing body."

She blushed and looked away.

"What are you so embarrassed for?"

She smiled nervously. "I don't know. It's just...it's just. I don't know. Having a guy talk about me like that is embarrassing."

"I think it's sweet that you are so shy with this, but please..." He pulled her chin toward him with his finger. "Please don't be embarrassed with me, okay?"

"I'll try," she said very quietly.

"Molly?"

"Yeah." She looked back down.

"Molly?" She wasn't going to look at him, so he did it for her. Putting his finger back under her chin again, he brought her face to his.

She could feel the fire in her cheeks; it tingled all the way down her neck to her chest. The conversation had hit that awkward point. She wanted nothing more than to run for the comfort of her motorhome, to shy away from the embarrassment. But the love in his face kept her rooted where she sat. She whispered before he could ask flat out, "I know what you're going to ask."

"Oh, yeah?" he said softly.

She shut her eyes. "The answer is no."

"Really?"

"No, never." She tried to look down again, but his fingers wouldn't let her. She finally opened her eyes to look at him. "So…now what?" she asked quietly.

Wow. She's all mine. Absorbed in his own thoughts and wanting to scream out that this beauty was his, he finally blinked. When he did, her face broke his heart. As hard as she tried, she couldn't mask the embarrassment and hesitation. Ashamed at his own selfishness, Carter smiled lovingly at her then leaned in to kiss her softly on the lips. Here he was, wanting to celebrate, and she was ready for him to drop her like yesterday's news. He kissed her again, trying to apologize.

"I think that's amazing," he answered quietly.

"Amazing that I've never been with a guy and I don't know what I'm doing? And you might have to be with me for a long time before I'm ready to have sex with you?"

His heart raced, thinking her first time might be with him that she might find him worthy. "Well Gorgeous, you've known exactly what to do so far. And you're worth waiting for. As long as you want, I'm not going anywhere. Honestly, I think it's amazing that I won't have to share that part of you with anyone before me." He gave her a small smile, trying to be calm when all he wanted to do was jump up and down with his fist in the air.

"Every time I look in your eyes, my heart stops for a second. You have the bluest eyes I've ever seen and a truly spectacular body, and…" He ran his fingers through her hair, letting the sheet of gold fall. "I just want to hold you and not ever let go."

She bit her bottom lip. "And when you do that lip thing you do, it about drives me insane. I know you do it when you're nervous, but it is so sexy."

Molly's eyebrows furrowed.

"You don't get it do you? You aren't even trying to be sexy and you are. How can you not have had guys beating down your door?"

She shrugged and a tiny grin escaped. "Have you *met* Brody? Then wait until you meet James. You'll know why."

"Thanks for the warning." Carter winked at her.

Damn, those ice blue eyes were beautiful. But it was that lop-sided grin that allowed her to be able to bare her soul. When he smiled, it graced his whole face and she could feel herself melt a little more each time. She pushed her nerves aside and continued.

"I've never really been looking for someone. I've been busy. I practically live on the road and I've met thousands of people over the years. But that's not how you find someone special when most of your conversations are ten words or less. I know I'm really old to be a virgin," she shrugged as she said it, embarrassed, but wanting to be open with him. "And I haven't really had some big plan to wait until I am married to be with a man, but I wanted to at least be in love with him."

She risked a look back at his face. She didn't want to scare him off with plans of forever. *I'm not hinting, I promise.* "For some reason, I just kind of thought that when the time was right, the right guy would just show up. Sounds so…storybook, huh?" She huffed out a breath.

"Kind of like a prince, huh?"

"Or like a knight in shining armor?" She smiled sweetly at him.

Carter continued to rub her leg. "I have to tell you…I kind of already knew."

"Knew?" She paused. "*Oh.* How?" Molly could feel her face warm, but she was interested in his answer, so she made herself keep eye contact.

"You made some comments last night that I picked up on. And at the track last night, I could tell."

"Tell how?"

"You're just…"

"Just what?"

"Just timid when we touch…and kiss…or when I talk about your body. And I realized that I spooked you a few times with jokes and comments, which, sweetheart, I'm so sorry."

Molly turned redder. "Is that a bad thing?"

"No, of course not. I think it's very sweet. I can just tell you're a bit shy and pretty nervous. Just like a second ago when I started to ask if you've ever been with anyone. I was pretty sure you hadn't, but you could hardly look me in the eye."

This was the part of the conversation that was going to put her all in. She blew out a breath and went for broke. She normally played her cards close, but not when hearts were on the line. "And that is exactly why guys don't come around. They know they're not going to get what they're looking for, so they don't even bother. At home I've got a pretty good reputation for being cold when it comes to men and dating. You add Brody and James in to the mix, and well, guys quit trying…which is fine. I'm not looking for a good time, Carter. I want more. I just want to be honest with you up front. I don't want to scare you off, but…" She shook her head.

She didn't know where her sudden bravery came from, but it all tumbled out. Molly knew her heart would hurt if he walked away, but she just couldn't invest more time without the truth. Every hour, every minute she was with him she got more and more attached. She just hoped that there was someone out there that could make her heart race like he did, because up until now, it had never happened. "But I don't want you thinking I've changed things on you. If you don't want to do serious, that's fine. But I'm not—"

He interrupted her with a scorching kiss before she got the threat out. With her face still cupped in his hands, he murmured, "Shh. Gorgeous, it's okay. Trust me, that *is* attractive to some guys, to me. I don't want one of those 'in your face, hang on you women' that tend to follow some of the guys around. That's not me. I'm excited that you're not in this just for the weekend and a good time. I want more too, Molly. I told you yesterday, I knew it the second we met. When I looked in your eyes, I knew. You're the one for me, I mean it. I don't play games and I'm not feeding you lines to get you in bed."

With his finger under her chin again, he pulled her face closer, looking into her eyes. She knew he was pleading with her to believe in him "Do you trust me?" He paused. "Do you believe me?"

The relieved breath she let out was audible. "Yeah, I can't explain it, but I do."

Chapter Six

"What do mean, you *are* going?"

Molly crossed her arms and lifted her chin in defiance. This was definitely one of those times when it sucked Brody was so much taller than her. All he had to do was look down at her and she felt like a child again. *Humph*. Well not this time.

She ran her fingers through her bangs and swept them to the side. "I mean. I. Am. Going. I *thought* I made myself pretty damn clear. Now, they invited you and Erin too, and Joe. I'd like it if you came with us, but only if you can be civil. I'm done with you embarrassing me. You're out of control, Brody."

"I'm calling Dad."

"What are you...*five?*" She shook her head in disbelief. "Whatever, Brody. Just decide if you're going or not. I'm going to go get ready." She turned, grabbed her clothes, and headed for bathroom in their motorhome.

They normally got along. And she was used to Brody *and* James being there. She had never even noticed it before; it was just the way life was. Maybe it was her. Instead of feeling protected, all of the sudden she felt suffocated. She really hadn't ever been interested in a guy before. That or maybe she hadn't had a chance to, now that she thought about it. Nobody ever got past the guard dogs. If it wasn't so damn maddening, she might find that humorous.

Leaning against the bathroom sink, Molly took a long look in the mirror then dropped her head. She didn't even bother to look up when she heard the soft knock on the door. She loved her brother dearly and fighting with him was eating her up, but on the other hand she knew Carter was worth fighting for. *What a mess.*

"Mol? Honey, you all right?" Erin peeked in when Molly didn't answer. "Oh babe, it's okay."

She never cried, but that didn't mean her heart wasn't being torn in two directions. She looked up at Erin. "I don't like this fighting with him, Erin. I don't."

"I know, honey."

"I understand he's got to play his role. But can't he trust me? I've never done anything to prove he can't."

"It's not a trust thing, honey. Not with you and not really with Carter. It's a 'he'll never be good enough' issue."

"That's not fair."

"I know it's not."

"We shouldn't even talk. I know he can hear me. These walls are paper thin."

"Na, Joey pulled him out the door. He said he needed to show him something on your bike so they went up to the semi."

"I like Carter. I really, really like him, Erin."

"I know you do, sweetie."

"No, I mean I *really* like him. Like, he might be 'the one' kind of like him. I'm falling for him."

"I know, Mol. I can see it, in you and Carter both. I think he's a good guy. Just take it slow, okay? I don't want you to get your heart broken. And don't worry about your brother, he'll come around, even if I have drag him kicking and screaming."

Molly snorted. She could see that visual in her head. She was finally able to take a breath and relax a bit. Erin always had a way of making her feel better. Even though they were about the same age, she'd always looked to her as a big sister. Molly and Brody hadn't ever butted heads on something major before, and they'd always been extremely close. She was worried this might drive a wedge between them that neither one of them could remove, but it wasn't fair he wanted her to be alone.

It was that final thought that pushed her over the edge. She didn't want to be alone anymore. Even in the most loving family in the world, she was alone because she didn't have that special someone to share it with. She smiled at her renewed sense of self.

Molly hugged Erin tight to her and said, "I know you will. Thank you for always being there for me. I love you so much."

"I love you too, sweetie." Erin pulled away to look at Molly. "It will all work out, okay?"

"Yep, starting tonight. You ready to go have some fun?"

"Just waiting on you, honey." Erin laughed.

Molly winked at her. Erin and she could be quite the handful together, and tonight would be one of those nights. If Brody wanted to make things difficult, then she could play that way. All it took was the right outfit. She didn't have access to her whole wardrobe, but she had enough with her to do the job.

"Okay then."

As she began to get dressed, she looked down at her jeans, her favorite, most expensive pair. *I don't have any idea what I was thinking when I brought these, but damn I'm glad I did.* Molly slipped them on over her black lace thong. They were just tight enough to be sexy. Over her matching black lace bra, she slid on a black tank top with a rhinestone cross across the chest. She would have chosen heels, but all of her heels were back home in her closet, so she threw on her little black ballet flats. She ran her fingers through her long golden hair and swept her bangs to the side and out of her eyes. She normally wore just mascara and a little bit of eyeliner, but they were going out, so she darkened the eyeliner and used eye shadow to make more of a smoky eye.

Molly looked in the mirror. *Yep, that's what I was going for.* The thought made her giggle to herself. She added a touch more lipstick and then threw it into her wristlet, along with some cash, her ID, and phone. She picked up her black leather bomber jacket and walked out of their motorhome. What she was wearing gave her the added confidence she needed to face Brody. He had always teased her that he hated that she was so beautiful, telling her she'd be easier to keep the guys away if she looked mousy. *Boy, tonight was going to suck ass for him.*

The narrowed eye of her brother proved that he was on to her. She threw him a cocky little smirk and tipped her head, indicating she was in it to win it. She continued to meet him eye-to-eye. There was no way in hell she was going to be the first to back down. She could see the tic in his jaw and his gray eyes darkened. Oh yeah, he was…pissed, big time. Well, it was just too damn bad for him.

Where most everyone else would stand down when he looked at them like that, Molly wasn't about to. He had obviously forgotten one thing. She was competitive by nature, just as he was.

She'd gone the extra mile to look good for Carter, the fact it pissed Brody off was just the icing on the cake. She didn't even hide the grin that swept across her face. "You ready?"

He snorted and turned. When Joey let out a chuckle and got the evil death glare from Brody, Molly lost it. Trailing behind the two men, Erin and she giggled the whole way to the bar where they were meeting Carter, Eli, and Jesse at for dinner.

Brody entered the bar around the corner from the stadium ahead of them, holding the heavy wood and glass door open for the girls and Joey. He hadn't hid his dissatisfaction about the evening. *Bummer for him,* because Molly was set on having a good time tonight. Molly's face danced with excitement as her sexy as sin man walked toward her, and she couldn't help but tingle all over like a high school girl.

Carter motioned for her to sit by Eli in the old wooden booth, and then he scooted in beside her, up close to her side. He put his arm around her shoulders and pulled her to him. "You look amazing."

"Thanks." She looked up at him with a smile.

He gave her a kiss on the cheek and moved to kiss near her ear. She felt the heat from Carter's touch and she wished she could be giddy over the tingles she felt all the way to her toes. But a fire burned her from her brother's eyes as he watched. She met his eyes with a stubbornness that she was done keeping under control. If Brody was a smart man, he'd see that the harder he tried to keep them apart, the more he was pushing them together. Her face softened as a wave of goose bumps spread down her bare arms. She was horribly ticklish and Carter's kiss near her neck did her in. *Damn.* Now he knew one of her weaknesses.

Eli smacked at him. "Dude, will you please stop kissing my woman? She's mine tonight." Eli winked at her. "Remember you said you were dancing with me tonight."

With her tongue in her cheek, she tried to keep the smile in. "Well, I remember you *telling* me earlier I was dancing with you tonight. How do you know if I can even dance?"

"I don't care if you can or not, you're not some girl hanging on me from the track."

"So," she said, crossing her arms, "You're using me, huh? Okay so, how do you know *you* can keep up with *me*?" Molly gave Eli a cocky smirk.

Erin was directly across from her, in between Brody and Jesse. She grinned at Erin, and then snuck a look at her brother. As he lifted his bottle of beer to his mouth, he gave her a warning look. If he was going to sit and stew all night, so be it. But she'd gotten to know Carter, Eli, and Jesse enough to be comfortable around them. They were good guys and she felt at ease. That was something that almost never happened. Plus, Erin and Joey were there and so far they were having a good time, joining in on the conversation.

Joey shook his head. "That damn attitude."

"Bite me, Joe." She snickered and looked back at her brother. He continued his disapproving glances between her and Carter.

She rolled her eyes at Brody and turned to Joey, giving him a kiss through the air.

Their whole table let out a collective breath as Dylan and a couple of his buddies pulled up chairs to their table. Molly was instantly put on edge, but tried to act like he wasn't even there. She couldn't figure him out. It didn't appear that Carter or his friends liked this guy. Why in the hell would he keeping coming around when no one bothered to hide that fact?

Jesse put his beer bottle down hard to get their attention. "Drinking game."

Grateful for the distraction, Molly smiled across the table at Jesse. Then his words hit her. *Oh man.* "I need food for this first," Molly laughed. Her last night with alcohol did not end up so well. Her brother must have not forgotten either; his snickering was way too loud.

"Shit. Food ain't gonna help you, girl." Joey wagged a finger at her. "You can't handle any amount of liquor."

"Ha…Ha…Ha."

"Yeah, how much did you have that night you passed out? What was it, three or so months ago?" Brody teased her.

What the hell? The butthead doesn't speak all night, but *now* he chimes in? Seriously? She was going to have to just kick his ass and get it over with. Molly was instantly red. "You had to bring *that* up, *again*?" She rolled her eyes. "It wasn't much, I was just tired."

Carter nudged her. "*Really*? So how much is too much?"

"Um…well. I don't remember."

"I do." Brody winked at her. "Two. Two freaking beers and she was out cold."

She would laugh. However, one, it wasn't funny. And two, it was embarrassing. And three, well, it still wasn't funny.

She narrowed her eyes across the table and shook her head. "See, you don't even know what you are talking about. It wasn't beer at all. And I keep telling you all, I was tired, not drunk."

"So, honey?" Jesse grinned, "If it wasn't beer, what was it?"

Ugh, shit. "Um." She stalled because knew there was way more teasing coming, as if her brother wasn't enough.

"*Yes*?" Eli drew out the word as he winked at her.

Molly closed her eyes and barely squeaked out the word, "Tequila," then put her head down on the table, ashamed.

Carter started laughing and rubbed her back. "Why in *the hell* were *you* drinking tequila?"

She looked up at the guys, she had nothing if she didn't have her pride. "James said I didn't know how to do a real tequila shot. So," she said as she shrugged, "I had to prove him wrong."

"Oh my God." Eli gasped as he almost spit his beer across the table in shock. "How many did you do?"

Molly snickered and handed Eli another napkin for the drops running down his chin. "Not many and I wasn't drunk."

"You're right, I forgot about that." Brody shook his head to disagree. "But, it was two shots and you were drunk. I was there, remember? You're just a lightweight. Admit it."

Damn man hardly says a word all night. Then he jumps in to embarrass the crap out of her? What did she *do* to piss off the gods above? She hoped he knew that old saying *what goes around, comes around*, because Lord have mercy — his ass was *hers*.

"No, I'm a cheap date."

Jesse nodded in approval. "Nice spin on it, sweetheart."

"I thought so." She smiled proudly at herself. "And I think it was three maybe four, with a beer first."

Carter squeezed her shoulder. "So, you don't do well at drinking games?"

She glared up at him, pretend anger in her eyes. "You're real funny, aren't you?"

He winked back.

The waitress brought another round and Joey pushed the bowl of pretzels toward Molly. "Here, Mol, I think you're going to need these."

"Okay, okay, game on," Jesse said loudly over the group's laughter.

Molly lowered her head, afraid of what lay ahead of her, but the scent of the man beside her, his warmth against her, made it all worth it. She snickered to herself, listening to Jesse's rules for the drinking game and laid her head against Carter's shoulder. *Yeah, it's damn worth it.*

Even with Brody's attitude, Carter was having a good time. Jesse's game had gone for a couple rounds when the DJ started playing a song that Eli said he really liked. Eli pushed Molly toward the end of the bench, which made Carter have to get up. "Dude."

"Get up. Come on, it's a good song. Let's go."

Carter glanced down at him. "Hunter, relax bud."

"Come on Mol, you're dancing." Eli shoved Molly again.

"Here we go again with this telling shit."

Eli pushed her again and she practically fell out of the booth, and Carter had to help her catch her footing. As he grabbed her waist, her tank top came up, revealing the back of her low cut jeans and the top of what was very obviously a black lace thong.

Jesse whistled. Carter followed at his line of eyesight. "Hey Frost, keep your eyes off my woman's ass please." Still, he couldn't help but smile.

"Damn it, Eli." Molly barely had time to stand and pull down the tank top, before she was propelled onto the dance floor. She fought the manhandling with little force though, giggling the whole way.

Jesse laughed, watching Molly being drug across the floor. "So, can she dance?"

Brody let out a breath. "Um…Yeah…" he said in what sounded like a deliberately slow, low voice. "She can definitely dance. My dad always comes with us if we go out and he's pretty cool. But I think she's why he always wants to go. He has this need to protect her."

"Damn, Sterling. Your girl can freaking move." Jesse grinned watching her

"I see that." Carter's proud smile spread all over his face.

"You're not the jealous type, are you?" Brody asked.

"Na, not with him, but maybe with a random stranger."

"Well, you don't have to worry about that. She never dances with strangers. Ever. She's kinda skittish around men she doesn't know." They all watched as she and Eli took turns teaching each other moves and laughing. "She just likes to have fun."

When the song ended, he hugged her to him and they started to walk back to the table, laughing like old friends. Even though he had his arm around her waist, another guy still approached her.

Carter watched her cling tighter to Eli as she shook her head no.

"Told you so—never."

"Okay, Mol, you're my official dance partner." Eli squeezed her waist as they got back to the table. "You can dance damn well for a white girl."

"You too."

82

"Oh no, baby. My momma may be white, but the woman can't dance. I got my style from my dad's side."

"Was that...*style*?" Molly motioned to the dance floor. "Out there? Really?"

Eli snickered at her teasing. "Oh, it's a good thing you're Sterling's girl. I'd have to beat your ass if you were mine." He swatted her butt playfully and kissed her cheek.

Carter stood up to let them in the booth, taking the opportunity to hug her close before sliding back in the booth. "I ordered you a salad," Carter said, still laughing. Molly's cheeks were flushed from her banter with Eli as she laid her had against his shoulder.

The waitress set another beer in front of her. "What are you all trying to do, get me drunk? I haven't even finished the first one yet."

Dylan started in again. "We gotta make it easier for our boy Sterling here."

Without missing a beat, she looked flatly at him. "Has liquoring a girl up ever worked for you Martins, or do you have to resort to drugging her?"

Jesse gave Molly a high five. "Ouch, dude, she got ya. Nice one, Molly."

"Martins. Don't *even* start tonight," Carter warned.

Molly did her best to steer the conversation a different direction, but her nerves were starting to fray. At least Carter didn't act like a jealous fool; he hadn't minded her dancing with his friends. And though he was showing restraint when it came to Dylan, he was stepping into the protective boyfriend roll seamlessly. She grinned to herself as she bit off a chunk of bread. The conversation and laughter danced around her, but all she could concentrate on was the man sitting beside her. His palm on her thigh, gently stroking her and leaving bites of electricity everywhere he touched. Molly looked up at him, catching his attention. Carter leaned in, kissing her forehead. A sweet gesture, but one that she felt down to her toes. She tried to take a deep breath and another bite, but it was so hard to eat when her heart was racing ninety-to-nothing.

They were all finishing their dinners as the waitress came back and set a tray of tequila shots and a bowl of limes on the table. Molly started laughing. "Who in the hell did that? Joey, that's not funny." She looked up at him, grinning. But he shook his head no and had his eyebrow raised with absolutely no smile on his face.

"Like I said, we gotta make it easier for our boy." Dylan smirked at her, throwing down his challenge.

She could see Brody and Joey were about to pounce on him. She gave Brody a nod, telling him to wait.

"Damn it. You...ass!" was all Carter got out before her arm went across him to hold him back.

"You did that?" she asked simply.

Dylan nodded, apparently proud of himself. "Gotta see how many it takes, don't we? He'll thank me later, I'm sure."

"So...these...are *all* for me?"

"Na, babe, I'll match you," he said with a cocky smirk on his face.

She stared unblinking at Dylan for several long minutes. "You'll only be able to handle one." She gave him a daring look, feeling Carter squeeze her thigh.

Dylan cocked his head to the side. "*I* can handle my liquor, sweetheart."

She shook her head. "It'll only take one. I *promise* you." Molly nodded at the tray. "You drink first."

"Why?"

"You'll want to leave after I do mine. You might as well get *one* in."

Dylan stared at her for a minute. Then he picked up a shot and raised the glass to Molly. He shot it, made a face as it burned going down, then turned the empty shot glass upside down on the table. "I believe it's your turn, *babe*," he said with pure arrogance in his voice.

She could feel the testosterone all around her. Between her brother and Carter, there was bound to be something more than just Dylan's nose broken tonight. She would do her best to finish him herself first.

She could play his game and win. There was absolutely no question in her mind. As much as she wanted to be herself around Carter and his friends, the sweet side of her had to take a backseat this time. James didn't raise a doormat. Molly looked straight at Dylan for several moments, feeling the other's eyes on her. She shrugged, daring him to stay. When he did, she smiled sweetly up at Carter, as she picked up his hand off her thigh.

"May I?"

"I'm all yours, Gorgeous."

Molly gave Dylan an icy stare to make sure he was watching her. "Eli, may I have the salt please, handsome?" Eli kissed her cheek as he handed the salt shaker to her. "Thanks, E." The sickeningly sweet smile she flashed Eli was purposeful, then her expression went cold again as soon as her eyes locked back on Dylan. As much as she wanted to laugh in his face, she couldn't. She had him right where she wanted him.

She turned Carter's wrist over and placed a slice of lime in his palm. With her eyes still on Dylan and making sure to make all her motions slow and deliberate, she started. Licking her lips, she brought his wrist to her mouth and slowly kissed it. She picked up the salt shaker and causally sprinkled a little salt on the spot she'd wet. She ran her hand through her hair slowly, sweeping her bangs off her face. Ready to go, she winked at Dylan.

Like a well thought out scene, she used all the drama and sex she could muster. Using her tongue to very seductively lick the salt off Carter's wrist, she shot the tequila, and then brought his palm close to her mouth to pick up the lime. She sucked out the juice from the lime and put it in the empty shot glass, then looked at Dylan as she licked her lips again. Molly kissed Carter's palm first, then his wrist, then batted her eyes twice at Dylan.

"Thanks for the shot. I'm sure Carter enjoyed it as much as I did. I'd have him tell you if it worked or not tomorrow, but I don't think he's the kind to kiss and tell." She gave Dylan a little cocky shrug. "Sorry."

Dylan glared at her. "Fuck you."

Molly did everything she could to keep her patience in check and her breathing slow, showing nothing but steel to her rival. With her eyes still locked on his, a full poker face and a voice that was knife's edge sharp, she left not a trace of uncertainty. "You already know that's *never* going to happen."

"I'm outta here." Dylan's chair scrapped across the floor as he pushed himself back.

Her calmness was apparently unnerving to him, she held in the smirk as she capitalized on his weakness. "After only one?" she asked in a cute, coy voice. She couldn't help but play with him like a cat with a mouse. And after two days of the asshole, it was oh so fun.

"You're a *bitch*."

Her arm instinctively went across Carter's chest again, but without breaking eye contact with Dylan. "Maybe..." She held stone still, at the last second she threw up a shoulder and winked. "But...I was right."

Molly threw him a little smartass wave as he and his two buddies turned to leave. She waited until they got out the door, then cringed and grabbed the nearest water, which happened to be Jesse's, and through gritted teeth, she hissed, "Oh my God, that shit burns."

Their table exploded. Carter shook his head, laughing as he watched her drink half the glass of water. "It does burn. How'd you fake that it didn't?"

"I sure as hell wasn't going to let him know it hurt." Molly laughed. "Sorry, cowboy."

Jesse laughed even louder than he already was. "Oh, honey, that's all right. That was too awesome, I'm just glad I got to witness it. I'd never of believed it otherwise."

Molly winked back.

"So am I to assume you've nicknamed me?" Jesse's warm smile crinkled his eyes.

"Yep. You wear the boots, you've got the accent. So yeah, *cowboy*, I did."

"Do you think he's ever going to learn not to mess with you? Cause at some point, I'm just going to take him out, just warning you all now." Joey started passing out the rest of the shots to everyone else. "And that asshole better have already paid for these. And you…" He pointed at Carter as he spoke. "You're damn lucky she held you back. I have a feeling George wouldn't be so kind if you pummeled that jackass. I think you got a free pass the other night. Let me take him, I've got nothing to lose."

"Thanks, Joey, but I don't give a shit. No one's going to mess with her," Carter said.

Joey stared a moment, then nodded.

Eli brought her knuckles to his mouth for a sweet peck. "Thanks for letting me be a part of that, even if it wasn't as good a role as Sterling's."

Brody's gaze narrowed in on her. "What…in…the hell…was that?"

"What?"

He slapped the table. "The whole sex kitten act. What the hell? Where did you learn…that?"

"Brod, I'm a big girl now." She answered nicely—on purpose.

"You aren't that big. Dad would shit."

"Then don't tell him." At this point, she was about to go off like a rocket. Her insides felt like a damn pinball machine. Between sitting close enough that only clothes separated her from Carter all night, this last battle with Dylan, and now Brody back on her ass, all she needed was the spark to set her off. And God help the person that lit that match.

"That is not what he meant by not knowing how to do a real shot! You lick the salt, shoot, and suck the lime. That's it."

"You're right, Brod...it's all in the lick...and the *suck*."

Carter slapped his hand over his own mouth and was about to die as Erin finally lost it.

"You! You taught her that didn't you?" Brody looked at Erin with the tears running down her face. "I'm going to kick both your asses, then laugh when Dad does it again. You should be ashamed of yourself, Erin."

Brody's outburst only made Erin laugh harder.

"Be nice to her, Brody, you big bully," Molly scolded.

The entire group was laughing hysterically, drawing attention from other people in the bar. Molly glanced around them, then back to her brother. She leaned closer over the table like she had a big secret. "Hey, Brod, we didn't practice body shots if that makes you feel better."

His jaw dropped back open.

"You think you're cute. Wait till Dad hears about this little stunt. Then we'll see who's laughing." He turned to Erin. "You quit laughing, you're just making it worse."

Brody felt the sharp pain in his forehead. The same one he got when he realized his jaw was clenched so tight he couldn't pass water through his teeth if he wanted to. He breathed in a slow breath through his nose and shook his head at his sister. She sat there smiling, just as pleased as punch. In any other instance this would have been funny. Hell, it would have been hysterical, but not when it was his freaking sister.

Chapter Seven

Carter's laughter finally calmed down from rolling hysterics to just inside of insane. He scooted out of the booth and held his hand out for her to follow suit. "Oh Gorgeous, you are so awesome. I love you."

Molly's eyes went big and she glanced at her brother. His eyes were as wide as hers and his jaw was on the table. *Yeah.* He'd heard the last three words fall from Carter's mouth too. *Shit.* Her head was spinning. Those three tiny words were weightless individually. But combined? Those little words held the weight of the world, and yet, Carter was acting if he didn't even know they'd slipped out.

He continued to laugh while pulling her close. "Okay, you're mine. I think you owe me a dance. Besides, I think with that evil glimmer in your eye and what's going on between you and Brody, there's no stopping until there's bloodshed."

Oh, there was going to be bloodshed all right. Did Carter not feel the X that Brody had just put on his back? He should feel it. Molly could sure as hell see it from a mile away.

Eli grabbed her arm as she and Carter slid out of the booth. "Hey. He didn't ask, either. Aren't you going to give him shit too?"

She grinned and kissed Eli's cheek before she slid the rest of the way out of the booth. She let his good humor and teasing bring her back from the ledge. One more step and she'd be freaking out about what Carter said.

As they made their way to the small dance floor, she waffled at least eleven times, going back and forth as she wondered if she should ask Carter whether or not he had said *I love you* on purpose. She hated not knowing what was going on if it involved her. There was a tiny piece of her that was a control freak. Eh? Maybe a little more than a *tiny* piece. Not knowing if Carter meant to say those words, or if he said it accidentally, or what if...*Oh God*. What if he said that and now he was waiting on her response? Crap. Maybe that was it. And she hadn't said anything.

She said I love you to all her close friends and family all the time. It was no big deal. But it was Carter and this was *such* a big deal. What if he was upset she hadn't said anything? Oh, God. She didn't want to have hurt his feelings. Did she love him? Maybe? Yes. Definitely—maybe yes.

Right before she was sure the men in white coats were going to come busting through the doors, Carter took her in his arms and pulled her close. Okay, maybe he wasn't mad she hadn't replied. She just wished she knew what was going through his head.

"So, you having fun?" He smiled down at her.
"I am."

The warmth he felt when she looked up at him with those deep blue eyes was hands down the best feeling he'd ever had. She was amazing. He could get lost staring at her.

"Okay, I have to tell you…you have no idea how hard it was to watch and feel you doing that shot and not just take you right then and there." He couldn't help the mischief in his teasing. "I'm talking, one arm swipe across the table, knocking glasses and bottles off, lay you down in front of God and everybody — and take you."

He knew he would embarrass her by admitting that, and he couldn't help but love the pink that flashed in her cheeks. But damn, the girl had just about killed him. It had been fifteen minutes and he was *still* hurting. He winked down at her smiling face.

"I'm sorry, it just couldn't be helped. But thanks for being a willing participant." She reached up on her tip toes to kiss his lips.

It was just a peck, as sweet as could be. But he wanted so much more. He took a sharp breath in, feeling the heated stare of her brother from across the room. The tension between the two of them had been palpable when they'd first walked in the bar tonight. And although Brody had laughed a few times and had even teased Molly, Carter could still feel the rift between them. With all his heart, he hated to be the cause of something between them. It was obvious they loved each other dearly, but as selfish as it may be, he couldn't walk away.

He hugged her close and she laid her head against his chest. "I know this is moving fast, but I just can't imagine a day without you." He kissed the top of her head and continued to rub her back while they danced to the music.

The pain in her eyes when she looked back up at him tore at his heart.

"I know."

"What's the sad look for?"

"Well, you realize how fast Sunday is coming, right?"

"I know." He sighed. "I'm trying not to think about it."

She smiled sweetly up at him. "So?"

He could tell she was nervous about her question. "So... what?"

"Well..."

"What happens next?" He let her off the hook and finished for her.

She bit her lip nervously. "You can read my mind, huh?"

He leaned down to kiss her gently on the lips. "I've been thinking the same thing." He leaned down to kiss her again, but more possessively than before. Her lips slowly parted and he took full advantage, his tongue slipping inside over hers, exploring her for several moments. His heart pounding, he finally pulled back to look in her eyes. "And, well, I think I've made myself *very* clear. So, Gorgeous, what happens next, is really...up to you."

It warmed his heart the way her face lit up; he could see the relief in her eyes, as if she really had anything to worry about. As far as he was concerned, she was his.

"So if I want us to continue on the way we are, then we just meet up again next Thursday in Houston?"

"It'll be a long three days, but that's my thought, yeah."

He cupped her face and started to kiss her, forgetting, or maybe just not caring that they were out on a dance floor surrounded by people, with their friends close and watching. He just needed her. He finally broke the kiss to look at her. "So?"

"Yeah?"

"You want to get out of here a little early? I can walk you back and we can talk for awhile, just the two of us."

She looked at him nervously. "All right."

"You can trust me, I'll behave."

She stared up at him. "I trust you completely."

"Hey cutie, want to dance?" Jesse asked as he ambled up to them.

"Just one, Frost, we're cutting out early." He reluctantly let go of her, allowing Jesse to take her in his arms. He walked back to the table, alone.

Carter blinked a couple of times, trying to clear his mind. There was something eating at him he just couldn't shake. He had a deep-seated need to watch over his heart, the one still laughing out on the dance floor with Jesse. He glanced back, watching for a minute as Jesse twirled her in a circle, her long, blonde hair flying as she laughed in Jesse's embrace.

He thought back to previous comments she, Brody, and the others in her group had made about James and his over-protectiveness. He couldn't fault the man. She had grabbed his heart in a vise barely over a day ago. He couldn't imagine how her father felt after twenty-six years.

Wait.

Brody said she moved in with them when she was fourteen. They referred to each other as brother and sister, but they weren't related. Not by blood anyway. She said there was history.

Eli pulled Carter out of his own thoughts as he slid back in the booth. "Looks like you lost your girl."

"What? Oh, she's on loan." He grinned then took a drink of her almost full beer. "Oh, that's nasty."

"You've been out there over twenty minutes. What do you expect? They got hot," Brody sneered. "Hey," he nudged Erin, who had her head on his shoulder. "You ready? I know you're tired." He glanced up at Carter. "I know it's still early, but Erin isn't feeling well. I need to get her back. Would you please see to it my sister makes it back to *my* motorhome, and sooner, rather than later?"

Carter understood the "you may be older, but I'm the big brother" look he received from Brody. It was loud and clear. He was also smart enough to know he'd better not screw this up. Brody had extended an olive branch, granted it was a forced hand due to Erin, but it was there. He also knew Molly well enough to know there was no way Brody was going to force her to leave before she was ready. Brody was stuck between a rock and a hard place. Carter wanted to laugh so badly he could hardly stand it. But he'd be the bigger person, if for no other reason than he got to spend more time with Molly *and* without her overbearing brother watching his every move.

"Yeah…we're actually going to leave pretty quick, too."

Carter held in the snort as he watched Brody silently signal for Joey to watch Carter and Molly. He held out a hand and waited patiently as Brody reluctantly shook it, then he waved goodnight to Erin before they turned to leave.

Carter stood back up when Jesse came walking back, chatting with Molly. "Thanks for dancing with me, D."

"Anytime, cowboy."

Carter watched the realization come across her face as she scrunched her eyebrows and pert, little nose up. He couldn't help but smile down at her.

"D?"

Jesse chuckled. "I'm not the only one with a new nickname around here. Hunter gave you one too."

"Oh yeah?" Molly raised an eyebrow at Eli. "You nicknamed me? Is it bad?"

Eli just smiled proudly as he stood to hug her goodnight. "Nope. You're our own little SuperCross Darling, *D* for short." Eli leaned to kiss her cheek and then squeezed her tight.

"Cute," Joey replied sarcastically. "Well, at least you're somebody's darling. You're just my big pain in the ass."

Molly stuck her tongue out at Joey playfully.

ॐ୶

Once again, Carter deliberately walked slowly, this time toward the stadium. He wanted to be alone with her and wasn't ready for her to call it a night. He was afraid that once they got close to the pits, her nerves would kick in and she would make a beeline for her motorhome.

"Did you have a good time tonight?"

She squeezed his hand. "Yeah, but I have to admit, I just like being with you. It doesn't really matter what we're doing."

Carter put his arm around her waist and pulled her close. "I know what you mean." Arriving at their entrance, security let them in. "I know it's late by your standards, but it's only about eight-thirty. Can we still go sit somewhere and talk?"

She snickered up at him. "Is that what you're going to call it?"

He tickled her waist. "Ha ha ha. You think you're cute huh?"

"Pretty much."

"Well, I have to agree with you." He winked down at her. "Come on, I know you want to get up early to run, but don't go yet. Please?"

"You've been a bad influence on me, keeping me up all hours of the night, drinking..."

He cut her off, "Wow, what was it, eleven last night and one beer tonight? Yep, that's me, a real bad boy."

"Yep." She swung around to face him and put her arms around his neck to stop him from walking. "You're the kind they try to protect me from, huh? Yes I'd like to 'talk' with you too," she said, using air quotes to be funny.

"You're a real comedian."

"Yeah, but you picked me, remember?"

"Yes, I did, didn't I, Gorgeous?" he said proudly and she just laughed. They continued to walk through the pits toward where the motorhomes were parked. There were a few chairs and tables set up in a corner that wasn't well lit, and he motioned that direction. He pulled in a subtle breath and mentally crossed his fingers. "We could sit there. Or...if you trust me...we could go to my motorhome." He could hear the hesitation in his own voice, but he didn't care.

He waited a second before asking again. He knew she was more than a little apprehensive, and by all rights. He expected that. He also found it very endearing. "So, what do you say? Do you trust me?" He could see the gears turning in her head. Holding her in his arms, he could feel the battle between her heart and her mind.

She glanced up at him, then quickly back down at the ground. "Yeah," she said softly as she looked back up, lingering on his mouth before her eyes reached his.

They continued walking to his motorhome. Once he opened the door for her, he could feel the stress radiating off of her. She had gotten very quiet, a complete one-eighty from her confidence in the bar. Carter half expected her to bolt before she actually stepped inside his motorhome. He had to silently tell himself to slow down. It was just so hard when all he really wanted to do was walk her on back to the bedroom and rip off those tight ass jeans and taunting little tank top. Instead, he held his breath and waited for her next move.

She hated that at twenty-six she was freaked out by being alone with a guy. Maybe because it was this guy, *the* guy. The one she had been waiting for her whole adult life. She was trying really hard to act like it was no big deal, but this whole situation was new territory for her. She knew she had to be the oldest virgin ever.

Maybe if she would have just gotten it over with when she was younger, there wouldn't be this pressure now. *That one guy, oh hell, out by the back creek. What was his name? He wanted me. Humph. Shit. No. That guy was a jackass.* No, Carter was the reason she had waited. Nerves and all, she wanted to find someone special. Through all the years of hanging out with other racers and meeting hundreds of fan, not one earned a second glance.

Then there was him.

One look in his ice blue eyes and she was mesmerized. One touch of his hand, she tingled on contact. The smell of his cologne, masculine and completely him, made her head swim. The way his voice melted over her, warm and relaxing, soothing her when she needed to be calmed. All of it. With a force stronger than Mother

Nature, she was drawn to him. She knew, waiting all those years, *he* was out there somewhere.

He turned a couple of lights on. "You want something to drink? I know you're not a big pop drinker, but I have juice and water."

"Um, a water would be great, thanks," she answered barely louder than a whisper. She was still looking around nervously. "This is really nice inside."

Like James's, it was more of a house on wheels. It was beautiful inside with a full kitchen, a nice little living room, and a separate bedroom with a door and tons of amenities, even a washer and dryer unit. She understood why he didn't fly back and forth all over the country, this was way easier. That's how James had done things when she'd raced, too.

Carter came out from the kitchen area with two bottles of water. "Yeah, I figure I want to be comfortable when I'm living it in most of the year. When we have long breaks, I just drive back to my folks and stay there." He motioned to the couch. "Here, have a seat."

He opened her water and handed it to her as she slowly sat down on the couch. He sat next to her, but crooked so they could see each other. She took a sip of the cold water, and then bit her bottom lip. Carter sucked in a deep breath. It was audible and she looked at him questioningly.

"You're going to have to quit doing that," he teased.

"What?"

"The lip thing, it is an absolute turn on."

Her eyes widened. "Oh…um."

"It's okay, Gorgeous, I'm teasing you. But it gets me every time I see you do it."

She offered him a tiny smile.

"Maybe next weekend I can take you out for dinner, just the two of us?"

"I'd like that." He reached for her hand, pulling it toward his mouth to brush his lips across her knuckles. He took her water and placed them both on the coffee table to free their hands. He held one arm open and used the other to gently pull her close. "Here, can I just hold you?"

Her heart skipped at least three beats and then threatened to quit beating altogether. She knew she could trust this man. Molly didn't know how she knew, but she could feel it. Deep in her soul, she knew she was safe in his arms, without a question.

A wave of tingles washed over her from head to toe as she scooted next to him. She slid as close as she could before he moved to adjust them, sliding one leg down the couch and pulling her in between his legs. Molly tried to take a couple of faint, calming breaths and hoped he wouldn't pick up on her nerves. She rested her back up against his chest and could feel his heart beating through her thin tank top. More like pounding, hard and fast. Molly grinned to herself. At least she wasn't the only one affected. He rubbed his fingers up and down her bare arms, sitting in silence for awhile. She snuggled back into his arms, wishing the moment could last forever. A sense of peace settled over her and she let her eyes slowly close.

"This is nice, isn't it?" he asked, his voice lower.

She smiled to herself again and nodded.

"I have to tell you this is the most relaxed I've ever gone into a race," he said.

"Really, how come?" She scooted into the crook of his arm so she could look up at him and see his face.

"Because of you, Gorgeous."

"Me?"

"Yes…" he drew out, "You."

He bent down to kiss her softly on the lips then lifted his head up to look in her eyes. His free hand moved to her face, gently stroking her cheek with his thumb. Gently, Carter eased her head back to kiss her again. She parted her lips for him and he slipped his tongue in her mouth to deepen the kiss. He started lightly rubbing her shoulder, and then down her arm and back up. Molly moved that same arm up, wanting to touch his face, unintentionally exposing her side.

The peace and tranquility she felt only a moment ago gave way to need. Her mind was spinning as she tried to assess what she was doing, but all level-headed thinking had vanished. In its place was a feeling she had never known.

Carter slid his hand down from her shoulder and eased it down her side. When he did, his thumb brushed the side of her breast. She sucked in a sharp breath at the touch. *Oh God.* She wasn't sure where the line needed to be drawn, she didn't know how far he'd try to push, but it just felt so right. He continued to lightly stroke that spot, just on the side. His kiss slowed, and then he lifted his lips completely from hers.

She slowly opened her eyes, even though they were so heavy, and a nervous little smile breezed over her face.

He took a finger and traced her jaw line. Molly focused on his eyes. Seeing the need and power in the pale blue, but also an understanding, kept her calm. Even though her senses were on overload, he had a quietness about him that relieved her fears, leaving only trust for the man who was holding her. His finger slowly started down her neck then softly he traced the neckline of her tank top. Her breath caught and she bit her lip, but she kept her focus on the eyes watching hers. She knew he was looking for signs. Cautiously testing her, but watching for the exact moment when it was too much, too soon. The trust she felt for him propelled her to want more.

Her breathing became choppier as Carter eased his hand down the middle of her body until he reached her waist. Her tank had conveniently crept up, exposing her flat stomach; his fingers started gently rubbing her soft skin. Then slowly, his hand started making its way back up, but this time, under her tank.

She knew there was a point in which she was going to have to tell him that it was enough. To not go any further—yet. She just wished she knew what that point was. As nervous and scared as she should be, as she normally would've been, she wasn't. She was anxious, but not nervous.

Instead, she adjusted to turn toward him and pulled his mouth to hers. Her breathing was louder and much faster now. He caressed her over the black lace until he found the front clasp. It popped open easily.

She didn't know she'd been holding her breath until it came out with a *whoosh*. *Oh my God. Oh my God. Oh my God.* She grasped for a deeper breath and kissed him almost desperately. She had been teetering on the line, and she was pretty sure she needed to stop this. But, *oh God*, she had never felt like this before. Her heart was racing and she felt like she was on fire, inside and out. She had been on the pill forever, but did that really work? Did she really want to be one of those girls that went to bed with a guy she'd just met? She had a million questions and only one answer. She didn't want him to stop.

Her hand slid down from his neck to his heart as his lips moved to her jaw line The next thing she knew, he was laying stretched out beside her with a leg draped between hers. Feeling for the hem of his t-shirt, she quickly pulled it up, needing to feel the warmth of his skin. Carter quickly helped pull it off, and immediately she tangled the fingers of one hand in his hair. The other she ran down his chest over each rippled muscle. Molly felt his pulse beat under her hand as she grazed his heart, making her way down his chest, heard him suck in a breath as her hand moved lower.

He must have pulled on a will power she wasn't sure she possessed, because Carter slowed the kiss. He propped himself up on one elbow, his breaths just as loud and out of control as hers.

"God, you are beautiful." He placed a soft little kiss on the bare skin just above her tank line.

Slowly, she opened her eyes, and tried to take a deep breath, but it caught again. That simple noise kept giving her away. She gazed in his eyes and let her hand wander over his chest.

He bent down to kiss her lips again. "I'm sorry, I got carried away. I didn't mean to. I really did just want to spend more time with you," he said, but at the same time, his hand was still under her top, caressing her breast, running his thumb gently over the tip. She pulled his face to hers to kiss him softly. He broke again. "Are you upset? I promised you. I told you I'd control myself, I'm so sorry, Molly."

Again she tried to kiss his apology away. "I could have stopped you at any point. I know, without a doubt, that at any moment I said no, you would have stopped. And without making me feel bad." She looked in his eyes. "I didn't stop you." Molly said slowly and intently.

He bent down to kiss her sweetly again, and smiled.

"Don't feel guilty, Carter. I have to admit to you, only to make you feel better…" She smiled. "I don't know if I—"

"I know," he interrupted, "But I also know you don't want to get carried away on a couch the first weekend we're together. I want your first time to be special. I want to take you somewhere nice, somewhere not surrounded by bike trailers." He grinned down at her. "I'll admit to you, I don't have anything here, anyway."

"Anything, what?"

"Anything, like…*condoms.*"

She could tell he was trying to be funny with the way he drew out the answer, and she couldn't help the fit of giggles that was about to burst out.

"And I don't want to just assume you're on the pill."

Between nerves, excitement, and the sudden attack of embarrassment, she lost control, the laughter unstoppable.

"What's so funny?"

"I thought guys kept boxes and boxes of those things around at all times."

He squeezed her breast that was still in his hand. "Ow," she laughed.

"You're in an awkward spot here to be making jokes, good looking. No. Not all of us keep them on hand. Just so you know, I've only been with a few women and only in long term relationships. I want to have this conversation, because, well, I think it's important to know sexual history, but...ah...not right this minute."

"Thank you," she replied grinning. "It definitely ruins the mood."

"But you appreciate my honesty, right?" He tickled her. Laughing, she tried to tickle him back, but he easily rolled on top of her and pinned her arms down above her head. Still laughing, she wiggled, but couldn't move.

Kissing her, Carter slid one palm down her back and they shifted to their sides, facing each other again with their legs tangled. His palm on the small of her back pressed her into him. Her stomach did another little flip-flop when she felt...*him*. She wrapped herself around him to answer. His kiss moved to her neck and jaw and she could feel his tongue on her skin, the bite of his late day whiskers brushing against her.

Out of breath, she whispered, "I think we're in dangerous territory."

"I know," he whimpered. He responded by kissing her more urgently than he ever had before. "I just can't help myself, I can't get," he said as he gasped for a breath, "enough of you."

Carter sucked in air, and Molly could tell he was doing everything in his power to keep himself reined in, something she greatly appreciated. She could tell he was being sensitive to her needs over his. He moved to kiss her lips, but more gently. "Will you just lie here with me for awhile? Please?"

She could feel his heart beat as she continued to rub his arm and back. "There's nowhere in the world I'd rather be."

And there wasn't. In his arms, she felt everything she'd been missing. He was powerful and strong enough to keep her safe, but gentle with her feelings. He was funny and loved to laugh but was fiercely protective of her already. And hot, the man was made for the cover of *GQ Magazine*.

She let out a sigh, content to stay in his arms.

Then her cell rang.

"Three guesses."

"I have a feeling I know who it is, Gorgeous." Carter sat up quickly so she could get up. "Could be worse, he could have just come knocking on the door."

Molly was laughing at Carter's reply as she answered. Without looking at caller ID, she knew who it was. "Yes?"

"Excuse me?"

"Oh good Lord, Brody. It's not like Carter, Jesse, and Eli are all in here having an orgy with me. It's just Carter and I and we're just...oh wait...hey, Carter, you forgot to zip your pants back up. Sorry about that, Brody...we're just talking."

Molly looked down at the phone that was silent. "Oops. Probably shouldn't have said that. I guess that was kinda like poking an angry bear with a stick, huh?"

Carter smirked at her as he quickly threw his t-shirt back on.

"I'd bet good money he'll be here any sec—"

The pounding on the door startled her, even though she knew it was coming. "Second. Told ya." Molly couldn't help it as another fit of nervous giggles escaped.

"It's a good thing you're cute, little girl." Carter tried to look stern, but Molly only laughed harder at the good looking man watching her with his wicked little grin and an ornery glimmer in his eyes.

Carter opened the door to reveal a fuming Brody who was leaning with one hand on each side of the door frame.

"Brody, we were just talking."

"And now...you're done."

Chapter Eight

It was almost seven a.m. and she was just about finished running. Molly had started with running up and down the staircases of the lower level and then moved to running laps on the track. She had been going for over two hours and was horribly hot and sweaty, even in just spandex running shorts and a sports bra. Her hair was pulled up in a pony tail, but around her face and neck was soaking wet. She had her iPod up especially loud because of the dozers and bobcat working on the track.

All of the sudden, she felt a tingle, a whisper across her shoulder blades. A few other workers had come in to help with the touch ups on the track since she had been there, but she stopped and looked around anyway. Seeing nothing out of the normal at first, she continued to scan the mostly empty stadium. Standing at the railing of the lower level seating, she saw the sexy as sin man smiling down at her. Relief and excitement both washed over her, and she jogged Carter's direction.

"Wow, you're up early," Molly teased him.

"Look who's talking."

"I really didn't want you to see me looking like this for at least a few weeks. You know, keep up the pretty all the time front".

She wiped her brow with her bare arm. Laughing, he grabbed her to hug her to him, running his palm down her back that she could feel was slick with sweat. Ugh, so much for showering before she saw him this morning.

"Good morning." He leaned in, placing a soft kiss against her forehead.

"Good morning."

"You look amazing, by the way."

"Oh, please..." Molly rolled her eyes. She knew exactly how she looked after she'd been running. Amazing wasn't anywhere close to an adjective she'd use. Red-faced, sweaty, her hair wet and stuck to her skin. She felt a shiver as a drop of sweat ran down the side of her neck and down her chest, disappearing into her sports bra. Oh yeah, she was a real beauty right now.

"You don't see it, do you? You don't even try and you're beautiful. I love that about you."

"Okay, you must still be drunk from last night."

"You'll hug me if I'm on the podium, right?"

"Well of course." She lit up. The thought of him on the podium made her heart soar. She would be proud of him no matter what, but they were both racers at heart. Winning was everything.

"There you go. I'm sweaty, dirty, and gross after racing."

"You like to be right, huh?"

"I always am." He winked.

"Okay, Hollywood, I'll let you keep thinking that a little bit longer." She giggled as his hands slid down to grab her ass.

Her pulse quickened at the shock of the public display of affection. She wasn't used to it at all, but the girly part of her liked that he was proud enough of their relationship not to hide it. She should be appalled, or in the very least surprised, but instead, she was completely giddy.

"I came to see if you wanted to eat breakfast with me."

"I'd love to. Let me grab a shirt first?"

"Ah man, and ruin my view?"

Her cheeks flushed instantly. "Not your view so much as everyone else's."

"Oh, good point. I don't want other guys checking out my woman." He laughed as he picked her up and swung her around.

"I love the sound of that."

"What?"

"Yours."

With his arm around her shoulders, they started walking. "You are mine, Gorgeous. You're mine for as long as you'll have me."

⤙•⤚

Wanting a quick minute alone with Molly before the evening got too busy, Carter hurried through a quick bite to eat for dinner. After they'd had breakfast together this morning, the day turned into a whirlwind. Something he was used to, but it frustrated him to no end this time. He wanted desperately to have more time with her, to get to know her even better. He needed to get his head in the game and his focus on the race tonight, but all he could think about was leaving tomorrow and not being able to see her again until next weekend. That thought was making him crazy.

He knew it was insane to be so attached to a woman he'd just known a few days, but he couldn't help it. He also knew if he said anything to anyone, they'd think he was a love-sick fool. At the moment, he didn't really care. That's what he was.

"Hey, man. Are you going to head over to see our girl soon?" Jesse asked as he pulled up a chair at Carter's table outside his factory rig.

"Yeah, I'm getting ready to head that way now."

"Well, wait just a second, if you don't mind. Hunter and I wanted to wish her good luck too. He'll be here in a sec."

"That's fine, as long as he hurries."

"So, what's the deal with her anyway?" Jesse's eyebrow went up.

"I like her, Jess. A lot."

"Yeah, we can all see that. How serious is it?"

Carter popped the last bite of his sandwich in his mouth on purpose. It gave him time to choose his words. He couldn't really remember a time when Jesse, Eli, and he hadn't been friends. As kids they only met up on the tracks, and as teenagers with promising careers, their time on the same tracks became more and more frequent. A friendship born of a mutual passion, then a mutual respect that followed. As they grew up, they each realized their world was relatively small when it came to people who understood them—understood that passion for racing and respected it.

As pros, their friendship was a necessity. It kept everything in prospective. They shared everything, the ups and downs of racing. Periods of time off due to injury and the frustrations that went with it, the trials of wanting to ride with the coveted red number one plate on their bikes and the stresses of keeping sponsors happy.

Now wouldn't be any different.

Carter didn't hide the goofy grin as he thought about his girl. He nodded at Jesse. "She's the one, man."

"Yeah, Eli and I thought so. You can see it. She's a doll, that's for sure. I'm happy for you."

"Thanks." Carter got up and threw his trash away as Eli walked up.

"I hurried."

"No prob, Hunter. I'm ready if you all are."

As they got close, Eli came to a skidding stop, grabbing Carter's arm to halt him as well. "Damn. How freaking sexy is that?"

Carter followed Eli's line of sight. He took in a deep breath then picked his jaw up off the concrete floor. "No shit. Oh my God, she's gorgeous."

Molly was simply standing there, talking with Joey outside their semi trailer, but it was what she was wearing that was driving the guys crazy.

Jesse shook his head. "No girl should look that damn fine in riding pants and boots."

"It's the unzipped pants and sports bra, dude. I know she's your woman, Sterling, but wow. That is pure sexy," Eli said in a slow appreciation. They continued to stand and stare at her, all three grinning to themselves like twelve-year-old boys. "She is just freaking ripped. Shit." Eli let out a breath.

Jesse hit Carter on the arm. "Damn, man. We were all sitting there that afternoon, how in hell did she pick you?"

"God only knows, but I pray she never changes her mind."

As the words were coming out of Carter's mouth, Molly turned and put her foot up on a chair and bent over to buckle the clasps of her boot. "Oh, wow." Carter smiled big.

Jesse elbowed Carter. "Apparently, she always wears a thong, Sterling."

"Quit looking." He halfway laughed, knowing they wouldn't.

Eli gave Carter a brotherly punch to the arm. "Ah, man, you know we're just giving you shit."

"Get your own woman." Carter elbowed Jesse in fun. "That goes for you too, Hunter."

The three of them continued walking the rest of the way to her. Eli put his arm around her shoulders. "Nice show, D." He wiggled his eyebrows at her, and then he kissed her cheek.

"What are you talking about?"

Jesse chuckled. "I didn't know watching a girl put on riding boots could be so...erotic."

Carter punched Jesse in the arm, but chuckled too. "What the hell, Frost?" He turned to Molly and winked. "Sorry."

"Y'all are pervs." Molly crossed her arms at the three men and shook her head in mock disapproval.

Carter couldn't help but grin like a school boy. "No, it was freaking amazing."

"Well, I'm glad I could give you all a cheap thrill. It apparently doesn't take much to entertain you boys, does it?" She grinned as Carter grabbed her to him.

"It's not my fault you're so damn hot."

She reached up to give him a quick kiss on the lips. "Nice save." She turned and walked to the chair she had left her jersey laying on a few moments before. "Ah man, D."

Molly gave Eli a raised eyebrow. "Seriously?"

She pulled her jersey over her head as she was walking back toward the guys. She'd purposefully left her pants unzipped so she could tuck in her jersey. As she finished, she looked up to see all three guys staring at her.

"Are you all thirteen?" Molly snickered as she zipped and clasped her pants. She looked back up to their grinning faces, then motioned to the floor. "Boys, go get something to wipe up all that drool. You're embarrassing yourselves."

Jesse shook his head. "That's okay, D, we don't care."

Molly rolled her eyes as Carter slipped his arms around her waist. "So, the nickname thing? It's going to stick, huh?"

Eli nodded. "Oh, yeah."

"All right boys and girls," Brody said out loud to no one in particular as he walked out of their bike trailer, reading the clipboard in his hand. "Time to head…"

Carter saw the disgust on Brody's face when he looked up to see him and his friends. He watched Brody's eyes wander over the arms he had around Molly. Tact wasn't something he was obviously concerned with. Brody seemed to have no problem making it apparent that he wasn't welcome around their trailer, or more accurately, around his sister.

Molly was either oblivious to the stare-down, or she just didn't want to start another round with him because she kept happily chatting with him. Pure joy and excitement shone on her face as she told Carter how excited she was to see him race. He squeezed her closer to him, watching Brody's eyes narrow. Carter kept his face light, masking the frustration that was verging on anger. He lifted his shoulder in a nonchalant shrug, letting Brody know once again that he wasn't backing down.

The phone ringing in Brody's back pocket broke their eye contact. Carter continued to watch Brody as he scowled at the caller ID before answering. He spoke for several seconds before looking straight at Molly with panic written all over his face. Carter locked in, watching every nuance, trying to gauge Brody's facial expression. This wasn't the same coldness that Brody looked at him with, it was pure fear.

Carter tried to rub Molly's back and keep her attention diverted with her head against his chest. Before he could tear his eyes off Brody, Molly caught on. Following his gaze, she looked over at her brother. When Brody instantly turned his back to them, Molly looked up to him for an answer.

"What's going on? Did I miss something?"

He tried to feign mild surprise to Brody's actions. "I don't know, Gorgeous. It's awfully loud in here. Maybe he's just having a hard time hearing."

Eli and Jesse bought him some time, announcing their good luck wishes and giving her light good bye hugs at precisely the perfect moment. "Hey, will one of you ask someone on my team to meet me down there with my bike? And have them bring my stuff too, please?" Over the top of Molly's head, Carter glanced at both men. The slight jerk upward of both their heads meant they understood something was up. "I want to walk down with Molly." He pulled her tighter to him without letting the silent conversation die.

"Sure, Sterling, not a problem." The slight rise of Jesse's eyebrow told him both men would be there if he needed help.

It amazed him how they could read each other's minute signals. Another nod to the fact he was as close to them as he was his own two biological brothers.

"We'll see you down at the gate in a few." Eli lightened the secrecy when Molly started clueing in to the three men. "Can't wait to see you ride, D." He patted her shoulder lightly before turning away.

Brody shoved his phone back in his back pocket of his jeans. "Let's go, grab your helmet and stuff."

His gruffness wasn't lost on either Carter or Molly, but the hurt look on her face as she silently questioned Brody sent a pain straight to Carter's heart.

"Let's go. Come on." Brody repeated anxiously.

When it was apparent Brody wasn't going to explain or apologize for his mood, she shook her head and turned toward the trailer. The instant Molly was up the two steps it took to make it in the door of the bike trailer, Carter marched over to Brody. "What's going on? Is everything all right?"

"Don't worry about it, Sterling. Don't you have a race to get ready for?" Brody huffed out and turned his shoulder to Carter.

Determined to get an answer, Carter moved so he was back in front of Brody again. "Something's wrong. Is everything okay with Molly?"

Brody furrowed his brow. "I've got it, Sterling. I said not to worry about it."

"I want to help if something is wrong."

"I don't need your help," Brody said through gritted teeth.

"Something is wrong, isn't it?"

Brody didn't answer. That silent admission chilled Carter to the bone.

The walk from the pits down to the track was longer than it ever had been in the past. Carter held Molly's helmet for her in one hand and he held her tight to his side with the other, listening to Brody's last minute instructions and reminders for her as they walked. He tried to catch Brody's eye several times, but could tell Brody was avoiding him at all costs. At least for the moment it seemed like Molly had either let the incident go, or she didn't realize that Brody was hiding something involving her. Carter hoped like hell it was the second of those two scenarios.

She was just coming out of her shell around him and his two best friends. The more she did, the more he adored her. The thought that something was going on in her family that could upset her had Carter's stomach in knots. Those kinds of phone calls were never good. Inevitably it was about a death in the family or some other terrible news like that. He knew Brody not telling her before she got on the bike was a smart move. That was one of the golden rules, never get on the bike if your mind wasn't one hundred percent there. That would be like playing with fire. He was scared to death to watch her ride, and he knew without a doubt that if she wasn't focused, she could get hurt. Badly.

When they got to Joey and her bike, Carter pulled her tight against his chest. He blew off his worries over the phone call and forced a lighter mood for her.

"Well, Gorgeous, you be careful out there, okay?" he whispered into her hair as he leaned in. He brushed a kiss over her neck before pulling away to look down at her. The smile she gave him was priceless, so carefree, honest, and innocent. He melted all over again. "You're really something, you know that?" He leaned in and placed a kiss on her forehead, shutting his eyes for a moment and dragging in an extra breath of her light perfume.

"I'll be careful, I promise. This stuff's easy. You be careful tonight, please?"

She pulled away and, on tip toes, gave him the sweetest little peck on the lips he'd ever felt. It seemed as if she hadn't cared that Joey, Brody, and Erin were mere inches away. She looked back up at him like they were the only two people in the stadium. She hadn't kissed him to prove a point to her brother, either. She'd given him the sweet token purely of love and it was written all over her face. Her smile reached clear up to her sparkling deep blue eyes, and it stole Carter's breath.

"I'll be careful too, I promise. I've got you to come back to now." He winked down at her grin and kissed her cheek. "I better go. I'll be waiting over there with the guys," he waved an arm at Eli and Jesse. Normally they'd have been back behind the scenes with their bikes, but there was no way in hell he was going to miss seeing her. Luckily his manager didn't balk.

Carter's stomach dropped at the announcer's voice. "And our next rider is a special treat for you all. She—" He clenched his fists at his sides and dragged in slow, deep breaths, trying with everything in his power to not hyperventilate. The announcer continued. "—started racing at the age of four and has won seven WMA MotoCross Titles. She then moved into the freestyle world, and her own personal trainer is the great Brody Noland." The crowd let out a huge cheer.

"Everyone, please welcome seven time WMA MotoCross Champion and two time X-Games gold medalist, Molly West." The crowd roared as he watched Brody give her the sign, and she rode down the stage ramp and onto the track.

The guys all looked at each other, then at Carter. "Did you know about the X-Games?"

"No."

"Well maybe if you'd quit making out all the time and find out more about her, we'd have known." Jesse punched him in the arm jokingly.

Molly raced across to the table top and launched into a perfect whip. Continuing around the track, she did a few tricks, most of which she was roughly twenty or more feet in the air. She rode down to the end of track close to where Carter and the guys were standing. Brody moved to her and Carter could tell she was waiting on his instructions.

Carter shook his head, "Ah, shit."

He had heard them discussing this part of the show earlier in the weekend. Brody wanted her to stop for a minute to grab a breath and let the anticipation of the crowd build before performing her last stunt.

"It's okay, she's got this dude." Eli patted Carter's shoulder.

"I know, I know. Just doesn't make it easier to watch."

Brody pointed to a couple of things and she nodded again at his directions, then he backed up. She hit the throttle and rode the perimeter of the track, eyeing the takeoff and landing. Molly sped up as she headed into the corner that Brody had mentioned he was worried about being slick, and then into the straightaway section. She raced full out toward her take off ramp. She sailed up about thirty feet in the air to do the rotation of a back flip.

Carter felt lightheaded.

Molly came out to land smoothly on the other side, facing the guys. She gave a small wave to the crowd and rode toward the stage.

Jesse laughed. "She is freaking awesome."

"No shit." Eli shook his head in disbelief. "I mean, how fucking cool."

Jesse shook Carter's shoulders. "Your girl is so amazing."

Carter let out the breath he didn't know he had been holding.

"She's fine, Sterling." Jesse put his arm around Carter's shoulders. "Just enjoy this. You're the only one with that bragging right."

"Exactly, none of you have to worry about your future wife falling off a dirt bike from however freaking high she was."

"It's so cool." Eli looked at him. "Hey, if you're not man enough to handle this…" Eli winked at his friend. Carter just shook his head, letting out another deep breath. He rolled his eyes and left Eli's comment hang unanswered.

"Did you say future wife?" Jesse teased.

Carter nodded proudly and with all seriousness in his voice, he answered. "Yeah, I did."

His heart was still hammering in his chest, and it had nothing to do with his not-so-accidental admission being caught and everything to do with the woman riding up to the announcer near the stage. They had talked about the tricks she could pull and he had listened to Brody plot out what he wanted her to do on this particular track, but hearing about it and seeing her do it in person were two very different things. Suddenly he had the need to call his mother and apologize for all the worry she'd lived with since the day he sat on his first dirt bike back when he was five.

Carter couldn't look away from her as Joey grabbed her bike and she hopped off. She took her gloves and goggles off, then her helmet. She pulled her hair out of her jersey that she'd tucked into her sports bra at the last minute. He had chuckled earlier as she explained to him with a dramatic flair how much she hated to ride with it out because it got tangled and in her face. As she let the sheet of gold fall down her back, the crowd let out another cheer, obviously realizing it really was a woman that had been on the bike doing all the amazing tricks she'd pulled.

The announcer walked up beside her, "First, let me congratulate you on all you've accomplished over the course of your career."

"Thanks," she answered in a shy, quiet voice.

She had told Carter this was the source of the biggest fight Brody and she had about doing this job—how Brody never could get it through his thick head how petrified she was to talk in front of people. Watching her from a distance, Carter couldn't help but see how child-like she appeared. She was scared to death, shuffling her feet, clutching her helmet to her like a safety net, and her voice was barely a whisper into the microphone. All he wanted to do was go rescue her.

"That was amazing. How'd you learn that?"

"With lots and lots of practice and with a great teacher."

Carter smiled, hearing the pride in her voice when talking about her brother. Even though the guy was being an ass to him, it was evident how much he loved his sister and Carter couldn't hold that against him. They would just have to work it out between themselves at some point, because he was not about to put Molly in the middle and make her choose.

"So you're saying, kids don't try this at home."

She shook her head and with a stronger voice pled with the kids in the crowd, "No, please don't."

"Well, thanks for being part of the night."

"Thanks for having me."

She grinned nervously as she walked toward Carter. He motioned for her to come closer to him. As she walked slowly to him, she bit her lip and Carter let out a sigh, loving that gesture and look of vulnerability on her face. He hooked his finger in her pants and pulled her the rest of the distance to him, then grinned at her, half proud, half wanting to choke her. "You pulled a fast one on me there, Gorgeous."

Molly giggled nervously as the rest of the guys started giving Carter crap, Eli laughing and smacking his back. "Sterling, that was freaking amazing, you be nice to her."

"You were already nervous, I didn't want to scare you more," she answered him. He could see she was anxiously stifling a fit of nervous giggles.

"Uh huh. It's a good thing you're so damn cute." He leaned down to kiss her then held her tight. "It was amazing and I'm very proud of you, but..." He pulled her away to grin at her, "you scare the absolute shit out of me."

The guys around them all started laughing. "I'm sorry. I don't mean to make you worry."

Still holding her at arm's length, he gave her a worried look. "It gets even worse, doesn't it?"

He could see the mischief in her eyes as she shook her head while biting her lip again. She wrinkled her nose. "Uh huh."

Carter grinned, letting her off the hook then pulled her close for another kiss. "I adore you, Gorgeous."

Chapter Nine

After a late night of racing, Carter and a handful of others often decided to hang around the pits and leave first thing in the morning instead of driving exhausted. Usually they chose to relax, catch up with each other, and simply enjoy a few minutes of down time. Like most nights after the races, several other riders, their wives or girlfriends, and mechanics had joined in.

The circle was growing rapidly and Carter watched as Molly slowly but surely sunk back into her shell, reverting back to the shy girl he'd met only days ago. With one hand, he tugged her arm, and with the other, he patted his thigh, offering for her to sit on his lap. He had honestly expected her to look to Brody first, an automatic gesture seeking his approval, but she didn't. Instead she smiled as she tentatively got up from her chair and sat down sideways across his legs. He knew she was tired, but when she melted against his chest, he thought he'd died and gone to heaven.

Eli walked up with his iPod and speakers. "Hey D, you going to dance with me?"

"Um, here? Seriously?"

"Why not?"

"Well, because everyone is just sitting around, and contrary to popular belief, I try not to make a spectacle of myself."

"You do?" Joey looked at her.

Molly flipped him off.

Joey chuckled at her nonverbal response. "Save that invitation for your boy."

"Classy, Joe. Real classy." She shook her head in disapproval. Carter and she both snickered when Brody smacked Joey on the back of his head.

"Okay." Jesse started their made-up game of Top That again. The objective was to show no hesitation when it was your turn to answer. The current subject for this round was song titles by the Beatles. So far Jesse and Molly were neck and neck. "So, what's another song?"

"What category was it?" Carter asked.

"You get side-tracked by Joey's comment, Sterling?" Eli smiled at him as Carter turned red, embarrassed mainly for the sweet soul sitting on his lap who tried even harder to curl into him. He wrapped his arms around her instinctively. Dylan and his fling of the night sat down to join in the rapidly growing circle. Carter felt Molly's breath on his neck when she tucked herself closer yet. He let out a heavy sigh and threw a warning glance at Dylan. He knew by not wanting to look at the man, she was trying to avoid him. He placed a kiss on her head and rubbed her back, comforting her so she'd stay put on his lap and not retreat to the safety of her motorhome.

"Rock ballads," Jesse answered, laughing at his buddy.

They all started again, throwing out names of good songs, trying to one up each other as to who could keep the game moving with the best song titles.

"Okay…new game," Dylan shouted out.

"Not your stupid injury game." One of the other riders shook his head. "Who wants to be reminded of being hurt and on the sidelines?"

"Oh come on, it's been forever since we've thrown that one around, and we have new people this time."

"What kind of stupid ass game is that?" Brody growled.

"Well," he started, "We all have had injuries and have the scars to prove it. We just shoot out our best ones to see who's toughest. I'm waiting for someone to beat the one that took out my knee."

Carter heard the sharp breath Molly sucked in when Dylan started describing the game. She began to discreetly sit up, keeping her head down. Carter's nerves went on edge, especially after looking across the circle of chairs to see Brody, Erin, and Joey all staring straight at Molly. Carter felt her tense up, and the more in depth Dylan's explanation got, the straighter she sat up on his lap. He could tell she was ready to bolt.

Molly sat stock still, and when general questions came her way, she shrugged her shoulder but never answered outright, seeming to let Brody and Joey do their best to field the game. Carter kept a firm and protective grip on her. He never let his eye contact drop from Brody and Joey, silently praying they would give him some bit of information or a signal—anything to clue him into what was going on.

About three rounds in, Dylan asked her directly about her shoulder. Carter had been wondering about the scar himself, but when he felt her suck in a deep breath and go stiff as she tightened her grip on his forearms, he somehow knew it wasn't from racing. Watching Brody, it looked like someone had sucker punched him.

Carter patted Molly on the back. "Hey, Gorgeous, I wanted to show you my calendar before you leave so we could figure out when you can meet me at my folks' house."

She accepted the opening and jumped up as fast as she could. Carter squeezed her to him as they walked away from the group that was making her so obviously uncomfortable—away from Dylan and away from whatever it was that had her so visibly shaken.

Carter had an arm around her as he guided her silently to his motorhome. He unlocked it and opened the door, leaving it open a crack after they walked in. Carter sat her on the couch, and Molly stared at her hands in her lap while he went and dug around in the fridge. She didn't say a word as he sat down beside her and opened a bottle of water. She waited as he set it on the coffee table in front of her. With all the courage she could gather, Molly looked up at him, her eyes brimming with tears.

"This isn't the way I wanted to have this conversation. I knew I'd have to talk to you about it soon, but not like this. Not so serious and not with me in tears. I hate crying, especially in front of other people, it's so...weak. I just feel so blind-sided." Molly's head dropped as she said the words, unable to watch the expression on Carter's face. She hated him seeing her this way.

Carter took her hands in his, and she wanted to look back up at him, but she was running the gamut of emotions—scared, shaken, distraught, every synonym in the book. Talking about her past was something she didn't do—ever. They hadn't known each other long enough or well enough to dump that kind of emotional baggage on his doorstep. Talk about trial by fire, this was going to send the man screaming for the hills.

She couldn't bring herself to face him, the shame was too heavy. "I don't even know where to start, Carter."

She felt her knuckles being lifted, then lightly kissed by his warm, soft lips. "Take your time, Gorgeous. It's okay. When you're ready, just start at the beginning."

Molly opened her eyes, only to watch the tears fall in her lap. Her eyes closed again with the deep breath she struggled to take in. "I didn't move in with Brody so he could train me, Carter." Even in her own ears, her breathing was jagged. She forced the next sentence out. It would be the hardest one, the rest would tumble out, if she could just get the first words out.

"I moved in with the Nolands to…" She paused for several long seconds. "To…escape."

She felt the tension in Carter drop on her like a lead weight. When she finally found the power to look up at him, the devastation on his face crushed her. She alternated between watching his Adam's apple as he swallowed hard and trying to decipher his horribly sad eyes. He didn't pressure her to continue, he just waited patiently for her next move.

She'd been drawn to him from the minute she met him. There was a connection so instant, so strong she could feel it with her entire being. For the first time in her life, she didn't try to wipe the tears away or flee the conversation. Instead she let her eyes close and her head drop and just let the story out.

"I started racing when I was very little. I grew up on tracks, like you, I'm sure. When I was nine, my mom died." She heard the sharp intake of air Carter took, felt him squeeze her hands, urging her on, but he stayed silent.

"After that my biological father, Ray, started drinking, a lot. Then he…" Her head lowered even further. "He started…um…" She looked up at Carter, her lip in her teeth. "He started smacking me around. Over time it just got worse and worse."

Molly went on, explaining to Carter how her maternal grandparents were already gone and Ray's parents didn't believe her. So she had no one. Molly continued with the whole ugly tale of all the hospitals and lying to doctors. How easy it was because she raced and no one ever really questioned it. They just assumed there wasn't any other reason for all the broken bones, arms, wrists — ribs, plus the countless stitches she'd needed over time.

"Finally one day Ray screwed up at a track. George worked on the amateur circuits back then, I'm sure you probably remember. Later, I found out he'd known and had been trying to get me help. He had a friend that was a lawyer and the two of them had set it up with James and Karen, they were just waiting on proof. One day Ray got really mad at the track and lost it. I guess George and his attorney had never thought it would end up that bad...that when Ray finally got caught, it would be so close. George said when I didn't show up for one of my heats, he knew.

"I never asked what happened at the track that day. All I know is that I woke up in a hospital several days later. George, his wife Eileen, James, Karen, and the lawyer were all waiting.

"They put him away on attempted murder. I think that last time was more serious than anyone really let me know. And I guess the surgery was pretty hairy. So he got put away and I got to live. I guess we're even." She took a shaky breath. "I owe everything to the Noland family, to George and Eileen. I have no doubt in my mind I would not be here today without all of them."

During the whole, ugly story, she'd been looking down, watching the tears fall and shaking as she held on tight to his hand. "Can you promise me something?" she asked in barely more than a whisper.

"Anything." His voice proved he'd been shaken to the core.

She looked back up at him, her eyes pleading. "Can you please not treat me any different than you have all weekend? I'm not fragile, Carter, I'm all healed. I have the most amazing family and friends now, and...and I have you. Please? Promise me?"

"Oh, baby." He pulled her to him. He held her so close to him that it was as if he was hanging on for dear life. "I promise. I promise to love and protect you too. Oh my God." He took a deep breath. "You really are the most amazing woman in the world. I just don't know how you got through all that, Gorgeous."

"I knew God had something better for me." At that admission, her tears started again. He held her as she cried and then cried some more, until at last there weren't any tears left. He left her side only to get a cold cloth and something for the headache that was throbbing. Molly finally felt some relief after over a decade of silence—silence that was completely of her own will. She knew the Nolands were there for her, they were her family. They cared for and loved her as their own and protected her with a vengeance.

It was just different laying out the whole sordid mess for Carter. As she lay on his couch drifting in and out of sleep, she felt him take her shoes off, place a pillow under her head, and cover her up with a blanket. When he sat back down next to her, he whispered loving words and gently stroked her hair until at last she fell asleep.

The door of Carter's motorhome was left open a crack, and Brody peeked in to see Carter sitting on the edge of the couch, running his hand through Molly's hair. From Brody's side, Erin pulled the door open a couple of inches further then grabbed his elbow. "She's asleep, Brody. Don't go in there like a bull in a china shop."

"Well, he should have brought her to me by now. What do you expect?"

"I expect you to calm yourself down and not to act like a total ass. I know it will be hard for you, but you can at least try."

Brody turned to his girlfriend with a curled lip and rolled his eyes. He didn't care if he acted like an asshole, a prick, or any other of the colorful terms Erin and Molly had thrown at him over the last three days. They could hate him for all he cared, but at the end of the day, Molly would be taken care of one way or another. It was his job, and he'd do it—not this guy.

Talk about shit hitting the fan. First the call from his dad and then that jackass Dylan had to bring up her shoulder. And just to make his life worse, Molly had to find herself a boyfriend. Wasn't that the damn cherry on top? A boyfriend. Oh, God. He rolled his shoulders at the thought.

He watched Carter lean down and kiss the side of her head and tuck the blanket up closer to her chin. Then he leaned over and grabbed his phone and keys off the table. Brody stepped back from the door when Carter went to push it the rest of the way open.

"Oh, good, I was just coming to find you guys." Carter climbed out of the motorhome and gestured to the sleeping woman on his couch. "She cried herself to sleep. I didn't want to wake her, especially with the headache she had."

"That's okay. Carter, thank you so much for getting her out of there. I have a feeling she told you everything?" Erin asked before she closed the gap and offered Carter a hug. Brody held in the glare as Carter nodded as he hugged Erin back.

"Are you okay? That's a lot to take in." She patted his arm.

"Oh God, don't worry about me. I can't believe she's been through all that. It broke my heart to hear her tell me. I knew there had to be something, some reason you were so protective of her, Brody. Well, both of you. But in my worst dreams, I never saw this coming."

"Yeah…well." Brody's attention darted between Carter and the open door. "Mind if I go on in? I need to get her home."

"Don't wake her, Brody. Really, she's fine here on my couch, she's sound asleep. She's safe, I promise." Carter raised his hands in surrender. "I won't touch her, but she's had a rough night and she just needs to rest."

Before he could argue, Erin chimed in. "Oh, Brody. Let her be. She's okay. We can trust him."

"How do you know?"

"Brody…stop it." Erin smacked his arm, scrunching her eyebrows. She wasn't joking and he could tell she was starting to really get pissed. It took a long time, but once Erin was pissed, she'd be hell to live with. And unfortunately, that was the last thing Erin needed with everything else. Brody let out a breath and conceded, only for Erin.

"Fine." The word was forced, just like his hand. Something he was getting damned sick of lately. "This is a one-time thing," he warned, before rattling off his cell number for Carter, watching as he entered it in his phone.

"There. I just sent you a text back, so you'll have mine."

Brody felt the buzz in his pocket. It did little to reassure him, but that was all he was getting tonight.

The guy had been perceptive tonight and gotten his sister away from the questions. He'd been about to do the same thing, he'd been watching for a sign from her then suddenly Carter had whisked her away. He'd been expecting Carter to come running for help, not knowing how to handle the panic attack Brody knew would be coming. He never did.

"Did she get really upset?"

"She cried from the moment I sat her on the couch until she just fell asleep on me. She was whispering one minute about something, the next thing I knew, she was asleep in my arms."

"But, like really upset?"

"Like the other night? No." Carter shook his head.

Brody saw the relief spill over Erin's face. "Oh, Brody, that's amazing. No panic attack."

Then he watched as she turned to Carter and gave him all the glory. "You have no idea how huge that is, Carter. That's all you. You just have no idea."

"I didn't do anything, Erin. Really, I was just there for her."

Brody wanted to scream.

Instead, he motioned toward the door. "You mind?"

"You don't have to ask. Go on in."

Brody went in and knelt beside her. He wished like hell he knew the right thing to do. He knew what the right thing for him was. Load her ass up and drive all night and tomorrow too, deliver her safe and sound back to their parents, and buy a lock for her door. Lightly running his knuckles over her cheek, he couldn't help but ask himself what the right thing was for her. The war inside him was raging.

Being the same age as her, being raised together, they'd both suffered the effects of James and Karen's parenting. They'd been what he'd considered overprotective of him as a kid, but when Molly moved in, that was taken to a whole new level, bordering on insane. The funny thing was, no one saw it at the time. Instead of he and Molly against his parents, he'd joined forces with them to make sure she was never hurt again. They were homeschooled, so that left just home and the tracks. At the track she was never alone. Ever. Looking back, Brody realized until this weekend she'd never fought it. She'd never complained once about being smothered or suffocated.

She had to have been. On one hand, Brody didn't know how else to act with her, but on the other, he knew damned well that he could never have lived like that if it'd been him. James had raised them both not trust other men around her.

He leaned down and whispered how much he loved her and then stood. He took the smile Erin gave him for what it was—pride. He stepped back out of the motorhome and shocked even himself by offering Carter a hand.

"Thank you…for taking care of my sister."

"You never have to thank me, Brody. She means everything to me."

Brody ignored the last part. "When are you pulling out tomorrow?"

"I'm not going anywhere until I know she's okay. What about you?"

Erin rubbed Carter's arm. "We can be flexible. Just let us know when she wakes up."

"Of course."

Brody took a deep breath and nodded before looking through the door one last time. He mumbled, "Thanks," once more, before turning to walk away with Erin under his arm.

For a minute, Carter watched Brody and Erin walk away. It was a long sixty seconds spent trying to wrap his head around everything he'd learned tonight. When he figured it'd been enough time and Brody wasn't going to change his mind and come charging back, Carter went back inside, shutting the door softly behind him. He grabbed the water she'd left untouched off the table and sat in the recliner across from her. Not realizing how dry his throat was, the bottle was empty in two long pulls. He sat peeling the label off the empty bottle for a long while, contemplating her childhood hell.

When at last he was blurry-eyed, he stood. Against his better judgment, he crossed the floor and cradled Molly in his arms. He laid her, still asleep, in his unmade bed and crossed to his dresser. When he turned back with the t-shirt, her eyes were open. "Hi, Gorgeous. I thought you'd be more comfortable in here. I'll sleep on the couch."

The sleepy smile warmed his battered heart.

"Here's a t-shirt for you." She sat up and he laid it down beside her.

"Carter?"

"Yeah, honey?"

"Would you? I mean, do you mind?" He searched her face as she stumbled for the words she wanted. "Would you sleep in here…with me?"

How did she know how badly he wanted just that? "Oh, sweetheart. Yes. I'll stay with you. Are you okay?"

"Yeah, I just…I don't want to be alone."

Carter pulled her to standing and engulfed her in his arms. "You'll never be alone again. I'll be right here, I'm not going anywhere. I promise." He let his arms slowly drop away. "You get dressed, I'll come back in when you're in bed."

He turned to give her some privacy when she reached out to stop him. He slowly turned back around, looking down at the beautiful girl staring back up at him. The moment stretched on as they shared the silence, in it an unspoken understanding. Molly bit at her lip as she slowly raised her arms over her head. Carter sucked in a breath, amazed at the trust she was placing in him. He lowered his hands to the hem of her tight fitted t-shirt and slowly lifted.

This wasn't at all the way he'd imagined how it would be the first time he undressed her. He took what she was offering—her last secret. The ones she could hide under her clothes. He tried to keep his face neutral, to keep the bile from coming up his throat. He had seen her in a sports bra, and she hadn't tried to hide before, but seeing her now was like seeing her for the first time.

He dropped her shirt to the floor and ran his finger over her shoulder, and her eyes slowly lowered with her head. He ran his thumb over the mark under her chin, and at last, she nodded. He continued to shower each trace of her past with gentle touches and light brushes of his lips. He unclasped her bra and slipped his t-shirt over her head. There would be time for looking at her body for pleasure. Tonight wasn't it. She had offered herself to him completely, vulnerable and open, a treasure he would never take for granted.

He helped her into the bed then crossed to the other side. Shucking his clothes along the way, he left his boxers on for her comfort and prayed he wouldn't embarrass himself. The instant he laid down, she rolled to him. Feeling her in his arms, albeit in less than romantic circumstances, still felt like home. She fit him. The whole of her, he wanted it all. When she drifted back to sleep, her breath on his bare shoulder, he knew he'd found the love of his life.

He traced patterns on her bare arm for what must have been hours. When at last he couldn't keep his eyes open another minute, he whispered the words he wanted so badly for her to hear, right before he thanked God she was alive and with him now.

☙❧

When she started to stir, Carter rolled from his back to his side and softly brushed the hair from her face. Her eyes fluttered open. "Morning, Gorgeous," he said quietly.

She gave him a small smile. "Hi," she whispered.

She cuddled up to him. "You feel so good next to me." She rubbed his smooth, bare chest with her fingers.

He drew in a long breath at the contact. "How are you doing this morning?"

She snuggled even closer to him. "I'm okay, a little embarrassed, but good."

"Well, you have absolutely nothing to be embarrassed about, baby." Carter hugged her tight, just wanting to keep her with him. He'd been sick to his stomach all night, between her past she'd told him about and not wanting to be away from her now even more because of it. Several times in the night, he'd squeezed her against his chest, needing to comfort himself.

"I'm sorry about last night, Carter. I sure didn't want to be crying uncontrollably to you the first weekend we met."

"Gorgeous, I'm just worried about you."

"I'm fine. I'm sorry, really." She took a deep breath and looked up. "Carter..."

"Yeah baby?"

"I really was going to tell you, just in my own way. You know, a little more casual, not like that. Not so damned dramatic."

"No. I have no worries about that. It was just hard to see you so upset."

"I'm really sorry."

"Molly, stop apologizing. I want you to be able to count on me for anything."

"Well, you have definitely proven yourself worthy."

He saw her actually smile for the first time and started to feel some relief. "How's your head?"

"Pounding."

"How about some breakfast and something for your head?"

She nodded, but cuddled up closer to him, kissed his chest, and shut her eyes again.

He grinned proudly. "I'm glad you're not rushing to get out of my bed." He chuckled lightly. "I was a little afraid you'd be kinda freaked out this morning."

"You took such good care of me last night and you feel so good to lie next to. Thank you, by the way…for everything. I kind of dumped a lot on you. I wouldn't blame you if you ran screaming the other direction."

"Gorgeous, I'm not going anywhere."

Molly looked up at him. A smirk of a grin appeared and he immediately felt better. "You know…when I thought about our first night together and how it would be, last night wasn't really how I pictured it," she giggled.

The sound of her laughter made the weight fall off his shoulders. "Oh, really?" He didn't try to hide the huge grin that split his face. "You've been thinking about that have you?" Her cheeks flashed red and the giggling continued instead of answering him. "Uh huh, I think you have."

"Well, do you blame me? You're hot."

Carter felt so much better after hearing her laugh and joke with him. "Oh, Gorgeous, I adore you." He sighed and stared at the ceiling, hating that this perfect morning was coming to a close. "Hey, Mol, we need to let Brody know how you're doing. He's been really worried, and the longer you slept, the more worried he got. He's sent two texts already."

She laid her head back down tucked herself close to his bare chest. "I don't want to move."

Carter's heart swelled. "I'm glad, but what if I do this?" He pinched her butt.

"Nope." She shook her head and chuckled.

"What about this?" He tickled her waist.

She wiggled. "Nope."

"Are you sure?" He started to tickle her with both hands.

She put up a good fight, wiggling and struggling, but started laughing uncontrollably, "Okay, okay…Uncle!"

"That's my girl."

"Just for that, I'm keeping your t-shirt." She pulled the collar up to her nose. "It smells like you."

"Baby, you can have it." He paused. "But…"

"Uh-oh."

"Yep, there's a catch. When we sleep in the same town, the shirt sleeps here." She snickered but he continued, "What do you think?" He wiggled his eyebrows at her. "Come on, Gorgeous, I'll be good, I promise."

"Well….you said, the shirt sleeps here. You didn't say anything about me." Laughing, she started to roll away from him.

He grabbed her and rolled on top of her. "I think you know what I meant."

"I don't know…I think I got you on a technicality."

Grinning, he slid one hand down her back to grab her bare butt, courtesy of her thong, and squeezed. "Oh yeah?"

"Yep."

"Well, Gorgeous, let me clarify this for you." He leaned down to kiss her. "I want the t-shirt with you in it. Stay with me next weekend. What do you think?"

A nervous smile played at her mouth as she looked up at him.

"I'll be good, I promise. I won't try anything. It's just that last night was so right, lying beside you, listening to you breathing, feeling your skin against mine. I liked knowing you were right here beside me. I want this, the laughing and talking in bed. I like this alone time with you."

He could see her struggling. The nice guy in him wanted to tell her not to worry about it, it wasn't a big deal. Every other part of him wanted to keep begging until she caved.

"Will you be upset if I ask for time to…think about it?"

"Not at all. If you don't want to or don't want to upset Brody, that's fine. I understand. I won't be upset." He winked down at her and saw the relief in her face. "I just wanted you to know where I'd like you to be, and that's with me."

The knock on the door made her jump in his arms.

"That's probably Eli or Jess wanting to check on you before they pull out." Carter gave her a quick peck, before hopping out of bed and pulling on his jeans from last night. "Ah, I guess I should have woken you, it's after eight and you didn't get your run in."

"I'd rather have been here." Molly smiled as she got out of bed, pulling on her jeans as well, but leaving on his t-shirt.

The knock on the door was louder the second time. Carter opened it, fully ready to welcome in one or both of his two best friends. Instead, it was her brother. Shit. If Brody would lighten up a little, Carter would meet him half way in a heartbeat. As it was, Carter felt like he'd snap in two from bending over backwards to try please the man.

"Come on in, Brody," he said, deliberately trying to keep his voice welcoming. "Hey, Carter? Where are my shoes?"

Brody's attention immediately went to the voice from the bedroom.

"They're out here."

"What in the hell?" Brody's head whipped back to Carter and his voice went to steel.

Carter was so taken back, he didn't answer. Judging by the anger in Brody's eyes, Carter's silence was apparently fanning the flames.

"Did she not sleep on the couch?"

"No. I didn't." Molly appeared in the main room, unflustered.

Carter only wished he could be so calm. "We didn't do anything, Brody. I promised you last night. I offered for her to sleep in the bed. I wouldn't do anything to take advantage of her."

"And I'm the one who asked him to stay with me, beside me. And that's what he did, if it was any of your business, but since it's not…back off, Brody."

Brody just ignored her and directed his anger at Carter. "I knew I couldn't trust you, man. You're just like all the rest."

"Brody." Carter wouldn't fight back, but he wasn't going to let him assume the worst by any stretch of the imagination. "I am not," Carter said, emphasizing each word. "I told you before, I will do anything to protect her and make her happy. I will never hurt her." He kept his gaze level, his breathing calm, and his voice low. If this ended badly, he didn't want Molly to have any reason to be mad at him.

"Enough." Molly's voice and tone had both men's attention immediately. "You're out of line, Brody."

"Dad is going—"

"Oh, don't you worry. I'm calling James the minute I step out of this motorhome. I know you were worried and upset about last night, something I appreciate, but you coming in here half-cocked, ready to start something, is bullshit. You want to love me, great. I love you too. You want to protect me, great. Saturdays around here can get crazy and I don't like crowds. You know that. So great, I appreciate the help. But when it comes to this…" Molly motioned between Carter and herself "You have no say, no jurisdiction, no comments, nothing. This is my decision."

She pointed at the open door. "We'll finish this conversation in a few minutes."

Carter watched her chest heave with the angered breaths she was taking. Later on, he'd have to remind himself to never piss her off. After that, he'd laugh his ass off at how the little, barely over five foot tall girl had brought her brother, who was almost a foot taller than her, to his knees. She was definitely a little spitfire.

Brody looked between the two of them and left without another word.

"Why? Why do you keep putting up with this?"

Carter took her in his arms and whispered against her ear, "Because I'm in love with you, Molly."

Chapter Ten

A couple of days later, her cell phone rang. Molly answered on the first ring. That phone hadn't left her side since the moment they'd pulled out of California last Sunday morning.

"Hi." Molly couldn't help but sound eager to hear from him. She had tried really hard the first couple of times he'd called to play it cool, not wanting to sound like a giggly little high school girl hearing from the quarterback, but she couldn't help it. When she saw his number appear, her heart sped up and her excitement couldn't be contained, so she'd given up. Now she didn't care, and judging by his laughter on the other end, he didn't seem to mind.

"Hey Gorgeous, how's my girl?" He chuckled.

"Better now. It's so good to hear your voice. How was practice?"

"Fine. We're getting ready to pull out and head to Houston."

"I can't wait. We're leaving early in the morning. Brody has the trailers packed, except for my bike since I need to practice one more time before we load it."

"I miss you."

"I miss you too. I can't wait for you to hold me again." She wasn't used missing someone, like half of her was gone. Sure, she'd been away from Karen or James over the years. Karen and James had stopped traveling with her when Brody had taken over her training after he'd retired, so she missed both of her adoptive parents. This longing she felt for Carter was very different though, it was so much stronger. She was having a hard time not crossing that mental line of being needy.

"Good...I'm glad. I have to tell you something."

She could hear the lightness in his voice, but still she was a bit skeptical. "Okay?"

"It's not bad."

"Uh huh?"

"My parents are coming in for the race this week. They were supposed to come for last week's, but something came up at the store."

"And?"

"And, I want you to meet them. Hang out with us."

"Oh, Lordy."

"Come on, it will be fun."

She took a slow breath, gathering some courage. "Okay. Can I ask you a question?"

"Sure."

"A question guys don't want to answer?" She may not have had any real world experience when it came to relationships, but she'd watched enough chick-flicks to know guys didn't like to be cornered. They usually stared with the deer in the headlights eyes, started mumbling incoherently, and ran out of the room. If the girl was lucky, by the end of the movie, he might come to his senses and carry her off into the sunset. Molly was pretty sure love in real life wasn't so easily wrapped up with a pretty bow.

"Yeah."

"What does this mean?"

"What does what mean?"

Damn. The man is going to make me spell it out for him. "Well, everything is moving so fast. And meeting the parents is kind of a really big deal."

"Can I be honest?"

"I only want honest, you know that, Carter." She could picture him grinning on the other end of the line.

The short time apart had made him miss her to the point it hurt. It also gave him time to think. After she'd laid herself on the line last Saturday night, he felt it was only fair to do the same. It might go a long way to reassuring her—he sucked in a breath—or it might scare the living hell out of her. He hadn't wanted to have this conversation over the phone, but they only got limited time alone at the track. That, and well, he couldn't keep it to himself another minute.

"I'm twenty-eight, Molly, almost twenty-nine. And that's really close to thirty. I'm ready. I've been ready. I've known that when the right girl walked into my life, I'd be ready to settle down...and I knew it when you walked into my life. I partied a little when I was younger, I'm over it. Now I have a career that I have to think about and I love it, but most women don't understand it. I've done the long distance thing before with a woman who didn't get it. I'm done trying to make up for the fact I'm always on the road, trying to make them believe that I'm not screwing around and cheating, having to buy their affection to make up for the fact I'm never around. I'm done with all that. On the flip side, I'm not a guy who just hooks up randomly on the weekends. I don't need embarrassing pictures of me showing up on the internet because I took a chance with a stranger."

That was a part of his career that Carter took very seriously, more so than the winning even. He was a role model, even beyond the scope of future racers, but to the kids that just loved his sport. He wouldn't do anything to damage his reputation. The thought that a slip in his judgment, even just one time, would give unwritten permission to a young person to repeat his mistake, that was unforgiveable. He would never let it happen.

"I want someone who understands my life and me. I want someone who can appreciate all the time I put into this, the practicing and the workouts and even the travel. This is harder than most women realize and I am tired of them thinking I'm just playing and telling me to get a real job."

"It is a real job, Carter." Carter could almost see Molly raise her eyebrows over the distance. "You had someone tell you otherwise?"

Carter smiled to himself as he continued. "I honestly didn't know if there might be someone out there who really gets it. I really didn't, but you walked up to our group that day, and I knew in that moment that my life was about to change. I know it feels like this is moving fast, but I'm not going to risk losing you because I didn't take the chance. You're everything I've ever wanted. You make it fun now. You're sweet and sassy at the same time. You're absolutely gorgeous and funny. And this will embarrass you…" He smiled to himself picturing her. He could only imagine how red her cheeks were becoming. "But when I kiss and hold you, it turns me on every single time."

He heard her suck in a breath over the line, and he pulled in a deep breath himself so he could continue.

"I love you, Molly." The words came out slow and deliberate.

He listened to her rapid breathing in the phone for what felt like eternity. "I know it's all happening so fast, but I know what I feel, Molly. I know this is right." He grinned to himself hesitantly because she still had yet to say anything, "I don't think I can follow the rules on this stuff, not with you."

Please say something, please say something, anything.

"I've never told another woman that I love her, Molly. You're the one, Gorgeous."

He could feel the sweat start to bead up on the back of his neck and his heart was racing like he had been running for twenty miles. His stomach dropped and he mentally cursed himself for not waiting until they were face-to-face to drop that line on her. He wanted to be there and see her eyes go wide with surprise, but then watch as the smile broke across her face, lighting up the whole room. He wanted to pull her into his arms and feel her heart beating fast at his admission.

"I love you too, Carter," she whispered back.

"Really?" He was bordering on sounding pathetic and he just didn't give a damn. The girl of his dreams had told him she loved him. To hear the words spoken back to him, it was worth everything. All the hours they'd been apart and the nasty looks and rude comments from her brother, those things just fell away. She loved him and nothing else in the world mattered.

"You have just made me the happiest man alive. I really have fallen completely in love with you."

"I have too, Carter." She paused, but he could tell she was gearing up. "So...can I, um, call you my boyfriend?" she asked in this cute, tiny voice.

Carter wanted to shout from the rooftops, he wanted to go caveman on her and throw over his shoulder and carry her off and never let her out of his sight. Instead he laughed into the phone, his happiness hopefully carrying through to his new girlfriend.

"You'd better. Because, Gorgeous, you're off the market. You're mine!"

"I like the sound of that."

His smile was so big his cheeks were starting to hurt. "I've heard you say that before."

"I mean it, too."

"Good. Ugh…Molly. I can hardly wait to see you again. This is killing me."

It was too. He had worn his cell battery down more than once, staring at the pictures he'd taken of her. There was one thing that was really bothering him though. In all their conversations since they'd last seen each other, she hadn't mentioned anything being wrong. Not that he wanted that, but after that incident with Brody and the phone call, he'd been on edge waiting for her to call with bad news of some sort. She hadn't. That had him worried. To make matters worse, he didn't want to come out and ask her outright for fear there was something going on, and that she didn't know about it.

He heard her sigh into the phone. "Me too, Carter."

"Well, Gorgeous, we're getting ready to hit the road. I won't call again until we stop for gas, so it will be awhile."

"I know. I hope today and tomorrow fly by. Thursday seems so far away."

"I love you so much, Gorgeous."

"I love you too, Carter. Be careful."

"Bye, baby."

"Bye."

He let out a deep breath. This was going to be the longest damn season in history. He had asked her flat out for the long distance relationship. It was better than no relationship with her by far, but telling her goodbye over and over was about to do him in. He could hear the sadness creep into her voice as she knew they were nearing the end of their calls. He hated that he was causing her pain of any kind, but the alternative was not an option.

৯৽৶

"There's my girl."

Carter's voice came from behind her, but before she could turn, he picked her up and swung her around by the waist. In that instant, all was right with the world again. She turned and smiled up at the man holding her in his arms.

"Oh, Carter, I missed you so much."

"I missed you too, Gorgeous."

She hugged him close, feeling the hard plane of muscles against her, smelling his now familiar cologne. With that, the stress of the last few days vanished. The rest of the men in her world seemed to be drinking out of the same punch bowl, because James, Brody, and even Joey were all losing it. Driving her crazy in the process. Their possessive glances and hushed conversations combined with their over the top smothering were wearing her patience thin. On top of all of that, she had missed Carter so much that her heart actually hurt. Her nerves were frazzled, her patience worn thin, and she was dead tired. She hadn't realized how tired she had been the last few months until she'd had the best sleep of her adult life. Probably in her whole life if she wanted to be honest.

That one night she'd spent in Carter's arms was worth more than gold in her book. Since that night, sleep was something that had eluded her almost completely.

She closed her eyes as she listened to his heart beating, his palm on her back, rubbing her gently, but keeping her pressed to him. She felt herself sway and forced her eyes open.

"Are you okay, Mol?"

"Yeah, just really tired, and really glad to see you."

"How about this, we'll go up to the pits and eat with Jesse and Eli, and then I'll walk you back here to your motorhome and you can get to bed early. What do you think? And tell Erin and Brody they're more than welcome to join us if they want. I saw Joey up by your semi as I passed it on my way here. We can holler at him on the way."

His words said one thing, but Molly could see the hopefulness in his face. If she had to pick one thing that was keeping her mind spinning at night, it was his offer. He'd asked her last week to stay with him for the weekend. She wanted to — more than anything. She had thought about it, weighed the pros and cons, made mental lists. It'd circled around it in her head so many times she was dizzy, but he wasn't pushing. She could tell he was waiting for her to make the first move, no pressure from him whatsoever.

If she didn't have this on-going struggle with Brody, her decision would have been made already. The guilt from disappointing him or, even worse, hurting him, was paralyzing.

"What do you think, sweetie? I know you have to be starving."

She looked up at the ice blue eyes. His lopsided smile reached clear up to his eyes, making the corners crinkle. Her heart melted all over again.

"I'd love that."

∂∽෧

Molly finished changing into a pair of tiny sleep shorts and a t-shirt, ready for bed. She came out of the bathroom in their motorhome yawning and ready to drop. They had stayed longer in the pits than she should have, but she wasn't ready to be away from Carter. She had been ready to get away from her brother's penetrating looks, though. The eye rolls, the snarled lip. She had had enough. She was embarrassed Brody was treating Carter so rudely, and she wanted to put them both out of their misery. She wasn't faking being tired, but it was an excuse to put an end to the evening. Brody's disapproval was the first thing she saw when she opened the bathroom door.

"I don't like you sitting on his lap."

"Brody, leave her alone."

Erin tried to run interference for Molly as best she could, and Molly appreciated it, but she also didn't want to cause an argument between Erin and her brother. Molly let out a breath and turned to Erin, ignoring her brother completely. "Good night, Erin." She bent to kiss her cheek and whispered, "Thanks," into Erin's ear.

"I love you, Mol."

"Love you, too."

Molly folded out the blankets on the couch and lay down, never once looking up at her brother who hadn't moved. He was still standing in the same spot he had been when she came out of the bathroom, leaned against the kitchen counter, his legs stretched out and crossed at the ankles, his arms crossed over his chest. To any other person, he'd look imposing. Molly just found him infuriating. However, she was too tired to argue with him. Well, tired, but also she'd reached that point where, although she loved him dearly, she was done. She was tired of his rude comments to Carter and she was tired of being treated like a child. She rolled over, hoping he'd get the hint and go to bed.

When she heard the soft click of the bedroom door, she rolled to her back and let out a sigh of relief. Molly stared into the darkness for over an hour. The green numbers on the clock on the oven moved slower than molasses. Before she changed her mind, she threw back the blankets. She looked at the two bedroom doors, both shut. Erin and Brody in one, Joey in the other. Molly crossed to the door of the motorhome, opened it quietly, and slipped outside.

Sitting in his motorhome watching TV, Carter thought he heard something. He turned the sound down to listen and heard a soft knock. He opened the latch and pushed the door open, looking down in the open doorway. The unsure smile and big blue eyes almost made his knees buckle underneath him.

"Molly, come in, honey. Is everything okay? Are you all right?"

"Your light was on, are you sure you were still up? Did I wake you?"

"No, baby, I'm up." He pulled her into his arms for a minute before pulling her by the hands to the couch to sit beside him. "What's wrong, Molly?"

"Nothing's wrong."

He could tell she was nervous. She'd sneak glances at him every few seconds, always with her lip between her teeth. Carter was sure she'd be twisting the hem of her shorts in her fists if he didn't have her hands already in his.

"Carter, I love you."

He brushed the hair off her face and tucked it behind her ear. "Ah, sweetie, I love you too."

"Carter?"

He brushed his knuckles over the soft skin of her cheek. "Yeah, baby?"

"I'm…"

She looked back down. Carter could feel her nerves, he was half afraid to move for fear she'd startle out of her own skin. He was starting to get nervous that something was really wrong. She could hardly look at him. His stomach dropped. Oh God. She was there to break it off with him. They were just getting started. He drew in a shaky breath, waiting for the words he knew were coming. Damn it, Brody. Carter knew he was going to try to drive them apart. Well, he'd been patient, he'd been the good guy, he had been the guy Molly needed him to be, but if Brody thought Carter would just let the love of his life walk away, then her brother wasn't just crazy. He was freaking stupid, because he wasn't backing down without a fight.

"I'm…um…I'm…ready," Molly said, barely loud enough for him to make out the words.

Huh?

He watched as she slowly brought her chin up, and at last her eyes met his, her lip in her teeth, of course. Those deep blue eyes blinked then went wide as she waited. Waited for him.

"Molly?"

"I've thought about it—a lot. I'm ready. I want to be with you."

Oh my God. Carter knew he had to be dreaming. Any minute he was going to wake up, in his bed—alone, but he could feel the warmth of her skin under his palm as he held her face in his hand. Carter ran his thumb over her lips then brought her chin closer so he could kiss her.

"Are you sure? This changes everything, Molly."

"I know."

He was trying like hell to keep his possessive side under control, but she was unraveling him thread by thread. "No. I mean, it changes everything. You'll be mine. No going back, you'll be mine—forever. I won't be able to let you go."

"I don't want you to."

"Are you really sure?"

"Yes, I am. I love you."

One thought stopped him. As much as he wanted to run to his bed with her in a fireman hold, he had to ask first. Unfortunately, he knew what the answer was going to be.

"Does Brody know you're here?"

"No, it's none of his business."

"He's your brother."

"Exactly. He's my brother, not my keeper."

"I hate that I'm coming between the two of you, Molly."

"I'm not going to lie to you and tell you things are fine. But Carter, I can't put my happiness on hold because he still sees that fourteen-year-old broken girl who showed up on his doorstep one day. We've both grown up since then, he just can't see that."

Molly squeezed his hands. "I love you, Carter…I want you."

"I know you do, Gorgeous, and you don't have to prove that to me. When I asked you to stay with me, I really only wanted to feel you beside me at night. Nothing more, no pressure, I promise."

"I know, and I'm not trying to prove anything. To you, to Brody, not even to myself. I told you, I've had several days to think about this, Carter. I'm ready. I wouldn't tell you that if I wasn't."

"Molly," he said quietly, his resistance fading fast.

She reached over and put her hand to his cheek and kissed him softly on the lips. "I'm sure," she said again.

Carter's heart took off in a mad dash and he tried to take a deep breath. This was not where he'd expected this night to go. The lower half of his body was screaming for him to hurry before she changed her mind, but he also understood the emotional weight on them both. He absolutely had to keep himself under control, since this would be her first time. He stood up and held out his hand for her then he led her down the short hall to the small bedroom and turned on the bed side lamp.

"I want to be able to see you, is that okay?"

She gave him a little nod. He turned and ran his hands up her arms, up her neck, to her face. Molly glided her hands gently around his waist and as she parted her lips, just barely, he slipped his tongue over hers. The two of them stood kissing for what felt like an eternity. He was going to take this slow.

Her muscles rippled under his hands as he skimmed his palms down her arms and made his way down to her waist. He was trying to gauge every sharp breath she took, watching for signals to stop. Just under the hem of her t-shirt, he ran his fingers across the skin of her stomach, weighing her reaction, before he inched the fabric up. Molly let the kiss go and raised her arms up for him to slide the top off. She'd been ready for bed, he realized, when he saw that she didn't have a bra on. He kept the chuckle to himself. She had wanted him, had come to him because she was ready. That was heady knowledge and his heart swelled at the thought.

Carter ran his hands slowly over her and her breath caught. "Are you okay, Gorgeous?"

In barely more than a whisper, she murmured, "Yes."

Molly tugged at Carter's t-shirt, and he helped her pull it up over his head. Immediately he grabbed her, holding her to close to him, skin to skin.

"Oh my God, you feel good." Carter rubbed her back, then moved her hair off her neck and leaned down to kiss the soft skin there, his other hand massaging her side. She sighed and kissed his bare chest. He pulled away an inch or so and ran a finger from her side to her stomach, along the elastic waistband of her pajama shorts. With little effort, the tiny shorts fell to the ground. She stepped out of them, leaving her in nothing but a sapphire blue lace thong.

"God...you are beautiful."

His hands slid around to squeeze her perfect ass as she rubbed her hands over his chest and stomach. He thought he would die when she ran her fingers down his torso to where his muscles sloped into a deep V. She attempted to undo the button-fly of his jeans, but couldn't work the buttons. He grinned. "Let me help you." He unbuttoned them, leaving the jeans hanging open.

Leaning over, he scooped her up. She kissed his neck as he laid her gently on the bed.

"I'll be right back," he whispered.

He really didn't plan on this, but he'd been damned sure to be prepared just in case. Carter went to the bathroom. Returning seconds later, he placed a condom on the night stand and watched as she smiled shyly up at him.

"Are you sure you're all right?" Carter asked again, and again she nodded. He pushed his jeans and boxers to the ground, and with her watching him, he walked around the bed to lie beside her. Carter tried not to let her wide eyes embarrass him. He knew she'd never been in the same room as a naked man before. The shock and innocence on her face was adorable, and he memorized it for a day when he was old and gray.

As Carter sunk onto the bed beside her, she laid back down. He propped himself up on one elbow and watched her face as he ran his hand from her cheek, down her neck, and over her body. He could feel her heart pounding in her chest as he caressed her breasts. Molly watched his face, just focusing on his eyes. He saw every flutter, every blink, and every time she opened them wide. She could hide nothing from him in those deep blues.

"I love you so much," he said quietly, then leaned down to kiss her gently on the lips.

He moved his kisses down her jaw and continued to let his mouth roam down her body. She sucked in a breath as he took her breast in his mouth. Molly let a small groan escape as his fingers slid down the middle of her body. Carter wanted to make this moment last. As his hands ran over her body, lost in exploration, her breathing became fast and choppy. He watched her eyes dilate as his fingers slipped under her thong. As his hand slipped further, her breath was sucked in on a hiss.

He lowered to kiss her chest again then watched her face for one last signal to stop, before he slowly pulled her panties down. Her eyes went wide once more, her mouth parted as the tip of her tongue darted out to wet her top lip.

Carter slowly climbed back up her body, letting her take a breath. He watched her eyes follow her hands as she moved them over his chest, up his neck, and to his cheeks. When Molly locked eyes on him once more, he saw what he'd been waiting for—desire. She was past the point of being nervous or scared. She was his. He lowered to kiss her lips, gentle but possessive. He couldn't contain that side of him another moment. He had warned her before that she would be his from this point on. When Molly's eyes fluttered shut, he pressed on.

She whimpered his name and that was all it took. He finally lost the control he had been fighting with since he laid eyes on her.

Knowing there would be pain before pleasure, Carter took what felt like hours to ease himself into her. He held still for a long minute, waiting for those big eyes to tell him she was okay. Molly didn't fail him.

When she opened them, her heavy-lidded eyes had gone from sparkling sapphire blue to almost black. He watched her chest raise and fall quickly with the short breaths. Her lips parted as if she were going to speak, but when he moved just a fraction the would be words fell away on a soft moan. When he moved again, her graceful fingers snaked up to his biceps and dug in, pulling him tight.

Carter leaned down, kissing her lips, taking over her mouth, devouring her like a starving man. When he felt her legs wrap around his waist, he drowned himself in her, over and over until at last he pushed her over the edge. She let out a high pitched noise before pulling his mouth back to hers and kissing him harder than she ever had. The need Carter sensed in her sent him tumbling after her.

With one motion, her legs fell off his waist, the grip on his upper arms released, and her arms fell to the bed as she sunk almost lifeless into the soft bedding. Looking down at her beautiful body with the shimmer of sweat dancing across her, she appeared completely at peace except for the hint of a satisfied smile on her mouth.

Carter dropped to the bed beside her and pulled her limp body to his chest. Instantly she snuggled into him, a perfect fit, like she understood that was where she belonged. "I love you, Molly."

"I love you too, Carter. So, so much," she whispered into the night.

Chapter Eleven

Brody woke the next morning with a rock in his stomach. Feeling the cold sheet beside him, he realized Erin must have been up for awhile. He ran his hands over his face and tried to wake himself up. Throwing on yesterday's jeans, he walked out to the kitchen.

"Hey, babe. How are you feeling this morning?"

When Erin looked up from the book she was reading, Brody could tell. He crossed to her and bent over to hug her from behind.

"I'm sorry honey. Hang in there, okay?"

She took a deep breath, but instead of answering, she laid her head against his forearm still wrapped around her.

"I love you so much. Can I get you anything? Crackers, toast?"

Erin shook her head no.

Brody had been about to stand back up when he saw Molly's iPod sitting on the table. He reached over and grabbed it.

"When did you get up, Erin?"

"Oh…I don't know…about six-thirty, I guess. Why?"

"It's a few minutes after eight. Molly should be done running by now." He walked over by the front door to look behind the recliner. "Her running shoes are still here and so is her iPod." Brody held it out as proof. "Damn it. She's not running. She's not even fucking here. Son of a bitch, she spent the night with him."

Brody's fist clenched and he brought it down on the back of the cushioned recliner in front of him. Not raised to be a violent or physical man unless he was defending himself or his own, Brody suddenly felt a rage like he'd never known. He'd told Sterling to leave her alone, he'd made it apparent he didn't approve, yet his sister was not where she was supposed to be. He dropped the iPod onto the chair and tightened his fingers into the padding until they all turned white.

"Now, we don't know that, Brody."

"Oh hell, Erin, really?"

"What's all the yelling about?"

Brody turned around to see the motorhome door opening and his parents walking in. Oh holy hell. There's no way. Why now? "Nothing."

Brody turned back to Erin, fully expecting to see the panic in her face at the unexpected guests. She was as calm as she usually was.

"We checked the track before coming here, Mol must be done running?" James asked.

Wanting to prolong the agony a little longer, Brody crossed to hug his mother, with Erin on his heels to do the same. "Why are you guys here, and so early?"

Erin's brow furrowed. "Is everything all right?"

James didn't answer. "Molly in the shower? We need to talk to her."

When Brody's eyes locked on his father's, James continued. "Things are getting worse. We need to tell her what's going on."

Shit. Their worst nightmare was coming true.

Brody knew if his parents had dropped everything to come, the threats must be getting more serious. He knew if he had eaten anything yet, it would be coming back up about this time. He rolled his shoulders and tried to stretch the knots in his shoulder blades. The stress was pulling him under.

James crossed the motorhome. When he knocked on the bathroom door, Brody dropped his head.

"James." Karen's head tilted. "We agreed. We were going to come and talk to George *first*. I don't want my daughter upset and riding a bike if we can help it. Don't you dare say a word to her, not yet."

"Karen."

"I mean it, James. Not a word until we piece more of this shit together. It's not safe."

"She's not safe."

"That's why we are here, James."

"You don't think she's going to wonder what the hell is going on? She knows all about that library I'm designing. She knows I wasn't going to be able to come in but for one race — maybe. Suddenly, I'm here..." He motioned between himself and his wife. "We're here and we won't leave her side? That won't be obvious at all."

"We're at least talking to George — first."

"Damn it, Brody. Where is she? I've knocked twice."

"She's not here."

"What do you mean, she's not here?"

"I mean, she's not in the motorhome."

"Well, where is she?"

"I don't know."

"What the hell is going on here, Brody? What do you mean you don't know where your sister is? We're dealing with something serious here. This is exactly why your mom and I came in. To help you watch her. Hell, we get here to find out something has already happened." James ripped his cell out of his pocket. "I'm calling 911."

"James." Erin placed her hand over his cell to prevent his dialing. "She's fine, at least for now." She waved an absent hand in Brody's direction. "He knows exactly where she is, he's just pissed about it."

"What's going on here?" James eyes darted between Brody's and Erin's.

Molly heard voices when she got closer to her motorhome. Great, this will be fun. The closer she got, one voice stood out crystal clear. She skipped the last few steps and opened the door. She was right, it was James and Karen too. Molly jumped into James's arms, not doubting for a second that he wouldn't catch her.

"What are you doing here? I've missed you so much." Molly kissed his cheek with a big, wet smacking kiss, always over exaggerating everything in a show for James.

James hugged her tight as she squeezed his neck, never outgrowing the affection they showered on each other since she was a young girl. He sat her back down on the floor and patted her back so she could go to Karen. As Molly crossed to Karen's open arms, the twinkle in Karen's eye made Molly giggle. She couldn't wait to tell her about last night. How special Carter had made her feel, how right he'd made the moment. Molly could feel the heat on her cheeks, but knowing Karen was happy for her made everything so much sweeter. She had finally found the one that Karen had always promised was waiting for her.

"Where the hell have you been all night?"

Brody's voice made her jump in Karen's arms. The tone and the strength, not something she was used to, had certainly never been used on her, at least…not from him.

The flashback hit her out of left field. Trying to catch her breath, she shut her eyes tight to block out the yelling behind her.

Brody had dragged her into trouble more than once as kids, James and Karen had gotten upset and even angry once or twice. Their silence was more powerful than if they had yelled, knowing she'd disappointed them simply crushed her. She had argued with Brody over the years over meaningless things, but always as siblings.

This was different. The authority he was trying to dominate her with sent her crashing into the past.

Molly blinked several times, trying to concentrate on Karen's face, trying to remain focused. Brody's anger was making it impossible.

"Brody, stop it," Karen snapped at her son.

"No, Mom. Her ass should have been on that couch last night."

Even though her back was still to Brody, she could feel the anger coming from him. She could hear how his words were said through gritted teeth. A shiver went up her spine.

Molly shook her head no. "Brody, you don't understand," she whispered. She repeated herself a little louder the second time and a third. "Brody, you don't understand" became a mantra of sorts, being said louder and louder each time. Trying to hear herself over the sound of Brody's voice.

"Enough." James's voice was louder than both of theirs.

Even though he was just trying to get their attention, when the added volume combined with the yelling Brody was doing, plus her own, in the small space it was too much for Molly. She reached out for Karen, clinging to her tightly. Molly desperately tried to stay above the wave of the panic attack, but the yelling was just too similar to the voice she heard so many times as a young girl.

This time was different though. Molly could hear herself trying to talk back, but the sound of her crying muffled her arguments. She knew she was safe, she knew who was holding her.

She just couldn't get the pictures of her past from replaying through her mind. Suddenly, she was too tired to fight him anymore. Molly sagged against Karen, defeated.

"Oh my God, Molly, I'm so sorry," Brody whispered beside her as his mother held her as tight as she could without making it worse.

"Damn it, Brody. You know you can't yell at her like that." Karen's words were spoken no louder than a whisper for Molly's sake, but they were sharp.

"I'm sorry, Mom, I didn't think. I was just so worried."

"You weren't worried, you were pissed off. I know the difference," Karen said as she glanced over at Brody and then turned her attention right back to Molly.

"Shh, Molly, it's okay, baby." Karen continued to stroke her hair and offer hushed words to soothe as Molly shook in her arms.

"You know, she hasn't had an attack since the first night we were in California." Erin said softly as she wet a cloth for Molly's face.

"Thanks." James took the washcloth from Erin. "Really?"

"Nope, and I'd bet money, it's because of Carter." Erin started to walk through the open motorhome door.

"Where are you going?" Brody asked over his shoulder.

"To get him."

"Who?"

"Carter."

"The hell you are. He started this. She shouldn't have been with him. If she'd been in her own bed last night, this would never have happened."

Brody's voice had risen again, sending another uncontrollable series of sobs through Molly.

"Karen, smack your son for me." Erin turned again. "I'll be right back."

Karen narrowed her glare on her son. "You know if you weren't so hell-bent on controlling her every move, you'd realize how much she loves him."

"Mom, she's only known him for a week. She can't love him."

"She does though."

The next thing Molly knew, she was being lifted. That smell, cologne? Carter's cologne? She could feel the hard surface below her cheek, warm and pounding. She moved her hand along the soft plane. Carter had come for her. She let out a breath and relaxed completely against him, held tight in his arms, feeling his heartbeat under her cheek. The pictures in her head stopped playing immediately. She could tell the yelling was done, but fighting the attack, fighting to keep from being drug completely under had worn her to exhaustion. She left her eyes closed and let Carter's soft whispers of love soothe her as she drifted off.

Carter had on his jeans from last night and nothing else. No socks, no shoes. He hadn't even run his hands through his hair, let alone shower. When he'd convinced Molly to stay and eat breakfast with him, all he'd done was thrown on the jeans he'd left beside the bed. When he'd welcomed a flustered Erin in his door, he hadn't even taken the time to grab his discarded t-shirt from last night before he ran to Molly.

After how wonderful last night and this morning had been for the two of them, it crushed him to see her so upset. Erin hadn't explained anything, but it was only a matter of a few yards between their motorhomes. All he had let her get out were the two words. It's Molly. At that point, he'd gone running.

Now as he held her to his chest, he took in the situation. He was in her motorhome, barely dressed, with Molly asleep on his lap. Not only did he have Brody to contend with, apparently today was the day he was meeting her parents. Talk about first impressions.

Now that he had her completely calmed down, he let out a breath, and dropped another kiss on her head before looking up.

"James, Karen." He started to hold out one hand and Molly whimpered in her sleep. He instinctively wrapped his arm back around her, forgoing formalities. They were kind of past that anyway. "I wish we could have met under better circumstances."

Karen sat on the edge of the couch and lightly rubbed Molly's leg. "Me too, Carter, me too. Thank you for coming so quickly. It's obvious how much she cares for you and trusts you. If anyone else would have tried to pick her up like that, she would have started swinging."

A piece of Carter wanted to be proud of Karen's compliment. He just couldn't though, not when it came at a cost to Molly. "Can I ask what set this one off?"

He watched Karen and James look at each other then at Brody. It was Erin's evil eye in Brody's direction that clued him in.

"I see," he said before anyone answered.

Heat briefly flared in James's eyes, but Carter didn't back down or lower his eyes from James's gaze. Molly had warned him early on about her father-figure. He'd been bracing himself for an amplified version of Brody.

Ten years from now they would all laugh about this day. He'd remind them about the way the two men stood, both leaning against the captain's chairs, legs out crossed at the ankles, arms crossed over their chests. The same penetrating gray eyes boring into him. He'd seen the same pose from Brody on more than one occasion in the short time they'd known each other. Carter was quite sure it pissed Brody off that the imposing stare-down didn't work on him.

He was also confident, that even though it appeared he had Karen's support and even Erin's, that the two men staring at him were united. It was very apparent they were on the other side.

Turning his head just an inch let him meet Brody's narrowed eyes. "Did you yell at her...about last night?"

Brody's eyes went wide for just a flash before narrowing once again.

Bull's-eye.

"You did this to her, didn't you?" Carter's voice was a hint over a whisper, not wanting to upset Molly all over again, but there was fire in his tone. "I've told you repeatedly, I won't hurt her. I've told you I'm not going anywhere." He dropped a cheek against Molly's head for a moment, just needing that connection, before he continued. Carter took a deep breath and leveled his eyes on her brother once again.

"If you have a problem, then you need to take it up with me—in private. I will not allow you to upset her like this again. I know she'll stand up to you, I've seen her do it. But make no mistake…you won't do this to her again."

James's chin came up just a fraction of an inch, even though the man had yet to speak. From what he'd heard from Molly, this must be a special occasion. The stories Molly and Brody had shared, while humorous now, gave him a newfound respect for anyone on the receiving end of James. The man was intimidating for damned sure, but there were three men in that motorhome, and he was the only one holding Molly in his arms.

The soft touch of Karen's hand on his arm broke both the tension and his eye contact with Brody. "She loves you, Carter."

"Quit saying that, Mom. How can she—"

Carter cut Brody's argument off before he could finish it. "I love her too, Karen, very much."

James took a deep breath in. Carter was gearing up for another round when George came through the open doorway. James put his finger to his lips. "Not here, George. I don't want to talk about this here. We haven't said anything to her yet." The hushed words were meant for George alone. Carter heard every word.

He waited for several long seconds, gauging the mood of the room and the sudden chill it just took. It was more than obvious that they didn't want Carter there for the conversation, either.

"I'll let you guys go. How about if I take her to my coach and lay her down, you all can talk here?"

Without looking at the men, Carter waited for Karen's approval. When she nodded and whispered her thanks, he felt as if he'd won some sort of battle.

"Erin knows where my motorhome is, I'll leave the door open. You're welcome anytime, just come in." Carter had found the golden ticket. Karen seemed genuine while thanking him and it was obvious how much she loved Molly. At least he had another ally. Poor Erin was starting to look worn down with all the fuss, and now he had someone fresh on his side ready to help defend him if need be.

Carter stood with Molly in his arms as if she weighed nothing. Slipping the two of them through the tiny motorhome doorway was something of a feat, but he did it without waking her or giving her a concussion. He grinned to himself as he pressed a kiss to her forehead and walked with a still sleeping Molly in his arms.

As he laid her back down in his bed, he couldn't help but feel conflicted. On one hand, he had Molly right where she belonged, in his bed. On the other hand though, her parents were acting very suspicious. He couldn't help the nagging feeling in his gut that told him something was very, very wrong.

Molly stretched. Something about the bed she was in and the way it smelled just like Carter, and the sheets were so soft and cozy. She felt around her and let her eyes open. *Carter's bed, how did I get here?*

She shut her eyes again for a long minute, the screwed up morning coming back to her. One minute she was in Karen's arms, dying to get her alone and talk. The next she was curled up in a ball crying. She shuttered again at the replay of Brody's voice, tone and words in her mind. He'd never done that to her before. Neither James, nor Karen had ever yelled at her like that. Only one man had. There was something so hauntingly similar in Brody's voice, the flashbacks had swept her away before she could even focus on reality.

She looked around the empty bedroom. "Carter?"

"Hi, Gorgeous. You're awake," he said, coming out of the bathroom.

Molly watched him zip his pants on the way. She breathed in the sight of the man standing freshly showered and in riding gear before her. "Hi," she replied, smiling. Damn, the man was sexy as sin.

Carter winked as he leaned down, bracketing her with his arms to kiss her. He sat beside her on the bed, lovingly brushing the hair from her forehead. "Are you okay? Do you want to talk about it? You have me worried, sweetheart."

"It was just...Brody. I don't know. He just triggered something. I don't even remember what he said now."

"Well, I don't know what all was said either. Erin came and grabbed me, and when I got to your coach, your mom had you in a pile of tears on the floor. I picked you up and you fell asleep in my arms. I suspected Brody had something to do with it, but we didn't get into. I didn't want to wake you up."

When Carter cupped her cheek in his palm, Molly grabbed it with both hands and held it to her tight. Things were falling back into place. Molly took a deep breath. These panic attacks were old, but now that she'd had two in front of Carter, not to mention the other night, she was starting worry he was going to freak out.

"I'm so sorry, Carter."

"What are you sorry for, Mol? You've done nothing."

"It's so embarrassing. I don't always know the triggers until it's too late. You're going to think I'm an absolute train wreck. Add to that my psychotic brother, and you have no reason to want to be with me."

"Yes. I do. I love you." Carter leaned down and placed a feather soft kiss on her lips, then another on her nose. "I'm not going anywhere, I promise." His face lit up. "Hey, you know what? Come with me."

Molly couldn't help but laugh at the excited man as he pulled her arms trying to get her out of the bed faster. Whatever he was up to, it couldn't be as good as staying in his warm bed, preferably beside him.

"I have to do sound testing here in a little while, but I want to give you something. I meant to as soon as I saw you last night, but I got so excited to see you again—I forgot."

He sat her on his couch and she tucked her legs up underneath her, trying to calm herself. She was the world's biggest child when it came to surprises and holidays. She watched as he crossed to the kitchen counter. When he turned, he held out the small green velvet box tied with a satin bow.

"You didn't have to get me anything, Carter."

"It will make me feel better."

She tried not to grin nervously at what that meant. Reaching up a timid hand, she took the box from him and waited until he sat back down beside her.

"Come on, open it." He smiled.

Molly slowly pulled the end of the ribbon and the bow fell apart. With the box still in her hand, Carter opened it for her. She tried to see the beautiful necklace, but looking through the tears made it hard to see the little platinum and diamond cross pendant.

"It's beautiful, Carter. Thank you."

Carter took the box and removed the necklace himself. Molly held her hair up and turned so he could put it on for her. "Na, it's selfish on my part, really. I don't like the thought of you doing what you do on a bike without a little piece of me with you."

She turned back to face him, her fingertips on the cross. Carter reached up with his thumb to wipe the tears rolling down her cheeks.

It was so surreal for her. In such a short amount of time, her life had changed so drastically. She always knew it could. Hell, in their sport you could be fine and walking one minute, then lying in a hospital the next. She lived with that knowledge every time she got on the bike. But to think about her life changing outside of riding, outside of bikes at all. To think that she'd become so attached to the man in front of her it felt like her next breath depended on his presence—that was frightening and exhilarating at the same time.

Carter watched as Molly continued to touch the cross against her neck. The simple, dainty cross on a short chain was perfect for her. He'd wanted to give her something—something that she could wear and think of him when they were apart.

He pulled her onto his lap, taking in the way her face was beaming at him. She was so sweet and so full of love. He couldn't believe he was so lucky to find her.

"Do you know how much I adore you?"

Molly smiled so sweetly, his heart melted. "I do."

Those two words rang loud in his ears and suddenly he was very aware. Carter could see clearly he was holding his future wife, he could see his future in his arms.

"Oh God, Gorgeous, I love you."

౿∾

Molly had her fingers laced with Carter's and as they walked to her motorhome, swinging their hands between them. She felt so light, carefree, and to be totally girly—she was completely in love. She'd never been given a piece of jewelry before, at least not something that wasn't from James or Karen. They were overly generous when it came to buying her things. She reached up to her neck again. This was different—this necklace meant so much to her. He could have given her a ring from a bubblegum machine, she didn't care. Anything from Carter was priceless.

The door to their motorhome was closed and a white envelope was taped to it. She pulled it off and opened the door.

"Where is everyone?" She looked around, only to find Erin inside.

"Um…they were just chatting with George. You know, catching up, since it'd been awhile since they'd seen him."

Molly raised an eyebrow at Erin. That was a story to sell someone else. They'd kept in touch with George all the time. Hell, he was the reason she was doing the preshow. Molly had wanted to introduce Carter in a way that was a little bit more normal than before. She shrugged at Carter, knowing he had to get to his test before long.

She slipped open the envelope in her hand. Opening the weird looking letter, she gasped at the first word—bitch. She had Carter's attention and he grabbed the letter from her in one hand and instinctively put his other arm around her waist.

"What the hell is this?" He held the letter up to Erin.

"Where was that?" Her eyes were wide, her mouth hanging open.

"Taped to the door."

"Oh, shit." Erin grabbed the cell sitting by her on the table. "Come here, now!"

Molly watched Erin nod, her facial expressions all over the board. Panic, anger, fear, and back to anger. "No, now. We just got one, here."

"Erin, what's going on?" Carter asked before Molly could form the words. Her mind was reeling. Carter had ripped the note from her hands before she'd read more than a few of the letters taped to the plain white piece of paper. But even with little to go on, she could tell it was a threat.

Carter's hold on her had gotten tighter and more possessive. At the moment, she didn't want it any other way.

The door flew open and James, Karen, Brody, George, and Joey all charged in. Molly watched as Carter instantly held the note out for James's inspection.

"Will somebody please tell me what's going on?" Molly's voice was desperate.

Carter swept her into both his arms, waiting for an answer.

Chapter Twelve

"Are you okay, baby girl?" James crossed to her after reading the letter. He bent his knees slightly to look in her eyes and ran his knuckles over her cheek.

Molly looked at the man she'd loved almost half her life. He'd been there for her, helped put her back together when they'd found her broken. James had protected her with a fierceness only rivaled by wild animals. She clung to Carter, but leaned into James's hand, a show of love for him as well.

"I'd be better if I knew what the hell was going on."

Carter pressed her against him, and she felt the strength of his hold in the palms spread over her back, the heat from his body burning her, but soothing at the same time. Molly laid her head back against his chest and kept one ear pressed to the beat of his heart, the hammering keeping her calm.

"James? That's not the first threatening letter you've gotten, is it?" Carter's hands tensed on her back as the question came out.

"We've got this, Carter. Don't worry about it." Brody's tone was dismissive. "You can go now."

"Not this time, Noland. No way."

Molly knew Carter would avoid arguing with Brody at all costs, but she was so relieved when he stayed. She tightened the hold she had around his waist.

"Stop it, Son. This is getting serious. We're going to need all the help we can get." Karen ran a loving hand down Molly's long hair. "Carter, Molly. Both of you—sit. We'll fill you in." She motioned to the kitchen table. Karen waited until Carter passed her, but Molly saw the harsh look her brother received.

Reluctantly, James began. "A few days ago, George called me at the office."

Carter interrupted James and looked over his shoulder at Brody. "Was that the call you received last Saturday?"

When he didn't answer, Molly impatiently urged him on. "Well, Brody? Was it?"

Molly watched, but her brother didn't answer.

Instead, Carter spoke. "I told you that night, I knew something was wrong. I offered to help then, Brody. Damn it. What if she'd been alone this morning when she'd gotten this last note? What then?"

The way her brother was treating her boyfriend was just one of a million things spiraling through her mind at the moment. She was so torn between the love she'd always felt for Brody and wanting to put on a pair of boxing gloves and go at him like the old days. At the moment, she'd do without the gloves.

In some perverse way, Brody being a jackass was helping. If Molly let herself concentrate on that anger and embarrassment, she was able to block out the bigger problem. The one that had a big red X on her head.

Karen rubbed her husband's arm as the four of them sat around the kitchen table. Molly could see the worry in her eyes, the circles underneath that she'd never seen before. That had Molly more scared than the note. James had twisted two paper napkins into bits and reached for a third, just to keep his hands busy. Molly had witnessed the nervous gesture before, years ago, when she'd been recovering in the hospital. She laughed, but no noise came out, thinking about how something so minor and obscure had stuck with her like that.

She watched the beads of sweat running in random patterns down the bottle of water Erin had placed in front of her. She heard the conversation, heard the words. Most of them weren't sinking in. Carter had one arm around her shoulders, the other on her thigh under the table. Every so often, one or both hands would squeeze her in silent encouragement.

"So there have been a total of five notes, right?" Carter asked.

"No." James shook his head. "Four notes and one phone call from someone who overheard a conversation that someone overheard and so on. They called George, but with such hearsay, there wasn't anything we could do but hope it was a rumor."

"But the notes, they're all like this one? Why go to the trouble of cutting and pasting magazine letters on copy paper? It just seems weird. Unless...maybe whoever is doing this has very recognizable handwriting. Like another rider?"

"Like a girl," Molly mumbled to herself, completely unaware she'd even said anything out loud as she peeled the label off her bottle.

James smacked the table with both palms, sending Molly about out of her skin. "I'll be damned."

Brody spoke for the first time in a long while, his face questioning, but a realization dawning, "Do you think?"

"I think it sure as hell opens up a new direction to look. Up until now, the police have had very little to go on back home."

"The first three were mailed to the house, right?" Molly felt Carter's shoulder jerk as he looked toward Joey when he began to speak. "So...obviously it's personal. Molly hasn't competed in over two years. She always raced clean, was always way out front, basically with no competition. So I think we really can rule out a racer. As for freestyle, that group was so laid back I just don't see any of them doing this. Again, too much time has passed, there's not some big competition coming up. You haven't set out to reclaim gold again. There's no reason. Plus, honestly, Mol, I don't see why anybody that is still competing would be willing to risk it all to go to jail when they get caught."

"Joe's right, baby girl, if it's a woman, it's somebody that is jealous of you, a crazy stalker fan who wants what you have, something. Or, it's someone from your past. I don't really see that as a possibility, though."

"Or a jealous ex-girlfriend," Brody said under his breath.

"I don't have an ex-girlfriend, Brody. Don't be an ass."

"Not you, Mol. Funny how the threats started just last week. And when did you two hook up? Oh, that's right...just last week."

"Fuck you, Brody."

It was a gut response. Something she'd never said to anyone close to her. He was over the line, and between his attitude and the situation she was learning about, Molly was about to snap.

"Molly Shea West." Karen's voice didn't raise much, but there was steel to it.

Molly's eyes went wide. The use of her full name like that was another first, the shock and disappointment on Karen's face hit Molly straight in the heart.

"I'm sorry, Karen. But I'm sick of that. I told you how he's been." Her apology to Karen was every bit sincere, but she continued on, her anger spiking again. Molly waved her hand toward the kitchen counter her brother was leaning against. "That's exactly how he's acted. It's awful and embarrassing, Carter doesn't deserve it. There's no reason for it."

"Brody, that was uncalled for."

"Oh, Dad, get real. You have to count it as a possibility. I was just the only one to suggest it."

"Even so, I haven't dated anyone in over a year. I'd be more than happy to supply the police with any names and contact information, though. I've got nothing to hide and I don't see any of the women I've ever dated doing something like this. I've had no bad endings, but again, I'll do whatever it takes," Carter said, looking at James.

"So what do you think we should do in the meantime, James?" George asked. "I think we should call the preshow until this is resolved."

"No." Molly whipped her head to see the seriousness in George's face. "I'm not going to let someone interfere with my job."

"Molly, honey, you know you don't have to work this hard. We've told you that for years." Karen stretched her hands across the table to take Molly's.

Molly looked at Karen, pleading for her to understand. "I'm not a little girl anymore, I have to make a living, and riding is it. I can't live off of you forever, and this is all I know." She shrugged and gave the familiar line. "It's like I always say, at least I'm riding the bikes and not posing naked on them."

Carter snickered and Molly let out a snort. She forgot he'd never heard her say that. Even with Karen's eye roll, that split-second of humor was refreshing, even if it didn't last.

"That's not why you don't want to cancel." Molly glanced across the table at James and waited for him to finish. "It's because you're a stubborn little shit and you never back down from anything...even if it's the right thing to do."

"Would you want me any other way?"

"I didn't raise a quitter or a doormat, did I?" James's face was conflicted half scared to death, half proud.

"Nope." The corner of Molly's mouth turned up, the grin never quite made it though.

"Well, the police seem to agree with you, for now anyway. If we can lure whoever this is out, they'll be able to catch them. In the meantime, we come up with the best scenario possible to keep you safe. I want you surrounded at all times. No arguments, little girl."

Carter kissed her shoulder. "She's not leaving my side."

Carter hadn't let Molly out of his sight since their conversation that morning. When he went to sound testing, she went with him. When he had to meet with his manager, she went with him. Her mother seemed to understand his need to protect her. They all needed to, but Karen saw what the two of them had together. She had been giving him silent signs of approval all day, a wink here, a nod there, smiling when she caught him squeezing Molly to his side.

James hadn't said much. There had been some mild laughter and joking about off the wall stuff, but as far as Molly and he were concerned, James was watching them from a short distance. Carter could tell his every move, every comment was dissected. He didn't care. He would go to the ends of the earth to prove to her dad that he was worthy.

They had decided to go out and eat somewhere close. At Carter's suggestion, Eli and Jesse were being told about the situation. He knew they would help in any way they could to keep her safe. That was where he and James seemed to see eye-to-eye. Doing whatever it took to keep their girl safe and unharmed.

When they broke off and each went their own way to get ready for dinner, Carter had asked Molly to come with him, to bring her stuff and get ready in his motorhome. Karen had tried to hide her pleased smile, but Carter saw the woman's eyes crinkle in the corners. James had taken in a deep breath, but kept his comments to himself, unlike their son, who spouted off every thought that came to his head. Carter didn't retaliate, didn't even say anything back. That earned him a light hug from Karen as she handed him Molly's bag.

Now he stood waiting against the kitchen counter for her to come out of the bathroom. As he peeled the label off the half empty bottle of water in his hands, he realized he was standing in the same manner that they seemed to catch Brody standing in a lot lately, minus the crossed arms and bad attitude. No, his attitude was fine, just like the dress he saw Molly carry to his coach.

"I wish we were going out to dinner, just the two of us, like I originally planned."

"I know, Carter. I'm so sorry," Molly said from the bathroom.

"No, Gorgeous, don't be sorry. I just wish none of this was happening to you. It scares me to death."

She didn't have an answer for that. She could hear the worry in his voice as he waited for her. Truth be told, if this would have happened two weeks prior, she'd have been a nervous wreck, but the strength of the man waiting in the kitchen was keeping her calm. Molly was nervous, scared, all the emotions that come with being threatened, but with Carter's presence beside her, it made the situation easier.

She adjusted the belt on her tiny sleeveless bronze silk dress. She didn't remember it being so short. Running her fingers through her golden hair, she let it fall back down to hit the belt, brushing her bangs to the side and out of her eyes. The sales lady was right, the bronze did look good with her hair color.

Molly picked up her tube of lip gloss from the bathroom counter. Out of nowhere, it hit her at that moment. She was getting ready in Carter's bathroom, his bathroom, surrounded by his things, his toothbrush, his razor, his space. She looked up to the reflection in the mirror. When Molly had woken up this morning curled into Carter's side, his arm draped over her side, keeping her close, she'd frozen for a split second. She must have tensed because his arms had tightened around her, pulling her even closer. The few conflicting thoughts she'd had about what to do next had vanished into thin air.

She'd never had the next morning moment. Yet, there she'd been, getting ready to make the walk of shame, minus the rumpled dress and heels. She had no regrets about sleeping with Carter, none at all. She loved the man, but she didn't know if she was supposed to get out of his hair quickly. Did she just slip her pajamas back on and wave goodbye, tell him see ya soon?

He must have sensed her uncertainty. Carter's arms had encircled her and answered every random thought and question running through her head. He had loved her through the night, but lying beside him the next morning, an understanding dawned on her. She was his. A warmth passed through her unlike any other feeling she'd ever had.

Carter, with his half lop-sided, half devilish grin had worked his magic on her. He had the charm of a school boy and the sin of a man. He convinced her to stay and let him make breakfast for her. She'd thought she was keeping her fears about facing Brody to herself. Apparently to Carter, she was transparent. When he'd bragged about his world famous pancake flipping skills, she'd just giggled and continued to stir the pancake mix. He had stood by the stove, waving the spatula around, telling the most ridiculous, made-up story of his awards and prestige for his pancake making abilities. When the very first one hit the floor in a splat, Molly had tears rolling down her face, laughing so hard she couldn't breathe.

Molly shook her head at the memory of their morning together, their first morning. It was perfect.

As she unscrewed the lid on her lip gloss tube, she grinned, almost able to hear the pancake land on the floor again, and hoped there would be many more mornings like that in the future.

Adjusting her cross so it could be seen over the neckline of her dress, she stepped out of the bathroom. She dropped her heels on the floor and slipped into the first one, but leaned on the wall to step into the second. Molly raised her chin up to see the look on Carter's face. Oh yeah. That was worth the price of the dress completely.

"Oh my God." He crossed to her. "You look absolutely amazing. Wow." He kept her at arm's length just to continue looking at her. "Again, I say, let's...not go."

Leaning in, he kissed her softly on the jaw, then below her ear. "You smell so good," Carter whispered by her ear. He gently pulled her hair to the side as he moved his lips to her neck. The simple move gave her chills every time he did it. Molly could feel his breath on her skin and she closed her eyes.

When he lowered his voice, it was so completely sexy. Although she was pretty sure he didn't do it intentionally, it always worked on her. "Please," he begged in between kisses. "Let me help you out of this dress, Gorgeous...please?"

"After dinner?" she whispered.

Her heart started beating faster. This was all so new. She wasn't used to the responses she was getting from him. He kept her close, cherishing her, but not smothering. No pressure, but at the same time, she felt wanted. Now that they'd had sex once, she assumed they probably would again. But, the way the man was holding her, she was wondering if that might be any minute now.

"Please?"

She knew he was turned on, but they really needed to go. "Honey, the sooner we go, the sooner we get back." She felt his tongue tracing circles on her neck and she couldn't help the whimper that escaped.

Carter moved his hands to her butt. Thanks to her lace thong, there was only a thin layer of silk between her skin and his palms. He pressed himself against her and there was no denying the man wanted her. Her head swirled with the knowledge that she was in the arms of a man that looked like he'd walked right off a movie set—and he wanted her.

"Carter." She whimpered his name.

"I know, baby. I know. You're just so damned beautiful…I don't want to let you go, not yet."

"You look very handsome, too." She smiled. "You get me every time I see you in your gear, but seeing you dressed up, you are…amazing."

She knew he was nervous enough without adding a tie, so he just opted for jeans with a white button down shirt and brown leather loafers. He had the sleeves rolled up and she ran her fingers over the muscles on his forearms. Molly didn't attempt to hold in the sigh. The man was built to perfection. She squeezed him. "And you smell terrific."

Carter knew exactly what went through his mind when he saw her come out of the bathroom, but he wasn't prepared for everyone else's reactions. The whistles instantly turned her red.

Eli came up to her first and hugged her. "D, you look beautiful," which was immediately echoed by Jesse.

"Thanks" she said, her voice barely able to be heard. Carter noticed immediately how uncomfortable she was, even with Eli and Jesse who she'd gotten to know.

She smiled nervously and looked to Carter. For support? He wasn't sure.

The restaurant was only a couple of blocks away, so the four of them walked from the stadium. It was a quaint downtown street with the street lamps already lit for the evening. The lofts and condos surrounding the area kept people bustling along the brick-lined sidewalk. Carter couldn't help but notice the heads Molly was turning while she hugged his arm tightly.

He grinned to himself, proud of the fact that he was the one with her instead of having to just watch her walk by. It wasn't lost on him that she was completely confident in riding gear, but tonight she was using him almost like a security blanket. Carter remembered back to earlier conversations the two of them have had about her looks. He knew she never flaunted her looks or used them to impress anyone. Now he could see she really was not comfortable with people staring at her unless she was covered head to toe in riding gear, and he realized then it was her skills she was confident in, not her looks. Carter grinned again and kissed her head as they walked.

"Hey, Gorgeous, I want to ask you something."

"Yeah?"

Carter looked down at the angelic face of the girl under his arm. The relaxed smile that graced her face made his heart swell. That smile he knew was for him and him alone. Carter took a breath and tried to figure out where to start. He'd been trying to work out exactly how to ask her, and given the circumstances, he wasn't sure what he would do if she said no.

"What do you think about staying with me?"

"What do you mean?"

He saw her peek over her shoulder at Jesse and Eli, like maybe they knew what he was talking about. They did, but both men just kept walking. Only at the last minute before she turned her face back to Carter's did Eli wink at her.

"I mean, sweetie, I want you to stay with me, in my motorhome."

The questions in her head were apparent on her face, but Carter held in his chuckle.

"Tonight?"

There was a slight scrunch to his face and he shook his head. "Not…just tonight."

"You're kidding, aren't you?"

"No, Gorgeous, I'm not," he said, now with a completely straight face. Carter wanted her by his side for so many reasons, but after the events of the morning had unfolded, it had become a need to have her beside him. He'd tried since the minute he met her to keep his protective side under control. That was over. Molly had given herself to him, she was his now to protect, to love.

"For how long?" She tilted her head to the side.

Carter could tell she was connecting the dots of his plan, but wanted reassurance, instead of assuming the answers.

"I would have waited, Molly, given you more time to get used to this, to us. Let your family get to know me better. Let Brody calm down. But there's not time for that now, sweetie. I want you with me, I have to keep you safe. I know your family can and will, but…that's my job now. I love you."

He watched her eyes go wide. She probably would have quit walking if he didn't have her under his arm. It was his momentum that kept her going. Before saying anything, she looked back over her shoulder to the other two men walking beside her, both smiled at her. Carter could see the silent encouragement in their subtle nods. He had discussed this with them in depth, and he knew how much Jesse and Eli adored her. They had both been shocked as all hell to find out what was going on. Their alpha sides had come straight to the forefront, ready to watch over and fight for their own.

Carter saw clarity wash across her face as it dawned on her, her eyes making their way between the three men, a soft, "Oh," emitted from her mouth, barely heard, but there. It was at that moment Carter saw she realized the men flanking her were there to protect her as well. They weren't just his friends, they were hers now too. Her mouth slowly turned up, the smile reaching her eyes at last.

"Thank you…all of you."

Her words were quiet, and if Carter wasn't mistaken, she was embarrassed to need the help. But she'd taken it without argument or force. Just a gentle understanding of how things were going to be from now on.

Carter had been waiting patiently for her answer. He kept his breathing steady, his face strong, but not demanding, yet.

"Yes," she whispered.

He leaned in and placed a soft kiss against her forehead. "Thank you, Gorgeous."

Molly walked through the heavy glass door of the restaurant that Carter held open, his palm on her back. Her senses were on overload, with her world spinning out of control, amazingly enough, she was at peace. She still had enough fear in her to keep her street smarts active, enough nerves to not let her guard down, but Carter had taken on the responsibility for her safety. With no drama or fan fair, he had let her know he was in charge and she had nothing to worry about.

She sat down at the large table with Jesse on one side and Carter on the other, and picked up the wine glass Karen had waiting for her. Oh, thank God. Karen always knew exactly what she needed. There had been more than one occasion when they'd sat in Molly's bed with a bucket of ice cream and two spoons between them, watching chick-flicks, usually after one of Brody's friends had made a pass at her and she'd been upset. Or after a rough day of practice with Brody, they'd run into the nearest mall and wander for hours, just to get her mind off of it. Now that she was older, the ice cream had turned to wine. The movies, they'd been replaced with bitching sessions instead. Molly loved the woman with all her heart.

Molly also knew Karen understood her new relationship with Carter. Karen was more trusting than the men in Molly's family. Maybe after she'd had another glass of courage, Molly would be able to tell them she was going to be moving in with Carter.

Moving in with him. Oh, wow. He hadn't said it like that, but moving in with him was exactly what he had asked for. And she had agreed. She blinked before her eyes went wide with the realization.

The second glass of wine wasn't sipped as she was taught was the ladylike thing to do. No, it was downed in one big gulp. The liquid warmed her body from the constant chill she now had, relaxing her mind from the never-ending spin, and dulling the fear she couldn't escape.

The intent of the meal was to discuss the situation regarding the threats and come up with a plan. After salad, dinner, and three glasses of wine, Molly was feeling pretty relaxed. When her piece of chocolate cake arrived, she slid the fork through it and held the first bite up for Carter to taste. She giggled, picking up a crumb off his bare arm that she'd dropped. Her happiness was a private party. The rest of the table had limited their liquor to almost nothing. That was just fine with her. She didn't really care at the moment. When George asked James what his game plan was, Molly happily announced that Carter had asked her to stay with him.

It wasn't like she was totally trashed, completely falling down wasted. She was just—overly relaxed. So when James's gray eyes turned on her at the same time as Brody's matching ones did, she smiled, quite proud of her new sleeping arrangements. As her hand made its way out of her lap and toward the half empty wine glass one more time, Brody cleared his throat loudly.

"I think ya probably should…ah…switch to water, sweetheart." Jesse whispered down at her.

A fit of nervous giggles escaped. "I'm not drunk, cowboy."

"No, but you're on your way, good looking," Carter said in her other ear. "I know you're stressed, Gorgeous, I'll buy a bottle for us to share later…I promise. Let's just get these last few details worked out, okay?"

"So, just how long were you planning on staying with Carter?" Molly looked back to James's face across the table. She cocked her head and re-ran the words he'd just said over again in her head.

Molly knew he was waiting on an answer. She was pretty sure she knew it. She couldn't remember. What was the question? Suddenly her cheeks felt very hot and she was tired.

James sat back in his chair and crossed his arms. There was stiffness to his voice, but it wasn't thundering. "Molly…?"

Oh, yeah. James. "Um, what?"

James shook his head with a raised eyebrow. "I asked you, just how long you think you're staying with Carter."

"I love you."

Karen lost it, her laughter starting the table in an uproar. "Oh, baby girl. This is why I always limit you to no more than one glass. Apparently, I wasn't paying close enough attention tonight. Carter, give me her glass, I'll drink the rest of it."

"To answer your question, James, I'd like to have her move in with me—permanently," Carter said as he pulled Molly closer, her head finding its way to his shoulder.

"After a week?" Brody hissed. "What the hell are you thinking? There's no freaking way."

"Brody." Molly didn't open her eyes. "You and Erin live together."

"Again, not after a week's time, that's bullshit." He turned to his parents, his voice louder than respectable in a restaurant. "Why are you acting like this is no big deal? What the hell is wrong with you two?"

Karen's chin came up, but her voice was calm. "Son, it's a very different situation. You were fourteen when you and Erin met. You started dating when you two were only twenty. Molly's going to be twenty-seven in just a couple of months. It's time. They would have waited, I'm quite sure, but with these threats, I understand Carter's need to keep her close to him. I understand that kind of bond."

"Not after a week, Mom. Don't you see how wrong that is?" Brody sat back, crossed his arms and basically pouted.

"It's no more wrong than you and Erin having a baby. You're not married, either." Karen's words were softly spoken, but said volumes.

Molly watched Erin's mouth drop open. She sat in shock. "I didn't tell them, Erin. I promise. I don't tell any of Brody's secrets."

In all honesty, Molly and Karen had talked about it, but Karen had known and not because Molly had told her. Molly kept Karen informed of how Erin was doing. She and Karen were both worried about Erin being out on the road so long, and she'd promised Karen to watch over Erin as best she could. Molly knew how excited Karen was to become a grandmother, and it was secretly killing her that they hadn't broken the news to them yet. Karen had felt so left out. That alone was reason enough for Molly to be mad at Brody. She didn't want Karen's feelings hurt and by them keeping something so huge from her, Brody was doing just that.

James turned on Molly, a slight chuckle to his words. "Secrets, Mol? So there's more?"

Molly's shit eating grin set the laughter going again. "Oh, there are so many. And so little time."

Chapter Thirteen

Molly sat at the plastic table outside the Noland Racing rig the next morning, sandwiched between Carter and Eli. Both men were closer than probably necessary on a regular day, but they weren't lucky enough to be dealing with regular days. Jesse, Karen, and James filled out the rest of the circle, all laughing as Eli and Molly went back and forth. The latest round of mock arguments was reaching epic proportions in the childish category as Molly tried to pick the spitball out of her hair that Eli had just shot at her.

"Stop it, Hunter, you big baby. It's not my fault I'm a better dancer than you. Suck it up." She ran her fingers through her hair with no luck. "Carter, help me. Did it fall out?" she said as she dropped her head so Carter could see.

"It's out, baby girl." James snickered

"Okay, D. You have to prove yourself tonight after the race, otherwise you can't claim the title of best dancer."

"Dude, I've danced with you already. I remember your moves…or lack of." Molly's eyes went wide as the comment slipped off her tongue. She bit her lip, waiting for the retort that was coming.

"Oh…Molly, you better run girl," Jesse laughed. "If there's one thing Hunter's more proud of than his racing, it's his dancing."

Molly started to scoot her chair out as Eli was getting up, but Carter stopped her. "No, Gorgeous, don't you dare leave my sight. Hunter, sit. You can't chase her around here, it's not safe."

Both Eli and Molly stuck their tongues out at Carter and launched into a fit of hysterical laughter together.

"Can you behave yourself, kids?" James looked between the two overgrown children. Molly snuck a look at Eli out of the corner of her eye, pretending to be covert. When he grabbed her around the waist, unexpectedly pulling her out of her chair and onto his lap, she squealed.

"Hey, Hunter, little tidbit for you…do with it what you may, but my girl there…she's very ticklish." James nodded at Eli.

"James, you big brat, I hope you remember Father's Day is around the corner," Molly snapped back, trying to wiggle out of Eli's grip.

James winked in response. "Hey, Sterling, can I talk to you?"

As Carter stood, Molly fought Eli's hold a little harder. "Wait, where are you going? Eli let me go, you big meanie. James, what do you want to talk to him about?"

"Hunter, hang onto her for a few minutes for me, bud," James said, inclining his head in Eli's direction.

"Wait, Carter." Molly held out her arms, wanting to save him from the ensuing interrogation slash speech she had a feeling he was in for. He leaned down and brushed her lips with a soft kiss, then another by her ear before he whispered into it, "It's okay, Gorgeous. I love you. I'll be back soon." As he stood, he ran his forefinger down the tip of her nose and over the lip she was biting. His lips made a small kiss motion in the air before he turned to walk away with her father.

She watched James put a hand on Carter's shoulder and squeeze as they walked further and further away. After they turned and she could no longer see them, she slipped off Eli's lap and looked to Karen for answers.

––

"So, I'm assuming you knew we'd have to talk sooner or later." James patted Carter's shoulder before he shoved his hands in his pockets.

Carter took a deep breath before answering. Mirroring James, he shoved his own hands in his pockets. "I assumed we would, yes, sir."

"You can call me James. There's no need to start with formalities now, son."

Carter nodded at the request and waited for Molly's father to continue.

"It's been a crazy week around our house, I have to tell you. First Brody calls all bent out of shape because you walked into my daughter's life and stole center stage, then we started getting those damned threats."

Carter silently acknowledged James, but waited for him to go on. He had been himself around James, but he hadn't been able to read the man yet. Karen was easy—she was sweet, kind, and very open with her affection for all of them. Even Jesse and Eli had been swept away with her loving, motherly ways. But James was more distant, watchful, and not so quick to accept him with arms wide open the way his wife had done.

"I'm not going to lecture you or tell you anything generic you don't already know. Obviously you know about Molly's past. You know where I'm coming from…and Brody, for that matter.

He's not always such an asshole, for lack of better words." James glanced over at Carter. "He's been an asshole to you, I know. I apologize. He's worried. We all are, Carter. You've admitted yourself how fast this relationship has taken off, but Karen's right, Molly's getting older. Erin has mentioned to Karen on more than one occasion how lonely Molly was becoming. She always did a great job of hiding it around us." James blew the air from his lungs as he shook his head, as if it was hard for him to admit it when he said, "I can see where she's ready to settle down."

The thought of his girl sad, upset, or as her dad said, lonely, broke Carter's heart. She had become his world in such a short time. Other than the times she'd been upset due to the threats and well, the panic attacks, she was so full of light, so funny and ready to laugh at anything. That was how he wanted to keep her. Carter was going to make it his life's work to always keep her smiling, whatever it took.

"I think the thing Karen and I are most concerned with is how she latched onto the first guy to come around." James shrugged his shoulder when Carter gave him a raised eyebrow. "I know that comes across sounding like I'm trying to be a jackass, but she's really never dated much. Look at it from our viewpoint, you meet and the next week she's…well…moving in with you?"

"I know we're moving fast, James. I didn't intend for things to be such a rollercoaster. A small part of it has to do with our chosen profession, it's so damned difficult to have a relationship on the road like this. I know…I've tried in the past, it doesn't work." Carter absentmindedly kicked a water bottle cap that was lying on the concrete floor. "The other part of the rush is the situation she's in. The thought of something happening to her, it scares me to the core, James. I know as her fath—," Carter caught himself.

"That's okay, son, she is my daughter. She has been since the day George called me when she was just eleven years old. We knew at that moment she was ours. Took us awhile to get her, but we finally did."

Carter smiled at the love in the other man's voice for Molly. It radiated from him.

"I know as her father, then, you understand how I feel. Obviously you've had more time with her, but I really love her, James. I know it sounds so freaking crazy for me to say that about someone I haven't known very long, but...I do."

He decided since he was putting his cards on the table, he'd go all in. Carter quit walking. He turned to James and waited for the words to form in his head. He blew out a breath and shrugged. "I wanted to wait and let you get to know me, for her and I to get to know each other even better than we already do. I wanted to do this the conventional way, the old fashioned way. That's not how the cards fell, but I will tell you, I'll do everything in my power to keep her safe, to cherish her, protect her and to love her. James, I want to marry her. I'd like to have your permission to ask her when the time is right."

Carter watched the older man's eyes flash in surprise, but he didn't eye him in anger and there was no longer any suspicion. He could see the understanding in her father's face as it became clear how serious Carter was about Molly.

"From what I can see, I think you're a good man, Carter. I've watched you with my daughter. You're good for her. She doesn't trust easy, you have that...don't ever break it."

"I promise, sir. I won't."

"I have to tell you, George has really been the one in your corner."

"George?" Carter raised his eyebrow.

He had known the man his whole racing life. While he respected the man wholly and would sit back and drink a beer with the man any time, any day, and would even go so far as to say George was a good friend, he was surprised at James's assertion.

"George and I raced together as boys. We've been friends ever since. Let's just say, he picked up on something when he introduced you and Mol. He's been keeping me posted ever since."

The smirk on the older man's face finally brought a blush to Carter's cheeks. "Oh, really? I'm pretty sure I haven't done anything to embarrass myself."

"You're all right." James finally grinned, and then his smile faded. "I know you know about Molly. You just have to realize what George would do if you hurt her. He's known her since she was just starting to race. He was there when her world was turned upside down. He was the one that saved her life and that man would kill to save her again if he needed to."

James took a breath. "And you can bet all your money, I'd be right behind his ass. That little girl means more to me than anything, Carter. George seems to think an awful lot of you, and that's high praise. Plus, you've won over my wife. That is a feat in itself. She doesn't let too many people get close to Molly. She's taken to you, and that's a compliment you can be proud of."

Carter wanted to ask some questions he wasn't sure he'd ever be able to ask Molly. They were on the tip of his tongue, but something stopped him. Part of him was afraid of the answers James would give him. Those were the answers that made him sick to his stomach.

"I have to apologize again for Brody, he has been an ass. I'm sorry about that. You've handled it with dignity, though, and I appreciate it. We don't need more drama added to the mix. Karen and I have been really over-protective of him and more so of Molly, but Brody's made it into an art form. He's been the one traveling with her the last handful of years. He's had to step up and keep her safe from the creeps out there. You were there that night with that Martins guy. Molly has to deal with that all the time. Brody's a little jaded and he's had a hard time seeing that your intentions are good. He's been through quite a bit with her."

Rubbing his hands over his face, James looked down. Carter could tell he wanted to go on, but didn't know if he should. For the second time, Carter didn't interrupt. He braced himself for what might be coming.

"When we brought Molly home, it changed Brody. I don't mean in the typical, become horribly jealous, fight, rebel kind of way. I mean, after she was stable enough to move and we got her home to Pennsylvania, he took her as his own. I think he understood how bad things had been for her. They may have talked about it, I don't know. She doesn't talk about it now, and back then, we wanted them to bond, so we didn't push him to tell us what they discussed. We let them have their secrets. We knew what kind of hell she'd been through from the little she revealed and from what the doctors and psychiatrists told us, plus what she spilled out in the numerous nightmares she's had over the years."

James looked back up at him. "Carter, you just have no idea. She was in pieces when we got to her. I'll never forget walking into that hospital and seeing her lying there so broken. Tubes coming in and out of her, the black and blue marks, all bandaged up. They told us they didn't know if she'd make it through the night."

The air left Carter's lungs. He shut his eyes as one hand went to his stomach the other covered his mouth. There was nothing he could say.

"You have to know this, Carter. If you want to love her, you have to know just how bad it was so you can understand where our love and protection comes from. So you can understand her. Brody's not trying to single you out, he doesn't hate you. He just fears if she's is out of our reach, that she's in a position to be hurt that badly again. We about lost her, Carter. She was so close. She doesn't know how close, but it was touch and go for awhile."

Without opening his eyes, Carter simply answered, "She knows."

"She told you?"

Carter opened his eyes to see the shock in James's face. He nodded. "She doesn't know exact details, but she knows she about didn't make it. She remembers certain bits of the time in the hospital."

"Oh my God, Carter, you don't know what that means."

He looked back at James. Carter actually had no idea what it meant. After what he'd just heard, he was nervous to find out.

"Carter, the fact that she told you anything means something. The fact that she told you details...means everything."

Carter tried to push the lump in his throat back down. The silence following James's words was knee-buckling. He had been standing still for most of their conversation, but the exhaustion hit him like a brick wall. He had no reason to be tired. He had slept like a baby the last two nights, even with the stress of the threats looming in the background. With Molly curled up against his chest, he'd slept peacefully. All he wanted was more of those nights.

Carter's heart ached for the little girl in the hospital, for George who had saved her life, for the family that had put her back together. Seeing her face in his mind sent fire through his blood. The love and laughter that she offered him now came from a woman healed and ready to move on. After several quiet moments between the two of them, James's words broke into his scattered thoughts.

"Well, Carter, I've said my piece, threatened to kill you like any good father would. Like I said, she doesn't trust or love easily. She's given you both. Please take care to never hurt her."

Carter needed their conversation to be over. He needed to have Molly back in his arms to hold. He hoped like hell he didn't break one of her ribs, because he planned to hold on tight and he was never going to let go.

"I give you my word, James."

❦

"Mom, Dad." Carter stood to welcome his parents. "You were supposed to call when you got here. I'd have met you at the bike trailer."

Molly smiled as she stood next to Carter, nervous to meet his parents and one of his two brothers. She glanced at her own parents, who were just off to the side along with Eli and Jesse, and then up at Carter. She watched Carter embrace his brother in a tight hug.

As Carter let his brother's hug go, he looked down at her. "Well, let me make the introductions here."

Molly's cheeks were pink as she listened to Carter introduce all the parents to each other. She tried to take a deep breath and made a conscious effort to not fidget. His parents seemed like nice people, smiling and making small talk with her parents. His mother, Connie, hugged both Eli and Jesse. They hadn't all been together in a while, but it appeared they had taken the two men as their own over the years, the result of many years spent trackside together growing up, those memories spanning two decades.

"And Mom, Dad…this is Molly."

She bit her lip as Carter placed her in front of him though he pulled her close enough that her back was pressed against his chest and his hands on her shoulders.

"Mol, this is my dad, Tom, my mom, Connie, and my brother Mike. You'll meet Sam another time."

Molly put her hand out to shake with them, but was dragged from Carter's hold and into his mother's arms. She found herself being passed from Connie to Tom and finally ended up in Mike's big teddy bear hold of an embrace.

Mike looked a lot like Carter. Same sandy blonde hair, same blue eyes, though they were just a hint darker than Carter's ice blue ones. He had that same warm smile that looked just a little bit sinful. The biggest difference was Mike probably had four inches on Carter's five foot eleven—added to that a good fifty pounds of rock hard muscle. It was apparent that both men worked out—hard. Where Carter was lean and ripped, Mike looked like a body-builder.

If Sam looked anything like Carter or Mike, the Sterling gene pool was blessed for damned sure. Even their father looked like an older version of them. Molly had always teased Karen and James for being a beautiful couple. Tom and Connie were definitely in that same category. Their clothes were tailored and well put together, and it didn't appear as if a hair was out of place on either of them.

Molly kept the grin to herself. It wasn't how she would usually walk around the pits of any track, but to each his own.

Mike squeezed her one more time before letting her go. She looked down at his hip to figure out what pinched her.

"Oh, I'm so sorry, sweetie. I forgot." Mike adjusted his badge hooked to his belt and glanced back down at Molly. "Did I get ya?"

"No biggie. Just didn't know what it was, that's all," Molly said quietly. She hadn't ever dealt with a police officer one-on-one before, other than for security. She was a tad nervous to talk to Mike. Something about him being a detective was a little unnerving.

With the introductions and hugs all passed out, everyone sat back down at the plastic table in front of the Noland's rig. Molly didn't hesitate to snuggle up against Carter's side when he pulled her next to him. He looked down at her, his face lighting with that smile when their eyes met.

"Well, I have to say, I can't believe I've got two of you to worry about now." Connie laughed.

"Mom, I will apologize now." Carter grinned as he ran his knuckles over Molly's cheek.

Connie waved him off. "Oh, honey, I'm teasing you both."

"No." Carter shook his head. "I never knew what you went through all these years until I had to sit and watch her. It kills me every time I see her sit on the bike."

"It does?" Molly's head tilted up so she could look up at Carter's face.

Sure, she'd worried about him and his friends, but she'd really not thought about it the other way around. Molly was so used to being on a bike, it never fazed her or even crossed her mind the he might be concerned.

"You shouldn't worry, Carter…this is what I do." Hugging his bicep, she laid her head against it. It warmed her that he was concerned, but on the other hand, she knew one of the reasons Carter and she had hit it off so quickly was the fact that they understood each other's profession.

"It's okay, Gorgeous. I know you love it, but I won't pretend for a minute that I won't be thrilled to no end when you retire for good," he said softly, before kissing her head.

"Oh, thank God. Someone is finally on my side after all these years. Carter, I give you permission to work on that, I'll help you on my end. Maybe between the two of us, she'll cave." Karen laughed.

Molly knew the tone. Her words were said in fun, but they were honest. It was not the first time Karen had made her fears known.

"Well, I hate to be the one to bring down the fun, but sweetie, I really need to ask you some questions now, okay?" Mike's face was sincere and Molly could tell he didn't want to make her uncomfortable talking about something they all wished they could forget about. But her safety was the reason he was here.

Molly squeezed Carter's arm closer to her and nodded. She wanted to pretend the whole situation would go away. Carter moved her off his arm so he could tuck her close to his side. She melted into him and waited for Mike to take out his pen and pad of paper. Apparently James and Karen had been working with the local police and the sheriff's department back home. So far, they had no leads. At least with Mike involved, it was someone they knew personally. Carter had insisted on contacting his brother when he found out what was going on, knowing she wouldn't be treated like a number. His brother had been a detective for almost six years, and Carter had mentioned some of his successes to her parents when he suggested asking Mike for help.

Her parents had jumped on board immediately.

With all four letters laid out on the table, Molly was able to read them for the first time. Their words had her shaking and her throat too dry to swallow. Carter must have sensed her fears becoming too much for her to handle. Without asking, he pulled her onto his lap and let her sink against him. Closing her eyes, she listened to the conversation around her, wishing she could just go to sleep and not wake up until it was all over.

"It's obvious one person constructed all four letters. And, Molly, I think you're right. I'm leaning toward it being a woman." Mike pointed his pen at the first line of each letter. "See how these letters are all lined up perfectly?"

"Yeah?" James replied.

"They cut letters out of the same type of magazine. Even though they are different words taped together in each letter, they're all lined up perfectly."

"Okay?" Carter moved in closer. Molly sat up so he could see what Mike was pointing out. "What's that mean?"

"It's a woman." Mike winked at Molly. "Just like she suggested."

"Are you sure, Mike?" James asked, leaning further over the table to get a better look. Molly turned her attention toward James and she saw the panic in his eyes.

"Well, you can never be one hundred percent until you catch the perp, but...yeah. I'm sure. They're too perfect. It's unlikely a man would pay that much attention to detail."

Mike stacked the letters back up, careful not to damage them. "Okay, sweetie, if you don't mind, I'm going to stick pretty close to you and just observe things. With me right on your heels, I know you're going to have trouble forgetting why I'm here, but I have my suspicions and I'm hoping to get this resolved quickly for you."

"Thanks for helping me, Mike. I really appreciate it."

He reached across the table for her hand. Molly tentatively put her hand in his. "You don't have to thank me, Molly. I want to be here. I'll do whatever it takes to keep you safe and get this case solved."

She lifted her chin to meet Mike's reassuring smile. Molly swallowed hard and nodded.

৵৽

Carter walked her bike toward the track for her. She glanced up to see him grinning at her. "What's that goofy look for?"

"I was watching you touch your necklace."

Molly shook her head, laughing under her breath that he'd caught her subconsciously holding her fingertips to the cross at her neck — again.

She appreciated that he wasn't using the action to make fun of her. It was a simple gesture that had become habit seemingly overnight. "It's my piece of you, remember?" She smiled up at him.

Molly's heart sped a bit with the expression on his face. It was a mixture of adoration and fear, mirrored perfectly by the words he whispered to her. "I love you. Be careful tonight, okay?"

"Always. Gotta get back to you in one piece." She giggled.

"Are you going to be okay here with Mike and Joey?" Carter slid his fingers over her jaw to cradle her neck in one hand.

Her heart skipped a beat for the man who was so lovingly trying to be in two places at once. She was standing by her bike backstage, waiting for her cue from Brody. Carter however, needed to be with his mechanic and his bike.

"I'll be fine." She let Joey grab the weight of her bike again so she could turn to wind her arms around Carter's waist. "We'll do just like we planned earlier. Mike will wait here with Joey for me to finish, then after, Joey will take my bike up to the rig and load it, and Mike will walk me to our parents. I'll be okay."

"I know you'll be watched over, I still just wish I could be here with you."

Carter pressed her head to his chest. She could tell by how fast his heart was beating he was anxious.

"You have to relax, Carter. You have to get your head in the game and focus on you. Focus on the race, okay? You won't do either of us any good if you get hurt."

"I'm okay, Gorgeous. I promise."

Carter sighed and looked behind him. "I've got to go." Leaning down, he laid a flutter of a kiss on her lips.

"I love you," Molly whispered, always hating to let him go, but it was time to get in the game.

"I love you too, Gorgeous."

Molly watched her man until he disappeared around the corner.

Brody tucked her hair down the back of her sports bra and waited with her goggles as Molly buckled the strap of her helmet. Molly could feel her brother's turmoil.

"You're going to be fine, sis…you and Sterling don't need to be worrying about all the rest of this shit…focus on your ride," Brody said as Molly situated herself on her dirt bike, the first hint of a smile she'd seen from him in the last week appearing at the edge of his mouth. Maybe there was a slim chance that her brother was finally coming around. She knew Carter had no reason to believe it based on how he'd been treated, but Brody really was a good guy — fun loving and loyal to a fault.

She nodded and looked out across the dirt track, forgetting the audience, forgetting her brother, forgetting even the threats. Molly revved the throttle and set out across the dirt.

Chapter Fourteen

It used to be that driving between races, from track to track to track was monotonous, but now that Molly was traveling with him, Carter was having a blast. It seemed like the weekdays were better for her with them on the open road. No one knew where they were, so they hadn't had any trouble. When they were on the road, it was as if a huge weight would be lifted off of Carter, and he found the time was spent enjoying Molly rather than worrying about her.

Carter talked to Mike several times a day, and Carter was beginning to think Mike's theory was unfortunately true. They had two more days until they pulled into the next stadium before they would find out. That was something that terrified the living hell out of him. Until then, they were at a private track, virtually off the radar and Carter was going to enjoy every last second of peace he had with Molly. He could practice during the day, Joey was there to help with his bike if need be and then after, they would sit and relax. Unfortunately, the hours were ticking by quickly, and before any of them would be ready it was going to be time to head to the next stadium. Back to harm's way.

Carter walked toward the open door of their motorhome on his way to grab a few beers for Brody, Joey, and himself. As he drew closer, he heard the soft singing. Leaning against the door frame, he stood watching Molly wiping down the kitchen counter, apparently lost in her own little world, singing away. She'd been trying to stay strong, pretend that the stress wasn't getting to her, and he hated that she felt she had to be happy-go-lucky for his sake, but Carter knew. Between the situation with the letters and the way her brother was acting about her new living arrangements, it was weighing on her.

It was obvious to even a bystander that Brody wasn't pleased with the provisions that James had agreed to. That was just too damned bad. Carter was rather happy with their travel plans. When he had asked Molly to stay with him, James had reluctantly agreed, on one condition, Brody follow.

James had covered his plan nicely, using the excuse of needing to have as many eyes on Molly as possible due to the threats. Inside, Carter knew for James it was a two-fold solution. That was okay. Carter knew he'd be the same way when he and Molly had a little girl someday.

In the meantime, Brody had backed off a little. Carter still felt the hard stares and there were a few digs here and there, but for the most part, it seemed as if Brody was beginning to accept Carter as a more permanent part in Molly's life.

Carter had just continued to be himself. He was normally pretty easy to get along with, and he just let Brody's insults slide right off his shoulders. Carter had no reason to act otherwise—he had the girl. Plus, he felt as if he'd begun to earn the trust and respect of her parents.

From behind, Carter watched Molly shuffling around, putting stuff away. Carter liked having her there, liked having her in his space. She fit without any awkwardness or weirdness. He grinned to himself as he stepped up into the motorhome, the beer long forgotten.

Carter laced his arms around her middle. With her hair up in a ponytail, he had easy access to the sensitive spots on her neck. When he placed a feather soft kiss on her skin, she melted against him. The sigh that escaped from her made his head swim.

"Let's go take a nap," he whispered by her ear.

"Is that what you're going to call it?" Her words were breathy and he could see her eyes had closed.

"Ah…my sweet, sweet smart ass." Carter chuckled against her skin at her retort as he squeezed her closer.

He spun her in his arms and lifted her onto the kitchen counter, placing himself between her knees. As he ran his hands up her bare arms, Carter felt her shiver in anticipation.

"I miss you." He dropped a kiss on her lips.

"I've been right here. You've been outside with the guys. How could you miss me when I haven't been gone?"

Carter could tell she was playing with him, and it was killing her to keep from laughing. He felt the smirk form under his lips, her delicious mouth curving at the corners. "I need you," Carter murmured.

"Well, now there's the honest answer."

He ran his hands around her backside and pulled her closer to him. She sucked in a breath, and he knew she could feel just how badly he needed her. Carter started to work his palms up under the tight t-shirt she had on, his hands traveling up the soft skin of her back. When Molly cupped his jaw in her small hands and laid her lips against his, he lost it and his mouth possessively overtook hers.

Molly whimpered.

"Got sidetracked from the beer, did ya?" Joey snickered.

Carter jumped, but didn't look up. Grinning to himself, he lowered his forehead to her chest and tried to get a hold of himself. "Nice timing, Joe," he said with laughter in his voice.

Joey shrugged. "I try. We could see you through the open door. Thought I better come warn you that Brody was getting a little…ah…hot under the collar out there watching you." His good-natured personality shined through his teasing words.

Looking back up, Carter tugged the crimson-faced girl to closer to him. "Thanks bud. Come on in and grab the beer, I'll be right there." Turning back to Molly, he winked. "Come sit with us, Gorgeous. Erin's back out from her nap."

"Oh, she took a real nap, did she?"

A mild snort escaped. "You're cute, little girl."

"I know." Molly giggled.

ॐ

Carter's stomach had turned itself inside out and upside down when they hit the city limit. By the time they drove up to the stadium, it was threatening an all-out revolt. He kept his fear to himself, not wanting to upset the golden-haired angel sitting in the seat beside him, keeping the small talk light and easy while he parked.

He was walking around the motorhome, making sure the automatic stops had lowered properly, when he heard the door open. He immediately looked up.

"Where are you going?"

"I was just coming out to be with you, relax." Molly smiled as she slipped her arms around his waist.

He tried to keep the stern look on, but her sweet, adoring face won him over. "Well don't forget you're—"

"I know," Molly interrupted him. "I'm absolutely not, under any circumstances, to be alone unsupervised. I'm not even allowed to walk to the motorhome to go the bathroom by myself. Babe, I know. It's okay, I'll stay with you, I promise."

"And?"

"And if you can't be with me, then I'm to stay with Mike. If he needs to check something out, he's to leave me with the guys or James and Karen. Carter…honey…I'm not going to do something stupid, I'll stay with you. I won't make it harder for anyone on purpose, just trying to be stubborn. I want to stay safe, too."

There was only a gentle understanding in her eyes. No frustration at having to be babysat, no anger at being told what to do, over and over by numerous people. Only the quiet resolve to do whatever she had to do. He was so proud of her for that. It was humbling to need people like she needed everyone right now and he knew what an independent soul she was.

"Ah, Gorgeous, come here." He threaded his fingers through the belt loops on her jeans and drew her nearer. "I love you." Carter tipped her chin up and brushed her lips with his. "I'm done out here, lets walk up to the pits and give your cell phone a break, what do ya say? Just let me lock up."

He placed the key in the lock, but turned to her. "Hey, by the way, they are going to go ahead and post security here and up by both of our bike trailers. I just need to let them know we're here now."

"How am I supposed to have sex with you tonight knowing that cops are outside listening?"

Carter shook his head and laughed out loud at the girl with her hands on her hips and a completely straight face. He could tell she was not kidding, but it was how fast the question came out of her mouth that shocked him. He just never knew what she was going to say and she always kept him guessing. She had shown him her true colors very quickly into their relationship. She had a quick wit, smart mouth, and sass to her that he adored. He knew she'd keep him on his toes and he was going to love every minute of it.

"Well, Gorgeous, I guess you'll have to not be so rough with me and keep the screaming to a minimum."

Her eyes went wide. "Me?" She huffed at him. "Are you serious? Me…ha."

"Ah, Mol, I love you," Carter chuckled and reached down to grab her butt as they walked.

"See. You can't keep your hands off me."

"Nope…never." He winked, and she finally broke and laughed out loud.

Molly spent a few minutes passing out hellos and hugs to George, Jesse, Eli, and her parents before she was able to finally sit down by Carter in the pits outside their bike rig. Word had spread like wildfire regarding her situation, even though they'd tried to keep it under wraps as best they could. It was a small, tight-knit community when it came to those that were injured or needed help. A few others had joined in their circle. A couple she'd met, others she hadn't. Although she was skittish about having several new people around her, Carter and Mike had her wedged between them tightly, so she felt safe.

"How did the week go, D?" Eli asked.

"Let's see. George called three times, James and Karen called…" She glanced in their direction. "I lost track of how many times you two called."

She patted Mike's arm. "This sweet one called multiple times a day. And Eli, that doesn't even include you or Jess. Add that to the five hundred and forty-eight texts I got, and well, there you go. But I do appreciate everyone checking on me."

"You're exaggerating." Jesse raised an eyebrow with that lopsided, cowboy grin of his.

"Oh, well, maybe a little, but still. Let's just say, I was well thought of." Molly wrinkled her nose.

Molly heard Carter turn and tell Jesse under his breath how impressed he was that Dylan's fling had lasted longer than six hours. She dared a glance in Dylan's direction and saw the girl he was walking with. Molly remembered meeting her the first weekend she had performed. She mentally rolled her eyes at Dylan. He'd been trying to come on to her that first night, and then had picked up the track bunny Saturday night in the pits, loser. That's exactly why she steered clear of men like that.

Normally Molly didn't pay much attention to people. She was fairly leery of fans, and anyone else for that matter, and tended not to maintain eye contact for very long when she was signing autographs. Needless to say, she never paid much attention to their looks, but this girl? It was going to be hard to forget this girl, even if she tried. Never mind the bad boob job that was making her already tight t-shirt strain or the heavily pierced ears and face—it was the hair. Molly would never forget it. She almost accidentally let the chuckle bubble out, but Karen would have her ass if she did. But damn. A bad bleach job was one thing, but she had added neon green and bright purple streaks to it. No, she was a memorable one, all right.

Her attention was torn away from the fashion disaster when out of the corner of her eye she saw her brother place a hand on Mike's shoulder. Molly turned to the two men, watching their silent conversation for several seconds. Turning back to Carter, she could tell instantly by his expression—they'd found another letter. Her heart sank as the ripple of fear worked its way across her skin.

"I don't get it. We just walked up there not more than fifteen minutes ago. Brody and Erin were parking their motorhome, right beside Carter's. When would someone have had time to tape the note to the door, and right in front of Brody? He could have come out and caught them at any second." Molly could hear the terror in her own voice, but she was too scared to try and cover it up any more. At least now she was back in more familiar surroundings, sitting beside Carter, at his table, she brought her knees up to her chest and dropped her head down.

"Whoever the hell this is has some fucking balls." James rubbed his hands over his face.

Molly's heart sank for a second time and for an entirely different reason. This was tearing James and Karen up. She knew they were beside themselves, not to mention what it was doing to Carter, Erin, and Brody. She'd had some crazy stalker notes in the past. She wasn't a celebrity by any means, but her face was out there. People knew who she was. This time, though, it was a whole new ball game. They knew where she lived and they knew her current schedule. Whoever it was, it was obvious they were following her. Now…she was terrified.

Molly jumped and grabbed the table when the door opened. Mike and George stepped into the motorhome to join their impromptu meeting, along with Eli and Jesse. Molly searched their faces for information, but could only see the worry in their tensed expressions.

"Here's the deal, for now." George pulled up a chair next to James. "It'll be a pain in the ass, but the first thing we're going to do is have Carter and Brody move these motorhomes up by the bike trailers. If we rearrange things and sandwich them between the two bike semis, we'll have one area to keep secure instead of four." George tipped his head to Mike for him to continue.

"There's an area big enough on the south side of the pits for all four trailers to sit side-by-side. We've already got the area being roped off now." Mike shifted eye contact between James, Brody, and Carter as he spoke.

Molly didn't care that they were talking about her or that she was sitting right in front of them while they did, she just wanted them do something. No, she wanted them to do everything they could so she didn't have to live like this another minute.

Leaning against Carter, Molly let her eyes close, willing herself to keep the tears welling up at bay. She had been successful up to this point, but now the dam was about to break. The warm hand that covered hers was soft as silk. She didn't even open her eyes. Instead, she squeezed the hand that had held hers so many times over the years, absentmindedly running her finger over the four carat rock on Karen's left hand.

Mike continued on with his directions. He was almost positive it wasn't a random fan, since the threat came only when people directly related to the race were in the building. Molly just couldn't believe that someone Carter raced with would do all of this. The only other option was that it could be someone who followed the circuit, either on George's staff or with the track building crew or possibly someone with one of the vendors or sponsors.

That made the list a mile long.

"So guys, if you'll get things moved now, we'll meet up again in…say…thirty minutes. I want to check on something and make a couple of calls. The local police are surveying the entire scene and I want to see if they've turned up any leads. Then I'll meet you all at Carter and Molly's motorhome." Mike reached down and rubbed Molly's shoulder.

She looked up to thank him, but no words came from her mouth. Instead, when her eyes opened and she had both Carter and Mike's worried faces looking back at her, tears broke loose and poured down her cheeks.

"Oh, Gorgeous, we're going to figure this out…I promise. I promise, it will be all right. Nothing's going to happen to you…we won't let it."

Carter pulled her on to his lap and Mike took her chair. Pinching her eyes shut again, she fought to get the tears under control, but wasn't having any luck. The big palm squeezing her knee was Mike's, she could tell. Molly slid her hand over his. She really hoped he knew how thankful she was that he was there.

"Sweetie, we're going to get this resolved. We're close. Hang in there for me just a little longer, okay?"

"Thank you, Mike." The choked whisper barely made it out.

る◌ふ

"Did you get her to sleep?" Karen asked as Carter came out of the bedroom.

It wasn't awkward at all to have his girlfriend's parents looming over him, in his motorhome, in his space. Since the last letter was found earlier in the evening, his motorhome had become a sort of ground zero for the secret meetings and discussions. Carter just wished Molly didn't have to hear it all.

When they'd traveled during the week, none of their conversations were about the letters or threats. Joey, Brody, and Erin had clued in early on as well. No one brought it up. The result had given Molly a breather and she'd been able to relax. During the week, she'd been the girl he'd fallen for, the sparkle back in her deep blue eyes.

The minute the last note had been found, she'd slipped into survival mode, quiet, distant, and almost child-like. He wasn't even sure she heard the conversations swimming around her. Most of the time, she had her head down or lying against something or someone with her eyes closed. It was breaking his heart to watch. Seeing her push her food around her plate, never taking more than a couple of bites, the way she jerked awake every few hours—all of it made Carter sick because the stress was making her sick.

When Mike quietly told him the police were coming by to update them, Carter stood and ushered her toward the bedroom, hoping she would drift off for the night and not have to hear any more for a little while. He exchanged her tighter fitting t-shirt for one of his and left her cotton leggings on. Carter hoped she'd be comfortable sleeping. He treasured those nights when she curled her naked body up next to him after he'd made love to her. Tonight wouldn't be one of those nights. Pulling the t-shirt over her head, he cringed at the expression on her face. Changing her clothes to help make her more comfortable was one thing, but it seemed there was nothing he could do to wipe that look of hopelessness from her face. Carter pulled her into his arms and held her. All through this last week on those nights when they'd been alone on the road, she'd felt strong, muscular, and warm. Tonight, she was a shell. Her skin was cold to the touch and she felt frail in his arms.

He wished like hell he could lay down beside her, cradle her to him, and make her personal hell go away. Carter knew better. He had to hear what the cops and Mike had found. So he tucked her in the bed alone for the first time. Pulling the covers up to her chin, he ran his palm over her long, golden hair, brushing the wisps from her face and waited. When her face relaxed and the grip on his other hand loosened, he knew she'd finally found sleep. Carter bent to kiss her cheek, and then he whispered into the dark his promise to keep her safe and to love her forever. The déjà vu moment hit him hard and stole his breath.

☙❧

"Sir…" The uniformed officer looked at James. "I can assure you, we're doing everything we can."

Carter watched her father nod, turn and walk back to the table to sit by Karen and comfort her. This was taking its toll on all of them. Brody finally had to take Erin next door to their motorhome. Between the stress and the pregnancy, she couldn't keep food down and was starting to look ill. Carter knew she was much more than just Brody's girlfriend to the family and his heart went out to her.

Neither Eli nor Jessie had left to hang out in the pits or gone to the meetings they were normally required to attend with their respective teams. So far, nobody was giving them or Carter any grief over it. It seemed the magnitude of the problem was on everyone's radar. Everyone wanted this all to end safely.

The rap at the door broke Carter's attention. Mike's posture stiffened as he spoke with the security guard standing just outside the door. When Mike held out his hand toward the guard, Carter knew. Another one. He couldn't find his breath as he waited for Mike to shut the door and come to the table.

"A stadium worker found this on a table they had set up by the East concessions. It was just lying on the table. The difference is it was addressed to Molly." Mike tossed the unfolded piece of paper on the table. "They're resorting to other ways to get the messages to her."

At Karen's gasp, Carter tore his eyes from his brother's and looked down at the letter. That first word never failed to spear his heart.

Bitch—
You're being watched
and no one even suspects me

The words chilled his blood, but not as much as it did seeing the letters taped on the envelope that spelled out Molly's name.

The terrified scream from the bedroom made him forget the newest threat altogether. Knocking over his chair as he jumped up, he went running. Molly was talking and mumbling in her sleep. As he took her in his arms, she screamed again and fought his hold.

"Molly, shh, Molly. Gorgeous, it's me. Wake up...Molly."

Carter continued to speak softly for several long minutes as her sobs turned into whimpers, holding her while she came out of the nightmare. Jesse flipped on the lamp and knelt beside the bed. Carter saw the panic in his face.

"Carter!" Molly's high pitched cry of relief grabbed him almost as hard as she did, as if she was hanging onto him for dear life.

"It's okay, Gorgeous, I've got you. No one's going to hurt you, I promise. Shh…shh…" He kept his words soothing, praying he could calm her and make her feel safe. He brushed the tear and sweat soaked hair from her face. Smiling a small acknowledgement at Karen, he took the cold, wet cloth from her hand and ran it over Molly's face. Her eyes never opened.

When she finally calmed and was almost back to sleep, he picked her up and grabbed the blanket, then walked out into the living room. With her curled up in his lap, he tucked the blanket around her and let her fall back asleep. For now, Molly was safe in his arms, surrounded by friends and family.

Chapter Fifteen

Molly sat on Carter's bed the next morning in her short spandex shorts and a black sports bra, lacing her running shoes. As she walked around the bed, she glanced back over her shoulder. At some point his bed had quit feeling like his and had begun to feel more like theirs. Molly smiled to herself. She'd have to remember to point that out to Carter. It wasn't even eight-thirty, but she had lain in bed as long as she could and this doing nothing was making things worse. She wanted nothing more than to go on a run. It always swept her thoughts away, concentrating on the pounding her body was taking, focusing on keeping her breathing regulated. It left her no room to think about anything else. Unfortunately, that wouldn't be happening. She hadn't been able run in days. She hadn't seen the inside of her home gym in more days than that, and with the season lasting another three months, it would be a long while before she did again. The Noland gym was one of her happy places and she missed it terribly, so she'd do the next best thing. Molly would just visit another of her happy places.

Carter had told her he needed to go check in with his manager this morning. James and Karen were going to stay with her until he got back and then they all planned to grab lunch at the bar and grill around the corner. Molly knew Carter's weekends were busy from Friday morning until the last lap of the main on Saturday night. Taking her away from the stadium to eat wasn't in his schedule, but he was doing it because he knew she needed the break. If Molly hadn't been convinced of Carter's devotion to her before, she sure was now. Their relationship was still so new, and a lesser man would have given up by now, but not Carter. Sometimes Molly still couldn't believe he was hers.

Molly was trying to pull herself together after the way she had fallen apart last night. It was something she wasn't proud of and didn't want to repeat, and today she just wanted to do something normal.

Molly pulled her cell off the charger on the nightstand. She dialed and waited for George to answer.

"I'm okay," she blurted out, knowing he'd be worried at the sight of her number on caller ID. Molly smiled to herself at the older man's worry and mock anger coming across as he yelled at her for scaring the crap out of him.

"Ah, George, you know I'm your favorite."

She almost worked up to a laugh as he continued to tease her. His voice had always calmed her in the past and it still worked now.

"Hey, George? Can I beg a favor? I know you've already done so much for me already this weekend, but will you let me do something?"

She listened with pride as he told her she could have whatever she wanted. Molly knew George would let her have the moon if she asked, but she tried to never take advantage.

"I just need to ride. I know they're not quite done with the track, but can I just have ten minutes, maybe fifteen? This is killing me. I've got to do something."

"Well sure, honey…just be sure you have one of the guys come along with you."

"Really? Oh, thank you, thank you, George. I promise I won't tear it up."

"You sure you're up to it?" he asked.

"No, I'm okay, really. I just need something, you know…normal…something to make it go away for a few minutes."

His silence told her he understood.

"I'll call Joey and have him get my bike ready and have James come with me," Molly said.

"All right, Molly…just be careful."

"Okay, George, and thank you."

"Any time, sweetheart, love you."

"I love you too."

Molly walked out of the bedroom and went straight to Karen and hugged the woman as tight as she could. Karen's floral perfume seemed an anchor of some sort, the scent never changing over the years, always the same, always there. Without words, she went to James's waiting arms. The man might work at his design table most of the day, but his form never showed it. He was probably missing the gym just as much as she was. Molly had always loved the differences between the two. They were a perfect match and one didn't go without the other. When she needed comforting, Karen carried a gentleness that calmed her heart, and James had the strength in his hold that always let her know everything would be fine.

She plopped herself onto one of the open kitchen chairs and waited for the questions. The sooner she got them out of the way, the sooner she could be sitting on her bike.

Karen's eyebrow shot up, and with her finger pointed at Molly, she gestured up and down at Molly's attire. "Um, sweetie…you are not going running. I'm sorry."

"I know."

"Why do you look like you're up to something?" James tilted his head, his probing eyes quite obviously trying to figure her plan out.

Over the years, she had seen that look more times than she could ever count. While Brody loved her dearly and he was an amazing man, he had been a mischievous kid. He never got into any major trouble of any kind, never had even a brush with the law, but the boy had given James and Karen a run for their money. Brody had always drug Molly laughing behind him, constantly leaving her on the receiving end of that very same expression.

Molly shook her head and giggled for the first time in almost a day. "You know, I thought you'd trust me better than that these days."

"Oh, baby girl, Brody ruined you there," James said as he laughed at the familiar line.

"And like I always told you…I was the good one."

"Was being the operative word there, sweetheart. That boy tarnished that halo of yours. We could always see through him, and you, my dear, were crystal clear. Just like now, I can see the gears turning in your head. You've got the start of your gear on, and I'd lay my money on the table that you think you're going riding."

Molly wiggled her eyebrows at the shit eating grin on James face. "Well, that's why they pay you the big bucks…you're so damned smart. And guess what, you're coming with me, wise ass."

Before he could argue, Molly threw her hand up. "George already said I could. He's waiting for me. Said to come up and see him in the tower when I got down there."

"You think you're cute huh, baby girl? Outsmart the old man?"

She tried to smile at James's teasing. Instead, she shook her head. "No. I just need it. Please? Will you take me?" Her words didn't hold the same humor they did only seconds ago. They verged close to a desperate plea.

"Oh, honey, yes, I'll take you down there. Did you already call Joe and have him start getting your bike ready?"

Molly nodded.

Karen gave her a sympathetic nod. "I'll stay here and wait for Carter and then send him down to the track if you're not already back."

"Thanks, Karen. I know he'd be completely panicked if we were all gone when he shows up."

"Well, I think that boy is a good one, that's for sure. And he's so stinking cute too." Karen's eyes went as wide as her smile.

Molly knew she was trying to bring her spirits back up. It was working. She grinned at Karen. "He's hot, that's for sure," Molly's tone softened, "He's so sweet, Karen...I just love him."

"I'm glad, sweetheart. You deserve it." Karen squeezed Molly's hand before standing. "You want something to eat?"

"Maybe after I ride?"

"Promise?"

Molly stood up and slipped her arms around Karen's waist. "Promise."

"All right, baby girl." James stood up. "Let me top off my coffee and I'll meet you in the trailer. Don't go down there without me."

"Are you kidding me? Hell no." Molly knew she was safe walking from the motorhome to the bike trailer, it was a matter of feet and she had cops watching their whole area, but there was no way in hell she'd venture any further than that.

She opened the trailer door and glanced over her shoulder. "See you in a few minutes." She blew him a kiss like she did every other time she left the house.

Molly was halfway between Carter's motorhome and her bike semi when she heard a girl laugh. She looked to the side and saw the neon green and purple haired girl walking in her direction.

"Damn girl. They've got you locked up tighter than Fort Knox."

Molly looked at Dylan's new romance and her lip curled up in a skittish smile. The girl's overbearing personality was a little much for Molly on a good day, much less this weekend.

"Oh, hi. I'm sorry…it's Maggie, right?"

"Marcie. But you were close. Where ya going? I'll walk with you. Dylan's off somewhere and I'm bored." The girl cracked a huge smile that sent a chill down Molly's spine.

"Um…actually I'm…um…getting ready to practice."

"Oh, well. I'll come."

Molly's heart began to beat a little faster. She just couldn't shake the girl. "Um?" Molly shook her head and backed away.

"Let me rephrase that." Marcie grabbed Molly around the waist with one arm, pressing the blade of a sharp knife to Molly's side with the other. "How about you come with me? We need to have a little chat."

The chills that had rolled down Molly's spine spread out and seeped into her veins. "Where are the cops?" Molly mumbled in almost a panic.

"See them over there?" Marcie nodded almost nonchalantly toward the table the two cops were standing by. "They just found another letter."

"You?"

"Yep."

"Why?"

"Just keep walking we're going to go somewhere we can talk. In private."

"How'd you know I was even coming out?" Molly asked as the safety of the four trailers disappeared behind her.

"I've been waiting for the perfect time. I could hear your phone call from the bedroom. Those camper walls are thin, you know?"

"How did the cops not see you?" Even though Molly knew she should keep her mouth shut, the questions continued to tumble from her mouth.

"They only walk around the back every once in awhile. Now quit asking questions. You're pissing me off."

Marcie increased the pressure on the knife, the blade digging in just enough to puncture the skin. Molly couldn't contain the high-pitched yelp.

"Even think about screaming and you're dead. Just keep walking and smile at the people that we walk by," Marcie said through gritted teeth near Molly's ear. She just barely loosened her hold. The two might appear they were old friends, though she dug the knife just a little deeper. Molly cursed the cold weather outside. If it wasn't the middle of winter, the crazy bitch wouldn't have that god-awful baggy coat on. Then the knife in her side would be visible to someone.

"Where are we going?" Molly's worst fear was leaving the building. If they did, then Carter would never find her.

"I told you to shut up."

Marcie continued to walk the perimeter of the pits, avoiding the majority of the people, zigzagging through the open spaces of semis. Molly was trying to gauge how much time had passed since she'd walked out the door, four, maybe five minutes? Surely James had made it to the rig and figured out she wasn't there. Molly knew without a doubt he'd expect the worst. That would mean he'd call out an all-out hunt. That glimmer of hope kept her breathing slow.

Marcie's direction turned one last time and Molly knew she was a goner. Marcie chuckled proudly at Molly's sigh of defeat.

Dylan's motorhome.

He always parked it by his team's bike rig. After all that had gone on, he'd done his best to not say two words to Molly…or Carter for that matter. She knew Marcie was right. No one would ever come looking there. Marcie pushed her inside and climbed in behind her and locked the door. Molly felt the trickle of blood flowing down her narrow waist, but was too terrified to check how bad it was.

Carter saw James come running at him, Joey and Brody on his heels. Mike came from the opposite direction and George from another. His hands started shaking so bad he could barely get his gloves off.

His mechanic had asked him to take his bike for a couple of laps after the meeting so he could test something. He should've told his manager to give him a few minutes—he should have gone to check on her first. The fear gripping him right then was so tight, he couldn't even get questions out. His throat went dry and choked shut, the rest of him paralyzed by fear.

Carter knew James had found the answer to his question on his face. "Shit! She's not here!" James shouted when he took in Carter's expression

"They have the building locked down and surrounded, she's only been missing less than ten minutes. She couldn't have gotten far," Mike said to them, before turning to the police officer standing by his side.

Carter finally found his voice, the shaky words tumbling out, "Wha…what happened? Where's Molly?"

He knew it had to be bad, the way they all converged on him at once. The next moments all passed by in slow motion. He didn't know which direction to turn, who to listen to first. All he knew was suddenly he was walking and then running...to the one person he trusted the least. Out of the corner of his eye, he saw Jesse running his way with Eli, the three of them ready to kill the one guy that had given Molly trouble from day one.

He didn't expect Dylan to come around the corner whistling. Carter's fist struck his jaw before Dylan could even ask what for. Eli had Dylan's arms behind his back, holding him for Carter's next swing, when Mike's wrapped his arms around his younger brother. The screaming and yelling barely registered as it echoed around Carter, but he only heard his own words that dripped with hate.

"Where is she?"

"Who?"

He fought Mike's hold, but his brother was trained. "You asshole! Molly, where...is...she?"

"I don't know."

"Bullshit! She's missing and you're involved."

Carter watched Dylan try to wiggle out of Eli's hold. Eli wasn't going to let that happen. Eli yanked Dylan back, his grip tightening on the smaller man's arms.

"Sterling, I don't know what the fuck you're talking about. I was just coming back from a meeting. I'll take you to my rig and coach. You can see for your fucking self."

Carter pulled from Mike's hold and took off running ahead of Dylan with Jesse and Mike right on his heels. Eli drug Dylan along behind. James and Brody had caught up just as the group of men descended on the spot where Dylan had parked. Mike motioned for the engine on the running bike to be cut.

The tell-tale scream of Molly's panic attack shook Carter to his core.

Mike turned and yelled at the cops that were joining in. "Cuff him." He pointed at Dylan who was struggling in Eli's arms.

"I didn't do anything." Dylan's words fell on deaf ears.

Carter took off in a rage for the motorhome door. "Carter, wait." Mike jerked him back by both shoulders. "You can't go in there."

Carter tried to shake him off. "Mike!"

"Stay here, let me do my job. We don't know what's inside."

"I know what's inside. Molly!" His voice was desperate.

A rage swept through him. His heart was on the other side of that stupid ass trailer door and he wanted nothing more than to kick the fucking thing in and take back what was his. She needed him. He couldn't stand by and let someone hurt her. He just couldn't. Carter could feel his stomach start to turn against him, bile rushing up his throat.

"Damn it, Carter. Listen to me. We don't know what we're dealing with. You go barreling in there—you could get her killed. Now…stay."

Molly saw the anger in Marcie fanning higher and higher. Now that the knife wasn't pricking her skin, she could breathe, though she could feel the panic building, threatening to constrict her throat. She held perfectly still, standing in the middle of Dylan's coach. She knew she was going to have to keep it together if she was going to make it out of there alive. She made a mental note of the layout, the type of windows, which ones would be big enough to crawl out of, anything she could use a weapon—if she got the chance.

"You don't remember me, do you?"

Marcie's words startled Molly and she blinked without responding as she stared blankly back at the deranged girl in front of her.

"Do you?" Marcie's face twisted in disgust as she took a step forward, demanding Molly's attention. As if Molly could focus on anything else.

"I met...um...you a couple of weeks ago. With Dylan that...um night." Molly tried to keep her voice steady, to keep the shaking to a minimum. She didn't want Marcie to know she was even more petrified than she appeared. But the fumbling for the words was a dead giveaway.

"No, bitch, before that," Marcie snorted. "That pencil dick was just the easy in I'd been waiting years for." Marcie pierced Molly with her glare. "I know you know who I am."

Molly looked at Marcie. She'd never seen the girl in her life. Her circle was pretty small and only included family along with the newly added Carter, Eli, and Jesse. No. She was damn sure she'd never seen this girl before.

"No," she finally answered meekly.

"The name Lynda ring a bell?"

Molly shook her head. There was only one Lynda she'd ever met, but that was years ago at an amateur's track down in Texas. The big-bosomed, bleached blonde with the big Texas curls held in place by a can and a half of cheap smelling hair spray. That lady was nice. She'd run the concessions at the small track. Molly had only talked to her once, maybe twice. Something stupid, like the woman giving her a popsicle for free when it was really hot one day. Molly shook her head at the recollection, not even sure why she remembered the woman's name.

"No. It doesn't."

"She knew you. She liked you, liked to give you snacks from the stand."

Molly's head spun. She didn't know what Marcie was talking about and she didn't care that some Lynda had liked her, didn't know why it mattered.

All Molly could discern was that she wanted out. She needed to be back in Carter's arms. She needed this nightmare to end.

It had to end.

She could feel it coming, the rapid beating of her heart, the struggle for a solid breath. She knew the signs of an attack. She tried to concentrate on Marcie's question. Molly's silence once again pissed off the knife-wielding maniac.

Marcie stalked up and grabbed Molly by the waist again, holding the knife to her throat this time. The scream that came from Molly was bone-chilling, even to her own ears. There was no way she was getting out of this motorhome alive. The threats and story started to play on around her. She could feel the wave building. It wouldn't be long before the panic attack took her under. At that point, she was a sitting duck. Molly knew this Marcie girl's anger would be pushed to the brink and she would be defenseless.

Molly tried to piece the words Marcie was shouting together, but they were not coherent enough to make much sense. Lynda was my mother…She loved Ray so much…You took him away…

The last few sentences rang louder than the rest, mainly because they were screamed in her ear.

"It was all your fault. You put him away. It was you. You killed her." Her words became desperate, disjointed. "The blood…it was everywhere. I was ten years old and held her while she died. I begged her to stay with me."

Molly held her eyes shut tight as a palpable rush of anger shook Marcie and she pressed the knife harder against Molly's neck.

"I was ten years old, bitch."

Molly's fear was crippling her, her words barely audible. "I didn't know."

"Well, my gramma always said, an eye for an eye, just like The Good Book says."

When Marcie's hold tightened even more, the wave crashed down hard on Molly. She screamed and her knees went weak. She felt the knife slice through the skin of her neck as she crumbled to the floor.

"I want S.W.A.T. on all sides. Have the ambulance drive in—no sirens. Nothing startles whoever is in there, got me?" Mike's commands were precise.

There was steel in his voice, not like the softness he used on Molly. Carter had never seen his brother in this mode, with this kind of power radiating from him. He could hear the racking sobs coming from the thin walls of the coach. Every second that ticked by was another moment that something could happen to Molly. He knew from the crying she was upset or hurt or both. Carter wrenched his fingers through his hair as he watched Mike working with the crisis commander. Why weren't they working faster? He needed them to hurry, to make it all end. Carter felt himself being torn in two. He knew his brother would do everything in his power to save Molly, but Carter wanted to go in guns blazing and kicking ass. Anything they had to do to save the girl inside. He paced a three foot line back and forth, continuously rubbing his hands over his face and up into his hair, all the while staring at the door of the motorhome. From inside, Molly cried out again, sending a fresh wave of fear through his body. He turned toward his brother. "God, Mike! Do something! Please!"

When soft arms wrapped around his waist, he closed his eyes and gripped Erin tighter to him. It was Brody's hand on his shoulder that he didn't expect, a sudden understanding of everyone's new roles in Molly's life. They were all in this together. There was no blame laid, no screaming at who should have been watching her. There were only silent tears and prayers as they all hung on every word and noise they heard coming from the motorhome.

The vicious story bled from just inside the walls, causing Carter to want to tear his hair out as he listened to the deranged girl blaming Molly for the choices her mother had made. It was a woman holding Molly hostage, just like Mike had assumed. A wave of sympathy hit Carter as a picture of a little girl holding her bleeding mother imprinted itself in his mind, that emotion melting like ice in his veins when the woman screamed, "An eye for an eye, just like The Good Book says."

Then all hell broke loose. There was no more waiting. The next two minutes of time went by in a flash, but like he was watching it through someone else's eyes. Like a movie. Guns were drawn, the door and windows were kicked in, and the screaming and yelling from every direction was deafening.

Then it was over.

He saw the green and purple haired girl. The words that fell from her lips as she passed by in cuffs would haunt Carter for the rest of his life.

"Ray should've finished her then I wouldn't have had to."

From inside the motorhome, Mike's booming voice called for the paramedics, but Carter beat them to the door. He fell to the floor beside his brother, not even registering his brother's warning not to move her. The only thing he focused on was her. "Molly...no," he mumbled incoherently as he scooped the bleeding girl into his arms.

Chapter Sixteen

The waiting room of the ER had been overtaken by their family and friends. Carter figured the hospital had seen its fair share of injured motocross riders over the years. There were three local tracks within driving distance and the SuperCross series came through every year. Carter was quite sure there had never been any other riders brought through the doors with Molly's injuries.

He was three shakes past becoming a basket-case. They wouldn't let him back to see her yet because the police had followed wanting more information. One look at Brody and her parents, and he knew he wasn't alone.

Everyone kept assuring him that she was going to be okay, but there was no chance he'd be able to relax until he saw those bright blue eyes.

Carter could tell Mike was trying to hurry things along, and he appreciated it. He didn't know what he would have done if it hadn't been for Mike, his brother, the badass. He inwardly smiled at the thought, but the motion never actually made it to his mouth. He vaguely remembered hearing Mike say something about calling their parents and something about them coming on the next flight. Maybe, Carter wasn't sure, but right then, he wanted as many people around Molly as possible.

His parents had fallen in love with her immediately. Even under the circumstances and the fact that Molly had been so withdrawn, they could tell what a sweet, loving person she was. Carter knew his mother was ready for him to settle down. She'd made it known how she was ready for grandkids from her boys. Mike's divorce two years prior had only fanned the flames. Sam hadn't been married a year yet, but their mother was on him. Carter would let Sam take the heat for awhile. He wasn't about to explain to his mother that Molly would have to retire first, and there was no way he was going to allow her to climb on a bike if there was even a hint of a chance she could be pregnant. Well, that and the fact he hadn't even asked her to marry him…yet.

The doctor came out and Carter jumped to his feet, along with her parents, Brody, and Mike. They all converged around the doctor, everyone's anxiety palpable as they awaited the news. The dangling cross in the doctor's hand caught Carter's attention. It was covered in blood. As the doctor continued to talk, Carter stared at the necklace swinging back and forth in the doctor's hand.

"She's sedated due to the panic attack. We're finishing getting her stitched up and bandaged. I'm running some fluids into her now, plus we've done a blood transfusion. She lost enough to be concerned, but nothing we can't take care of here. We'll monitor her for a few hours then let her wake up on her own. If she's doing okay, we'll release her as long as she's got someone to stay with her through the night. I'll write a script, I have a feeling she's going to need a few sleeping pills just to get her through the next few days at least."

Carter drew in a deep breath, listening but unable to look directly at the man. He was transfixed on the blood-stained necklace—her blood. It shouldn't have been there. She shouldn't have been in Dylan's trailer. He should've protected her. That thought superseded all others. The guilt was crushing.

"Oh, here, I almost forgot." The doctor held up the diamond cross. "She's a lucky girl. The way she fell against the knife and the cuts she sustained, it could have been a whole lot worse. The chain was laying over her carotid, it kept the blade from slicing through."

"That little chain?" James questioned.

"Based on what I've seen of knife wounds, her attacker hadn't purposely tried to cut her neck, yet. Molly must have fallen down, probably as the panic attack hit its peak. The cuts were more of a scraping motion against the blade. What little pressure that the blade had against her skin cut her right over where the carotid lies…" The doctor lifted his chin and tilted his head as he gestured to the area. "They're deep, but not life threatening. Somehow the carotid wasn't even nicked. So yes, that thin, little chain protected her. That…or the cross hanging from it did. Depends on how you want to look at it. As a medical professional, I have to tell you the facts. As a man, I believe in miracles myself."

Carter felt her parents and Brody all look at him. After a long few seconds, he held out his palm and watched as the doctor lowered it into his hand.

"As soon as you are all done out here with the police, feel free to come on back. She's still out, but I know you're all anxious to see her. The nurse will show you how to take care of her wounds."

"Wounds?" Carter's voice shook.

Carter watched the doctor's mood go somber. He took a deep breath and nodded. "There's several. I'll go over everything with you when you get back there."

"Thank you, Doctor," James said.

Carter stared at his hand. The tiny cross, a piece of him she always wore. He closed his eyes and fisted the cross in his hand.

Brody's voice broke into his mental self-berating. "She's tough…she'll be okay, Carter."

He should have been ecstatic at the encouraging words from the one person who tried to keep them apart. Instead, he lashed out.

"She shouldn't have to be tough. She shouldn't be here. She shouldn't have been in that trailer! I should have protected her. I should've kept her safe. I promised." He glared at Brody and gritted his teeth. The words came out in anger—anger at the whole situation—but mostly anger at himself. "I promised you…I promised her." Carter had let down the one person he cared about most.

As Carter began to withdraw, he noticed Mike closing in, ready to console him, brother-to-brother.

But it was Brody's arms that went around him first. The shock would hit him later, he was sure. In the meantime, he grabbed onto the lifeline Brody was throwing him.

"I'm so sorry, Brody. I'm so sorry. I should've been there."

"Carter."

Brody pulled away. When Carter thought it was safe to finally open his eyes, he looked up to meet Brody's face, waiting for the I told you so, waiting for the hatred to come bubbling out.

"Carter, you saved her life."

Carter shook his head. "No…I didn't."

"You did, though. When you found out about everything, you demanded your brother come help. Without him…well?" Brody shrugged. "You did that. You knew who could help her and you made it happen…even when I fought you. And you were the one who went straight for Dylan's trailer. You saved her, Carter. Thank you."

With tears welling in his eyes again, Carter looked at the outstretched hand. He gripped it hard then looked up. Brody's eyes matched his own. It was an understanding, a common ground.

Brody was offering his blessing, in so many words. Desperately trying not to cry, Carter squeezed his eyes shut tight and nodded.

❧

Carter stood by Molly's head, never taking his hand off of her as visitors came in and out of the small room. The nurse shuffled people around as she attached a new bag of fluids for her IV. Carter watched quietly as she checked the bandages for excessive bleeding, took her vitals, and typed notes on the computer by Molly's bed. Molly had yet to stir, but they weren't concerned. The doctor and nurses kept assuring him that the more she slept the better, that her body needed that healing time.

He needed her to wake up, though. He needed to know she was going to wake up. Carter needed to know she didn't hate him.

"Carter, honey—here, sit." Karen pushed down on his shoulder as she nudged a chair under him. He looked up at her with a grimaced smile of appreciation. "When Jesse and Eli get back, you're going to eat. They offered to go get something and you need it."

"I'm okay, Karen, really." His argument was a whisper.

"You're going to need to keep up your strength. She's going to need you the next few days."

"I hope so."

"Carter?" Karen moved closer to him. "Hey, look at me." Her words were soothing, but he understood the no-nonsense tone in them. "What do you think is going to happen? That she'll wake up and blame you?"

Carter's head dropped. "I don't know, Karen. I just don't know."

"Damn it, Carter. This was not your fault. Brody's right, you saved her. You are the one that brought Mike in. You're the one that knew he could help and made it happen, even when my son stood there arguing. Mike went in with his gun, but you brought Mike in.

You saved my daughter, Carter. For that...I'll be forever grateful. To Mike and to you."

Carter heard Karen's words, but he just couldn't let himself believe them, not until he could hold Molly and see in her eyes that she'd forgiven him.

He glanced up at the clock again. It felt like the hands never moved. Carter rolled his shoulders and shifted in the hard plastic chair. He was stiff, but there was no way in hell he was moving. Hearing the sharp intake of air, he whipped his head back to Molly's face. Gently, he brushed her bangs off her face and held his breath as her eyes fluttered partway open.

"Hey, Gorgeous," Carter kept his voice at a whisper. He wanted her to wake, but if she was going to drift back off, he knew the doctor said she needed it. He ran his knuckle over her cheek. It was so much colder than normal. "I love you."

Watching her try to swallow on what must have been a horribly dry throat, combined with the injuries to her neck, was just heartbreaking. "Oh, baby, you want to try a sip of water?"

Molly barely nodded, but he understood.

Using the straw to get some water for her, he let a few drops drain into her mouth, and watched her try to swallow again. Better, but still visibly painful. He repeated the motion a couple more times until it looked as if she was done, and then he sat and gently stroked her hand and arm around the IV site. She blinked several times and he could tell she was trying to fight sleep. He rushed to get his words out before her eyes closed again.

"Molly, I'm so sorry. I should've been there. I'm so sorry, Gorgeous." His ragged plea for forgiveness was said on a choked back sob.

"Shh." She was barely able to be heard above the beeping of the machines she was hooked up to, her words raspy and hard to make out. "No Carter...it's okay. Wasn't...your fault. I love you." She attempted a smile.

His relief came out with a whoosh. He knew she had struggled to get the words out, but even with her being under the pain meds and trying to come out of the sedation, he felt them and he knew she meant them.

"I love you, Molly...forever."

He lowered his head until it was on the bed beside her and draped his arm over her leg. He continued to run his finger carefully over her hand and fingers until he felt her lift them. When she threaded them through the back of his hair like she had done so many times before, he lost the battle against his emotions. Silent tears fell against his will and dripped onto her blanket as he gripped her necklace in his other hand.

ॐ‑❧

"How did you sleep, Gorgeous?" Carter asked as he brushed her bangs off her face.

Molly stretched gingerly, the pain over various parts of her body a cruel reminder of yesterday's hell. The alarm had gone off several moments before, and she knew Carter needed to get up, but she refused to let go of him. She wanted him with her for just a few more minutes, or maybe forever. Curling into his side, she snuggled in and hoped he'd stay in the warm bed with her.

Last night after she'd been released from the hospital, everyone had come back to the motorhome to eat take-out for dinner. As spacious as it felt on a regular basis, the small space had closed in fast, but it seemed no one had wanted to leave her side. Sitting on the couch wedged between Carter and Mike had felt like the safest place in the world. Molly had quietly listened and watched the conversations going on around her. Tom and Connie had come in last minute to support her and their sons. They all needed comforting. With the threat gone, everyone had seemed to relax and let go, and Molly sat in contented silence and listened to the old tales being brought out against Carter, Eli, and Jesse. Molly had known they were trying to take her mind off of the horror and it had worked. She couldn't help but laugh when Mike threw in some added details to a few of the stories that had seemingly slipped past their parents, conveniently.

Molly had even quietly teased back, smiling up at Mike beside her. Molly had grown quite attached to the gentle giant who had saved her life. There weren't even words to describe her gratitude. Though she'd tried, they just didn't seem like enough. But sitting there last night between the two men who were now her personal heroes, listening to their childhood stories while she shared some of hers, had made the evening perfect. Low key and quiet with humor mixed in, and safe.

No one had woken her as she'd slipped in and out of sleep, tucked under Carter's arm. Being surrounded by her friends and family had allowed her to relax enough to finally find peace.

Molly knew that this morning her parents would be anxious to hear if she'd slept through the night without a nightmare. She'd sensed how hesitant they were to leave her last night even though it was clear they completely trusted Carter with her care.

Molly was just as relieved as they were going to be that she'd made it. She'd woken twice, but neither time with a nightmare. Both times Carter's strong arms had tightened around her and pulled her back against his warm chest. He'd whispered soothing murmurs and words into the darkness, and each time she'd fallen right back to sleep.

Molly kissed Carter's bare chest and pulled away to prop herself up so she could see him. "I slept fine." She smiled down at him.

"Good, I'm so glad, Gorgeous." Carter pulled her close for a quick kiss.

"I guess I should let you get up, huh? You know I don't want to. I want to stay in bed all day."

"I know, baby, me too." Carter grinned and she could see the relief in his eyes.

His eyes weren't sad and heavy like they had been yesterday. It was a new day, time to put it all behind them as best they could. Their families were supposed to come back over for breakfast and then they'd planned to hang out in the pits and enjoy race day. Carter had been doing so well this season. Molly could only hope that yesterday wouldn't harm the second place standing he was in. She'd have to make sure he stayed in the game.

Molly could hear bikes being kick started and revved all around her, the drawback to parking so close, but really, she loved that sound, loved the smell of the pits, loved it all.

She was ready to ride.

Mentally preparing herself for battle, Molly knew there were going to be some men who would try to stand in her way. She grinned to herself, ready to take them all on.

"What's the shit eating grin for, Gorgeous?"

Busted.

Well ding, ding, ding—round one, now only James and Brody to go. Crap—she hadn't even thought about Karen.

Here goes nothing.

"Um…well, I was just trying to decide…I think I'll ride without my chest protector on. I'm afraid it will rub the stitches in my side." She bit her lip and waited.

"Excuse me?"

"And I'm going to see if James will mind…I think I'll leave the neck brace off too, just this once. I won't pull anything too dangerous. I'll be okay."

"What the hell are you talking about? You really think you're riding? Tonight?"

If Carter's eyebrow went up any further, it'd reach his hairline. Molly giggled at the mental picture.

"Honey, I really don't think you should push it."

Damn, that was easier than she'd expected. After years of battling like this with James, she knew which words to clue in on. He had said think. Bingo.

"I'll be fine. I really need to, Carter. I know you of all people understand that, right?"

Carter took in a deep breath. Molly knew that signal. He was almost there.

"Okay, Gorgeous, if you think you're up to it."

"I am, I promise. Now you can help me convince James and Brody."

"Oh, no." Carter shook his head, his tongue in his cheek. "You're on your own with them, baby."

"But…"

"You thought you were playing me? I'm smarter than you think, apparently." Carter started laughing. "And don't think for a minute I won't start calling the boys to vote against you. You might make it past your dad and Brody, I'm not sure…I doubt it. But just in case you do, I highly doubt you'll convince Jess or Eli. And then there's always Mike."

Molly lay back on the pillow, contemplating her next move. George.

"And don't even think about, George," Carter snickered. "I can see the steam coming from your brain, it's working so hard. Nice try. I only agreed to give you false hope."

"You're a mean boy." Molly crossed her arms over her chest. The longer she lay there, the harder it became to hold in the laughter. "Mean, I say."

"But you love me."

"Well, yeah. You did kinda save me and all. I kinda…owe ya," Molly said with mock aloofness.

"Hmm…owe me, huh? I like the sound of that."

The humor in his voice made Molly weary. She had gotten to know Carter's ornery side. He could still be that twelve-year-old boy she'd heard stories about last night. Molly lay very still. If she had been standing, she would have thrown her shoulders back and chin up, ready to take him on. She wasn't in a position to look that cool. Unfortunately.

"Well? Spit it out, boy."

"Boy?"

Shit. That sin-laden grin that danced across his face was a doozy. And damn it all to hell, it got her every time.

"Yeah…boy."

"All right, little girl." Carter winked. "The way I see it, I love you. And even though at first you were staying with me while…you know…" He waved his hand dismissively through the air. "It was something I needed you to do. We don't have that excuse anymore."

The conversation and playful banter had just taken a ninety-degree turn going way too fast and skidded into something else. Suddenly, Molly felt like he wasn't teasing anymore and a tingle rushed across her skin from head to toe.

"I want you to move in with me permanently, Molly. I want you with me because you want to be here now. Not because we need it. I know, even though it feels like we've lived a lifetime over the last few weeks, it really hasn't been that long. I also know it feels like I'm rushing things, but Molly…I love you."

Carter propped himself up on his elbow, his head inclined in emphasis.

"This isn't a proposal yet, but only because I need to get the ring from my parents house. It was my Grandmother Sterling's and it will be yours. That's how serious I am."

She'd had drugs in the emergency room yesterday, maybe they were still in her system. Molly wasn't sure she was hearing the words he was saying, because it sounded an awful lot like he was proposing.

"We can take it as slow as you want. I just know you will start to feel better day-by-day and I don't want to get to the point that that because you've healed, you think you need to move back in with Brody. I don't want you to wonder how serious I am. I want you with me and not just until you're healed."

His voice was steady, his face happy but entirely serious. Molly took a long look, reading every line, every nuance. She was looking for…she wasn't sure what. Maybe he was teasing? But he wasn't laughing. He had a reassuring smile, but nothing more. Suddenly, she realized he was waiting for an answer.

When she didn't say anything, he continued, "I told you when I made love to you that first night, it was going to change everything. You're mine. I wouldn't have let you go, but after almost losing you yesterday…" Carter shook his head. "I can't bear the thought of being apart from you. I won't risk losing you a second time."

He wanted her.

After everything she'd put him through, put Mike through, Carter wanted her. Nightmares, scars, panic attacks, her crazy brother and all, he wanted her.

Molly was in awe. "I love you."

"I love you too, Gorgeous. So much…I always will."

His mouth turned up in that lop-sided, sexy as sin smile that pulled at her heart, but it was his eyes this time. They were beautiful and so full of love. She melted.

It didn't matter what happened from here, she knew she would always be his.

He had leaned in over her, and she raised a shaky hand to his jaw and stroked the early morning whiskers. "Yes."

It was an answer to moving in with him, but it was so much more than just that.

৵৽৽

They were having their own private party in a secluded corner of the pits. Emotions were high, the adrenaline still pumping. The track had been a challenge tonight, very technical.

Carter excelled on these tracks. He wasn't a mudder and usually lost ground in points when he rode outdoor tracks with bad weather, but he made up for it on tracks like tonight. Taking another second place finish went a long way to securing a top three finish for the season. He wanted that coveted red number one and Molly wanted it for him. They still had a long season ahead of them, though.

Eli had edged poor Jesse out for third, but Jess could have hung onto some points if it hadn't been for his bike in the sixteenth lap. Out of nowhere, he had no power. They were all thankful he wasn't mid-air clearing a triple when it happened or he would've been taking up the bed in the hospital that Molly had occupied yesterday.

In their sport, a bike failure could be life or death as far as points and wins went. They had faced death yesterday. So in the grand scheme of things today, a bike failure was minor. Jesse was fine and that was all that mattered.

Molly listened to the laughter around her. The liquor store across the street had been raided and no one was giving her any trouble as she reached for the bottle of white wine closest to her. She laughed with this story and that story. She even let Carter put a piece of pizza on her plate, a total splurge. His face lit up when she took a bite. Molly rolled her eyes at him and took a second bite of the warm, gooey goodness. Alcohol and pizza, what was the world coming to? When Molly caught the knowing smile of Karen across the circle, she realized what they'd already put together.

She hadn't run in over a week and she was eating something other than grass, as Brody put it.

She had finally accepted herself.

She wasn't trying to outrun her past anymore.

The man she loved knew about it, had witnessed the evidence it had left behind. He had lived through it and stood beside her when it had come back to haunt her.

Molly finally realized what Karen and James had been trying to tell her for years. It wasn't her fault. She didn't do anything wrong back then, just like she didn't yesterday. Bad things happened and she'd lived through them — but she didn't cause them and she couldn't control it.

Molly looked at the pizza in her hand. She didn't need to try to control anything anymore and her past didn't control her. Carter had lifted that burden from her — had helped her see.

She didn't have to hide anymore.

He must have sensed her breakthrough, and when she glanced at him in the chair beside her, he nodded. "Figured it out, didn't ya?"

Molly looked back across the circle to see Karen and James holding hands and smiling at her. Karen mouthed, "We love you" and James winked.

Carter pulled her close and kissed her forehead.

"Yeah…I did. Because of you."

Carter's thumb crossed beneath her eye, wiping the tear that escaped. Finally though, it was a happy tear. Molly sucked in a breath at the loving smile on Carter's face. She was so at peace; she didn't even startle when someone squeezed her shoulder.

"Sis, can I talk to you?" The sheepish smile on Brody's face was one she remembered well. She'd seen it every day since she moved in with him. Up until a few weeks ago, anyway.

"Sure, Brody. Everything okay?" Molly blinked back another tear that was threatening to fall and stood up.

Brody didn't speak. Instead, he turned and walked a few feet away from the group, apparently waiting for her to follow.

As soon as Molly got close enough, he reached out and pulled her into his arms. He towered over her, but he bent to tuck his face in her neck, whispering his words into her ear, "I'm so sorry, Mol."

"It's over, Brody. It's okay…I'm okay." For the first time, she knew she really was.

"No…not that. Well, that too. But…" He stood back up. Molly could see the sincerity in his eyes. "I'm so sorry about how I've acted about Carter."

Molly drew in a deep breath. Seeing the nerves in Brody's eyes, she could sense he was waiting to find out if he could be forgiven. Like there was a chance he wouldn't be.

"Brody, I understand. There's nothing to forgive."

"But there is, Mol. I was a jackass to Carter and to you, too. He's a good guy, I see that now."

"You didn't know that in the beginning. I didn't either, for that matter. I'd just…sensed it. You were right to try and protect me, especially with everything that went wrong."

"I know, but I'm talking about before everything went to hell. I was rude and pretty hateful. He didn't deserve that and neither did you. I'm sorry."

"Brody, from the day I moved in with you, you have been my protector. You were my best friend, my confidant, my partner in crime even." She grinned and saw the slight smirk tug at his mouth. "We've been inseparable for almost thirteen years. You're my twin. I wouldn't have it any other way. You were nervous of his intentions…Carter understood that, especially when he found out about everything."

Brody shuffled his foot. Molly understood his need to apologize and she appreciated it.

"I'm…um…Brody…" Molly hesitated then decided just to be straightforward with her brother. "Carter sorta asked me to move in with him. Or I guess, stay with him, I mean."

He nodded. "I know."

"What do you mean, you know?"

"Carter came to talk to Dad and me this morning before his practice time. He told us."

Molly took in the half smile on Brody's face and tilted her chin. "Did he…tell you…everything?"

That made Brody chuckle. "Yeah, he asked our permission, both of us. If that's what you mean?"

Molly bit her lip. "Yeah."

She knew he was keeping her in suspense on purpose, just to be a mean brother. Brody was back to being fourteen again. Finally, he snickered.

"We told him yes. Both of us told him yes. He'll take care of you, Mol. I'm just going to miss you so damn much, you're my little twinny."

As tears formed in her eyes, Brody's hand came out for their secret handshake they'd made up as kids. By the final swipe of his hand against the back of hers, tears were rolling down her face.

"I'm always going to love you, Brody. You're my brother."

"And you're my sister. Forever."

He gathered her into his arms. The brother she loved so dearly was back. She took a breath in, but hadn't heard Carter approach until she felt his palm on her back.

"Everything okay?" Carter asked.

Molly glanced up to see the lop-sided grin on the face of the man she'd fallen in love with. Before she could answer, Brody did.

"Yeah, Carter. You've made my sister happy. Everything's just fine."

With his final words, Brody kissed her forehead and pulled out of her arms. Then he stepped back for Carter to take his spot.

Epilogue

Molly looked around the hotel room. It was simply heavenly. Ready for bed in her tank top and sleep shorts, she flopped onto the big, fluffy bed like a teenager. Now if Erin would just hurry back with the snacks.

The knock on the door made her grin. She had specifically requested chocolate and pop. The two girls were having their own private celebration. Molly climbed back off the bed and hustled to the door to let Erin back in.

"Did you forget your key or did you get so much you couldn't..." Molly asked as she was pulling the door open. Her confusion stopped her.

"Aren't you going to let me in?"

The danger in his voice sent her stomach to the ground. She tilted her chin, still trying to figure out what was going on. "What are you doing here?" she asked, a nervous giggle escaping.

"I missed you, Gorgeous."

Molly glanced down both sides of the long hallway. Erin was going to be back any second, not to mention that their family and friends were scattered all over the hotel.

"Are you going to make stand out here in the hallway...?" He motioned around him. "And talk to you from here?"

"Carter. You're not supposed to see me."

"That's tomorrow...in your dress. This is tonight."

Carter had proposed shortly after her attack. He had taken her to an amazing restaurant near the stadium they were at for the weekend. Tucking her in a dim corner, the two of them had just relaxed. She hadn't been expecting it when he leaned in close and began to whisper words of love and promises as he slipped his grandmother's ring on her left hand. It still shocked her when she peeked down at it. The princess cut two carat sapphire was beautiful, and the diamonds surrounding the sapphire on all four sides sparkled as the light glimmered off of them. The platinum band looked delicate on her narrow finger. She loved everything about it. Carter still hadn't shown her the matching wedding band and the suspense was making her crazy. After he had proposed, Carter had surprised her with a small engagement party. The entire family had been there, including Jesse, Eli, Joey, and George.

Molly's mouth watered as she made a slow pass over the sex in jeans leaning against the door frame. Low slung 501s, snug t-shirt with his muscled forearms visible, his hard planed chest straining the soft cotton. Not to mention the hint of facial hair from the long day. Damn, the man was hot and he knew it. When her eyes made it past the smile that got her every time and up to those baby blues, he winked.

"You're so bad."

Carter chuckled. "You still haven't invited me in, Gorgeous."

Molly backed up and opened the door wider. As Carter walked through, she once again peeked into the hallway before shutting the door.

"Are you afraid you're going to get in trouble?" Carter snickered as he pulled her into his arms.

"Erin will be back any second. She went to get snacks."

Carter shook his head, the sinful smile tugging on his lips. "Sorry, Gorgeous, your snacks aren't coming."

Molly's face scrunched. "What do you mean? And why aren't you at your bachelor party? We're in Vegas, I thought you guys were hitting every bar and strip club open."

"I didn't want to. We ate, hit a bar, and Brody and I ditched 'em."

Molly's mouth dropped open. "You left James?"

"Eli and Jess were going to take him, my dad, and everyone else to one more bar, but I think your dad was ready to come back and see your mom." Carter wiggled his eyebrows and Molly giggled.

"I don't need to know that."

Still grinning, Molly glanced back at the door. "So where's Erin?"

"You girls made it too easy. We caught her down in the lobby. I stole her key card and Brody kidnapped her."

Molly feigned anger at her loss of snacks, her eyes narrowing, arms crossing over her chest. "What about my chocolate she was supposed to bring me?"

Carter laughed. He dropped one of the arms he was holding her with and reached behind him. Molly'd bet her laughter could be heard from two doors down as he whipped out the plain chocolate bar from his back pocket.

"I missed you, Molly. I haven't slept without you by my side in four months and I don't want to wake up on the most important day of my life without you in my arms." Carter squeezed her around the waist, tugging her closer. "Erin and I are going to switch places before we all meet for breakfast."

"You're going to keep me up all night, the night before our wedding?" Molly tried to contain her smile so she could continue reprimanding the handsome man holding her. "I'm going to have dark circles under my eyes in our pictures."

"And a smile."

Molly lost it at his quick retort. "You are so, so bad."

"That's why you love me."

"Damn straight."

Molly gasped when Carter suddenly scooped her up in his arms and threw her on the bed. She bounced twice, her peals of laughter apparently contagious. Carter was laughing as he tore his shirt over his head himself.

"So, it seems to me you boys got lucky. What if Erin hadn't been in the lobby? What were you going to do then?" Molly asked with more than a hint of sarcasm in her voice.

"Ah, my sweetheart…don't you worry. Brody and I had a plan."

"The two of you make me very nervous. You've gotten really close and I'm not sure I trust you with him."

Carter bracketed her head with his arms. The sinful smirk came across his mouth as he shook his head. He dropped a kiss on her lips. "You shouldn't."

Molly could see the fire in his eyes as he slowly pulled her shorts down her legs. As he inched her tank top up, she raised her arms for him. She could see the rapid rise and fall of his chest, hear his breathing become jagged as he slowly removed her panties, like he was unwrapping a treasured package. Once he had her undressed, he pulled back and stood. Molly couldn't move as she watched his eyes roam over her, darkened with desire.

He unbuttoned the fly on his jeans and pushed them off. The sharp intake of air Molly sucked in was audible. Her gaze traveled slowly over the man whose body she now knew so well. She had felt every ripple of every muscle, felt every inch of smooth skin over the steel beneath it. He was beautiful. Not what a man wanted to hear, but he was, simply breathtaking. Underneath it, though, was the heart she'd fallen for.

He climbed on the bed next to her and wrapped himself around her, the heat of his skin burning her. His lips brushed hers lightly.

"This is the last time I'll ever make love to you as Molly West. From now on, you'll be Molly Sterling. You'll be mine." There was an edge to his voice.

A ripple of need rolled up Molly's spine. "I've been yours since the night we met." Her admission came out breathless.

Carter kissed her harder the second time, the possession in it not masked. His tongue passed over hers for a few delicious seconds before he made his way to her jaw and down her throat.

He slowed.

His lips gentled over her newest injuries. Carter never kissed that side of her neck roughly anymore, it was always with love and tenderness. Unspoken, but there, a simple acknowledgment of what he'd almost lost. Then, as usual, he let the moment go and moved past it. She had never asked him why. She didn't have to...she knew.

His mouth continued down her chest, over her heart that was now pounding, to her breasts. Molly ran her fingers through his hair as he took the first in his mouth. She arched back with closed eyes as he moved to the other, the fire in her climbing higher and higher, need quickly eclipsing want.

"Carter," she begged through a whisper. He was the only one that could give her what she needed now.

His mouth moved lower still, his kisses soft again. His lips settled on her stomach. Her hands moved to his shoulders, and she felt the deep breath he drew in, felt his words spoken against the tight skin of her abdomen.

"No more condoms."

She ran both hands up his neck, settling her fingers on his cheeks. The shake of her head was slight. Dragging her eyes back open, she looked down her body to see his face, his chin still on her stomach, but his eyes locked on hers.

"No more pills," she whispered.

His mouth made its way back up her body, this time on a mission. Each pass brought him closer and closer to her. It would be another first of sorts. This time, there would be nothing between them. She would feel him for the first time.

As Carter settled himself between her legs, he touched her cheek in silent understanding as he slowly slid into her body. The air that was in her lungs escaped as a hiss through her teeth. Not from pain, but impatience. Molly needed him now and the man was driving her out of her mind. There was no point in hurrying him, though. He never failed to give her what he knew she needed. A sheen of sweat glistened on her skin while she waited.

Tonight the wait was short.

"Molly," Carter said under his breath, and then he started to move.

Immediately she felt herself splintering into a million pieces. Her eyes shut so tight she swore she saw stars. When she went tumbling, a high-pitched noise escape from her mouth, right before Carter took it over, kissing her faster and harder. Nipping at her, taking what was his, before slowing and taking more care with the lips he'd just punished, then quickening again. Carter dug his hands into the mattress on either side of her, and she felt the strength in the one last push, heard the grunt of power that came with it. Then he collapsed, sweaty and breathing uncontrollably on top of her.

"I love you, Molly Sterling."

Carter's declaration was barely heard. Molly tried to grin at her new last name and hoped he could hear her return the words. "I love you too, Carter."

〜〜

She grinned as she looked into the full length mirror, watching the three women move around her.

They had decided for a quick wedding. She was completely uncomfortable around a lot of people and Carter knew that. Instead, he insisted on a small, intimate affair with just their closest friends and family. Carter's family was huge and she hated the thought that it might cause a rift. Their destination wedding had solved that problem. His only request was that it was sooner rather than later.

Molly had had absolutely no problem with that.

Finals week was the first week in May, the last race of the season, and it all ended in Vegas, a huge event with easy access to a wedding. Karen and Erin had quickly put together the small wedding. No attendants, no flower girls. Just the two of them in the small chapel that looked like it belonged in a little country town somewhere, surrounded by those that loved them.

Molly had pinned up the sides of her hair, leaving a sheet of thick gold hanging straight down her back. It was already warm there in May, so she had opted for no panty hose, going with only a white lace thong that she knew Carter would love and a white lace strapless bra underneath the dress.

She yawned as Erin, Connie, and Karen helped her carefully step into the white strapless silk dress with a sweetheart neckline, and pulled it up. The dress had little fabric covered buttons running down the back and a sash that was wide in the front and narrowed in the back to tie in a small bow, leaving the ends hanging long. It was a simple dress, plain almost, but with the full skirt and short train on her tiny little frame, anything else would have been too much.

Karen attached the elbow length veil in place with a small Swarovski clip. Taking a deep breath, Molly turned around for their approval, and was immediately smothered in hugs and kisses.

"Don't make me cry." Gentle laughter escaped her mouth as she tried to hold back the tears. "I have on too much mascara."

"I love you so much, Mol." Erin said as she hugged her tight. "You mean the world to me. You and Brody are my best friends. Remember, the three of us against the world?"

Molly smiled through the tears at their familiar motto. "Yeah, how could I forget? That got us into more trouble."

"No, your brother got us into trouble." Erin laughed and yawned.

Molly grinned. "Well he's not here to defend himself. So yeah, we'll blame him."

"I was there," Karen said as she hugged both girls. "He is to blame."

Giggles burst from both girls again, and Molly had to dab beneath her eyes, trying to fix her mascara. "Why can't this be waterproof? The stinking package said waterproof."

Both girls yawned again at the same time.

"Why are you girls both so tired? You can't stand up there on the alter yawning, Molly." Karen's chin tilted in suspicion.

Molly bit her lip. They were pretty sure they'd made a clean get away this morning. Carter had sent a text when he got to Brody's room and promised her he hadn't run into anyone. Erin had said the same. But when Erin yawned again, they both lost it. Molly was sure their laughter could be heard out into the small church.

"Girls, shh." Karen waved her hand downward as she looked toward the door of the changing room. "What's gotten into you two?"

Erin mouthed "into" to Molly and Molly lost it, the little dirty inside joke sending her into a hysterical tizzy.

"You had boys in your room last night, didn't you?" The anger on Karen's face would have been more threatening if she wasn't fighting laughter so hard. Even with her hands on her hips, her face gave her away as it turned redder and redder.

Karen leveled her eyes at both girls, or at least attempted to. When Molly couldn't stifle the yawn, the suppressed laughter started bubbling up all over again. That was the problem. Molly had a nervous giggle anyway, and once she started, it was like hell trying to get it to stop.

Karen shook her head. "So who did the sneaking?"

Both girls shouted their defenses at the same time, "The boys."

Connie raised her eyebrow. "I had a feeling my son was to blame." The crooked grin of the older woman barely hid her amusement.

Molly brought her hands up in surrender. "Technically, I never did anything wrong. I stayed in my room the whole night."

Erin's eyes went wide. "Well…I was kidnapped."

Both mothers' eyes rose.

Karen shook her head and finally chuckled, letting Molly know she thought it was funny. "We'd better put you back together. You have makeup running everywhere now."

Erin took the tissue from Molly's hand and wiped off another smudge. It reminded Molly of the old days, when they'd do each other's hair and makeup. It had been a friend triangle that ended perfectly — Brody, Erin, and her. Finally after so many years growing up as friends, Brody and Erin had made it official. Now her two best friends were going to make her an aunt.

"Well, Mol. I'd better go find your brother and my seat. Who knows what those boys are up to? With all four of us in here, there's no one to contain the madness that might be happening out there. I love Carter, Eli, and Jesse, but man, you add Brody to the mix, and those four together are one hot mess."

Molly grinned and looked at Connie. "I'd say Mike could keep them under control, but from what I've seen — he and Sam just join in like little boys. What is it with good looking guys? They're all freaking as ornery as hell."

Erin shook her head and blew Molly a kiss as she walked out the door. Connie grabbed her purse and a couple of tissues.

"Ah, let me have one more." Connie chuckled as she leaned in to hug Molly carefully. "All right, sweetie. We're so happy to have you in our family, Molly. Tom and I love you." Her words were cut off as she started to tear up, and she waved her hand in front of her face to try to get herself together. "I'll leave you two alone. See you in a few minutes."

When Connie disappeared out the door, Molly checked the clock on the wall for the four thousandth time and let out a breath, bit her lip, and put her finger to the cross at her neck.

"Nervous, sweetheart?"

"No, why?" Molly whispered.

Karen didn't even have to speak, Molly could tell be the look on her face. Karen's smile widened even more when Molly dropped her hand.

"Oh. Yeah, I guess so."

"It has nothing to do with marrying Carter, does it? You're nervous about walking down the aisle?"

"You know me too well." Molly grinned and walked into Karen's open arms.

Karen adjusted the veil. "He makes you happy, doesn't he?"

"More than I thought possible."

"I'm so glad, that's more than we could have ever hoped for. You've turned into an amazing young woman, Molly. James and I couldn't be more proud."

"I wouldn't be here today without the two of you. I will never be able to thank you enough."

"Oh, baby girl, give me grandchildren and we'll be even."

"Done." Molly smiled. "Karen?"

"Yes, sweetheart?"

"I've been wanting to ask you something for a really long time, but never knew how."

"What, honey?"

"Is it…would it be okay…um—"

"Sweetheart?"

"Well, I just feel like you and James are more than a couple who took me in when I needed help. I was wondering if maybe it would be all right… I mean, would it be weird if I called you Mom and Dad?" Molly asked, unable to hide the hesitation in her voice. She had wanted this for so long, but it was such an awkward request. The more time that went by, the harder it became. Her stomach rolled once as she bit her lip and nervously waited for Karen's response.

The embrace she received from Karen was answer enough, but undeniable in the excitement bubbling out of Karen. "Oh my…sweetheart, you've just made me happier than I have ever been. We'd love that! We just never suggested it because we thought it might make you uncomfortable. We've always considered you our daughter, you know that."

Molly shook her head yes, not trusting her voice. If she spoke now, she'd end up starting from scratch with her makeup.

A knock at the door startled them both. "Five minutes."

"Oh, Molly, I love you, so much." Karen dabbed both of their eyes with a tissue.

As hard as she tried to keep them from escaping, the tears of joy rolled down her cheeks in a fresh wave. Molly hugged Karen again, holding on tight. "I love you too."

"I better go get Jam—I mean, your father." She flashed a watery smile at Molly and then walked to the door, blowing her a kiss before pulling the door shut and leaving Molly standing in the room by herself.

Carter stood in his black tux, pulling at his collar. His friends and brothers had been chatting and joking with him, trying to keep him calm, but all he wanted was to be by her side, and even more so to have her in his bed. One by one they all shook hands and left to find their seats with their wife, girlfriend, or date, leaving him with just James and his father. James reached out his hand to his future son-in-law then pulled him into a tight hug.

"You're a good man, Carter. You take good care of my baby girl."

"I will, sir."

"I know you will." James smiled.

"I know it's been quick and we've been through a lot…it's been kind of a whirlwind, really. Thank you for trusting me."

"Well, I do trust you, Carter. She's happy, as long as you keep her that way, that's all I can ask."

"Thank you, James."

"Well, I better go get my little girl. I'll meet you up at the altar." James nodded at Carter as he walked out of the room.

"Well, Son." Tom straightened his son's black bow tie.

Carter took a deep breath. "I love that girl, Dad."

"All right then, let's go make her yours."

James tapped on the door and peeked his head in. "I heard my daughter is ready to get married."

Molly turned back around to face him and watched his mouth drop open. "Wow, you look beautiful, baby girl."

Molly could see tears form in his eyes as she walked into his arms. "So…you talked?" Molly grinned.

"To your mom?" James smiled, his pride evident across his face. "Yes. I've never been more proud of anything than to be able to call myself your father. You and Brody are the best two kids a man could ask for."

Molly hugged him tight, smelling the familiar cologne she'd bought him for Father's Day last year.

"You know when I signed that contract with George, I never dreamed in a million years you wouldn't come back home at the end of it." Molly watched James attempt a smile, but it didn't quite reach. "You sure about this boy?"

Molly knew he was teasing, but she couldn't help but feel that twinge of fear. She wouldn't ever go back to live in her old bedroom. She'd never again wake up and drink coffee with him and her mother on Saturday mornings. Things were going to change. She was excited about her new life with Carter, but a piece of her was homesick already.

"Yes, I love him."

He gave her a little smile and his words were tender. "I'm not ready to give you away yet."

It seemed as if her father had just had the same realization she did. The dress just made it all so real. She'd had the same moment when she saw herself in the mirror for the first time.

"You're just sharing. I'll always be yours…" She paused. "And Mom's."

Molly heard the breath James took and hugged him tight when he pulled her back into his embrace.

"Well, let's go take you to your boy. He's about to wear the carpet thin from pacing. I don't think he can wait another minute."

The two of them walked to the doors of the little sanctuary in silence, each lost in their own nerves and thoughts. They stopped just outside, both taking one last deep breath.

"I love you, baby girl." James kissed her cheek before pulling the veil over her face.

"I love you too, Dad."

The doors opened and everyone stood. She saw Carter at the altar as she waited for her cue. She let out her breath, put her shoulders back, and lifted her chin, glancing at James. He nodded his reassurance, and the two of them started down the aisle. She gripped his arm tight, needing his strength one more time. Molly kept her eyes glued on the handsome man at the end. Not trusting her emotions, she didn't dare make eye contact with Karen.

Molly got half way to the altar and saw Carter's mouth drop open, then that slow, sexy grin that had won her heart on day one came across his face. He winked at her as James helped her up the three steps to stand by his side.

James said his line then held her hand out for Carter to take. Molly glanced down at her hand in his, then back up to his smiling face.

"You look gorgeous," he mouthed to her. She just smiled back.

Her heart was about to burst, first from the conversations with Karen and then James, and now to be marrying the love of her life. She didn't hear much of the ceremony until the minister led them to the written vows.

She turned to face Carter, who had tears beginning to well up, which immediately caused her to lose her own battle with tears.

"Molly, we haven't known each other for very long and we've been through a lot. But I knew the day I met you I'd marry you. I knew I'd found my perfect match. When I'm with you, I feel like I can do anything. And no one can make me laugh or challenge me..." He grinned at her. "Like you do. I love you more than anything in the world, Gorgeous." He squeezed her hands.

Molly took a deep breath, hoping it was somewhat subtle. "Carter, I remember the day we met, too. Seeing that slow grin come across your face as you shook my hand, it stole my breath. Then I looked in your eyes and I fell in love with you that very moment. You've been by my side through some very tough times and never wavered. I feel loved, cherished, and protected when you are by my side. I love you."

He mouthed, "I love you," back to her and she felt the tear roll down her cheek.

The minister continued on through the short ceremony. Her heart soared as she heard Carter say the words first. The shortest sentence known to man, but one that meant so much. One that meant everything.

"I do," she said, smiling sweetly at Carter.

"And by the power vested in me by the state of Nevada, I declare you husband and wife. You may kiss the bride."

Carter's palm slid along her back, pulling her closer. He told her I love you one more time, before he tipped her chin up with his other hand and her lips met his for the first time as husband and wife.

~∞~

The small, private room of the restaurant had been transformed into a princess's dream, quaint and romantic with white lights and greenery everywhere. The aged brick walls gave an old world Tuscan feel to the Italian restaurant. In the middle of the rustic wood floor was a space big enough for their first dance and the father-daughter dance she would share with James. Carter wasn't sure how Karen had found it, but for their catered dinner, it was perfect. She had put together the most perfect wedding and reception for her daughter and Carter appreciated it. It wasn't some elaborate affair that Molly wouldn't enjoy because she couldn't relax.

Instead, Molly bounced around, being passed from one hug to the next, and Carter watched her, laughing the entire time. She was stopped once again by Eli and Jesse. Carter could tell they were teasing her about something, and he smiled as Jesse took her under his arm in mock protection from Eli over who knew what. Judging by the plate full of food in Eli's hand, it was to keep Molly's dress clean. But Carter couldn't care less if the dress ended up covered in food, as long as she had fun.

Mike swooped in from behind her, scooped her up, big dress and all, and carried her giggling to Carter's table.

"Here, I brought you something, brother." Mike chuckled.

"Thanks, I'd been missing her." Carter grinned as he pulled her closer to him. "You need to eat, Gorgeous."

"Especially if you're going to keep up with mom on the wine," Brody teased.

Jesse sat down on Brody's other side and Eli by Erin, the seven of them rounding out this new tightly woven group.

"You know you could tell Sam and Lindsay to come sit with us." Molly looked over her shoulder at her other brother-in-law.

"That's all right, sweetheart. Lindsay's still sucking up to her mother-in-law." Mike winked.

Molly's jaw dropped. "Mike."

Mike shrugged his shoulder. "What can I say? Everyone knows you're the favorite."

"Mike." Molly's cheeks flamed.

Jesse wiggled his eyebrows. "So…I want to hear more about this kidnapping scheme."

Both Molly and Erin turned five shades of red as their table erupted in a round of laughter once again.

The teasing, eating, and drinking continued well into the night. Carter got his first dance with his new wife then barely held it together as he saw the tears trickle down her cheeks as she danced with not only her father and her brother, but now also with Mike.

Jesse and Eli both came up behind him, one on each side as Mike twirled her once and pulled her back against his chest.

"You're a lucky man, Sterling." Eli squeezed his shoulder.

"Trust me," Carter said as Molly reached up on tip toes to kiss Mike on the cheek and then headed his way. The smile on her face lit up the room. "I know. I'll treasure her every day that I'm alive.

CPSIA information can be obtained at www.ICGtesting.com
Printed in the USA
LVOW042323240512

283239LV00003B/1/P